EXTRAVAGANCE

BROADWAY BOOKS

NEW YORK

◆

EXTRAVAGANCE

A NOVEL

Gary Krist

Designed by Gretchen Achilles

ISBN 0-7679-1330-2

"Hark you, Mr. Broker, I have a parcel of excellent logwood, block-tin,
spider's brains, philosopher's-guts, Don Quixote's windmills,
hen's-teeth, ell-broad packthread, and the quintessence
of the blue of plumbs.

TOM BROWN
Amusements Serious and Comical

PROLOGUE

"INDUSTRY," THE BEEKEEPER SAID, "is the only true path to God's grace."

I watched from a distance, standing under the rattling leaves of a poplar tree. The man, despite his pious words, looked more devil than angel to me. He wore thick gloves and a wicker helmet draped to the shoulders with dusty burlap sacking. His leather apron, wax- and honey-smeared, clung to his chest like an eelskin.

"Nothing is earned except by good, honest labour," said he, testing the weight of each throbbing hive. "The Bible has it so"—and here a smile showed in the gap between the pleats of burlap sacking—"but pray don't ask me to say precisely where."

He plucked a dish of smouldering grass from the ground and swept it round the first straw skep, painting the hive with his sweet smoke. A few lone bees emerged to buzz about his covered head, but though I looked for the rest to turn angry and swarm from the hive like seamen from a burning sloop, the bees inside were still. I wiped a trickle of sweat from my lip and—heart jumping, thinking it a bee—slapped an ant from my moist bare thigh.

The beekeeper turned his head and smiled again. He was a large

1

man, beefy and bulb-nosed, with the stance and slow movements of a bullock. In the heat of the spring afternoon, his cheeks shone wet and ruddy beneath the wicker helmet. He had the smell of beeswax about him—of beeswax and smoke and horseleather—which I liked. I had seen him once or twice in the town, and knew him to be a man of many trades: a lockkeeper, a grower of potatoes and roots, a street-corner Dissenter, and now a honey-man. I never knew his name.

He put aside the smoke-dish and lifted the skep from its wooden platform. This caused some mild perturbation in the hive, and I took a step back, though I stood distant enough to be safe, I thought. Then he reached within and brought out a comb, brimming with amber honey and deep-cobbled by bees. "There's them that will kill the bees to harvest their honey and wax, but I've not the heart for that," said he. He took a goose feather from his belt and gently brushed the bees from the comb.

"What's your name, boy?" he enquired of me then, eyes upon his work.

"William Merrick, sir."

"And do you go to school, William Merrick?"

"I do. Though I have a tutor as well—my older cousin, an educated man—whose attentions I share with my brothers."

"And does this cousin teach you your Bible verses so you have them all by heart?"

I hesitated, wondering if it were best to lie and be caught out, or else to speak the truth and risk his disapproval. "Mr. Dooling—for such is my tutor's name, sir—he owns a fine old Bible, bound in red morocco. He puts us to reading it whenever he needs an hour to himself."

The beekeeper laughed then—a deep, rasping growl. "You answer like a Norman, Master Merrick. Which is to say, you answer not at all." He placed the brushed honeycomb into a bucket and reached in for another. "But I was a boy once, too. I know there's better games than Bible-reading."

The time was early May, and the spring had run long and hot that year, with little rain. The grassy hills beyond the Exeter road showed sere and brittle in the sun, grazed by sheep and wild ponies kicking up the dust. Freed from lessons by the heat, I spent my afternoons aimlessly, scraping at the countryside for amusement. I chased hares, played jousting knight against the cattle, made daring leaps from haylofts, and bathed in the warm oily waters of mossy ponds. I was nine that year, and well-mannered—when it suited me.

"Have you tasted honey fresh from the hive, William Merrick?" the beekeeper asked. He was engaged now in brushing another comb. Bees clung to his arm, the feather, his helmet.

"No, sir."

"Come here, then."

I shifted on my feet. I was yet damp from my bathing and the shirt clung to my narrow, knobby chest. A bee, I knew, had thirst like any other creature's.

"Are you afraid?"

I nodded, and hung back.

He laughed. "That's a good lad. A little fear is not a bad thing when working with the bees. But there's fear and there's panic, y'know. Calm is what matters to the bees. Calm without fear is a peril, and fear without calm doubly so. But the man who can hold both at once within his breast will not be harmed. Do you believe me, William Merrick?"

"You are the honey-man, sir, and ought to know."

He grunted in satisfaction. "Good, good. Then there's something remarkable I wish to show you."

He replaced the skep on its platform and picked up the bucket of honeycombs. "Come along, then, if you're not too frightened."

He started down the hillside toward a gathering of barns and out-houses in the fields below. Curious now, I followed, skirting the little village of hives, yet keeping a distance from the beekeeper, too, as his clothes and bucket still shed strays at every swing of his arm. In a minute, we had reached his honey house, as he called it. He placed the bucket inside and peeled off the wicker helmet and shawl. His grey-black hair was matted and tussled like a wren's nest atop his head.

"There comes a time," he said to me, "when bees, like men, must set out to try their fortunes in a new place. And, like men, they can easily be led. Or misled. Do you understand my words, boy?"

Impatient as I was with this didactic way of speaking—and ea-ger to see the promised amazement, which I hoped might be some horrible, dead thing—I asked him: "Will you tell me next that men, like bees, can sting?"

He looked up sharply. But then, deciding my answer had no scorn in it, he merely shook his head. He shed his gloves and tossed them upon the hot yellow straw. Then he took from his pocket a few balls of beeswax. After first kneading them soft, he pushed them into his hair-clogged ears and nostrils. "You're a clever boy, William Mer-rick," he muttered—somewhat incomprehensibly, with his nose so stuffed. "Mind you don't overvalue your cleverness. To the soul it can be killing as the canker to the rose."

He beckoned me round the corner of the honey house. Again I followed, until we came upon an apple tree in the yard. It hummed like a church choir, and its limbs seemed as if wrapped up in a kind of furry pelt—which I recognized all at once, and with a start, as a swarm of bees, unhived, clinging to a joint in the boughs.

I stopped cold, but the old man went on toward the tree. As I watched, he reached into the seething mass and slowly pulled away an object—a small cage or box that had hung there by a leather strap.

"The queen," said he, as he slung the box round his own neck, bees and all, and took a few steps from the tree.

He turned to face me. " 'Tis simple as a proverb: They follow the object of their desire."

I looked on, astonished, as a cloud of bees rose from the apple tree. They moved across the intervening space, gathering then on the old man's aproned chest, his blown cheeks and stubbled chin. I gasped, seeing the future content of all my midnight horrors there before me, but the beekeeper only gave a nod.

"The calmness, William Merrick," said he, draped in that shawl of blind, teeming life. "You must learn the calmness, and thus conquer the fear."

I put a hand to my dry lips and—sighing—fainted dead away.

SEPTEMBER

PRIMARY

OFFERINGS

CHAPTER I

IN SEPTEMBER OF THE YEAR 169-, I, William Tobias Merrick—twenty years old and possessed of more sense and education than prospects—was sent from my father's house at Exeter to live with my bachelor uncle, a prominent wine merchant of Wapping, near London. It was thought that I, being the fourth son in a family whose brickworks would only comfortably support three, might learn something there of the shipping trade, my uncle's connexions in this area being quite extensive. Neither my father nor my uncle saw fit to consult me in this matter. Having assumed that any young man should welcome the chance to work amid great seagoing ships, they regarded my opinions as settled beforehand. Thus it never came into their consideration that I disliked the sea above all things, and had once resolved, during an intolerable bark crossing from Cardiff to Portishead some years past, never to set foot on the boards of a ship again.

Wapping—as viewed from the horse cart sent to fetch me upon my arrival day—seemed a foul and smoky place. Ships of all sizes lined the blackstone wharves along the Thames, groaning under rank-smelling cargoes of charcoal, wool, indigo, tea, and all else imaginable that a seaworthy craft might hold. The high street, such as it was then, was thronged with a considerable array of humanity—watermen and sailmakers, lightermen and coopers, not to mention members of the other trades, both respectable and not, associated with large river ports. As one reared amid the quiet lanes of Exeter, I knew at once there would be novelties here to fill a year of idle Sundays. And see them I would. Suspecting my uncle to be a man much engaged in his business—and one who might regard his obligations to me as more sentimental than actual—I anticipated his having but little time for my supervision. Thus did I hope to be left largely to my own devices, free to set off into the streets and there occupy myself in the manner of any young man new to the city and eager to take a Dutchman's draught of life—that is, I would take myself to the coffee-houses and the theatres and the taverns, though without much idea of what precisely I would find there.

I was at this time a healthy, energetic fellow—well-made but slender in form, restless in manner yet still more so in my thoughts and aspirations. Through my father's generosity, I had conducted early studies with my home tutor and at the Rev. Charles Tuffley's school in Exeter, though it was no one's true expectation that I should pursue a clerical preferment. For I was victim to what my father called an *Excess of Animal Spirits*, and it was quite apparent to all that life in a Devonshire vicarage would hardly be consonant with my nature. I fancied myself in any case a *Deist* (much to the Rev. Tuffley's dismay), and would probably have refused a bishopric at three thousand a year if one had been offered me. Nor, however, was I any more usefully engaged during a year at Trinity College, Cambridge, where the tutors could speak of naught but Plato and like ancients, for which I had but little patience. Why, I would wonder aloud, if there be a *Form* in Heav'n for every thing we spy on earth, how is there money? Money is for buying what one has not, for filling a perceived lack, so how can there be money in a realm where all is completeness and perfection? To this my Cambridge tutors had no answer but scorn. And so I did not thrive at university, and was soon sent down. I returned to Exeter, where I remained a year before being sent on to my uncle at Wapping. But this last proved all to the best, inasmuch as I had another design—one that rendered my residence in Wapping, so short a distance from the City of London, exceedingly desirable to me. For I, William Tobias Merrick, had every hope of making my living not by the shipping trade, but by what seemed to me the only adventurous profession available to a man of intelligence and enterprise but little fortune—*viz*, as a *Stockjobber*.

'Twas my old friend, cousin, and occasional home tutor, Joshua Dooling, who had planted this seed in my breast. He it was who gave me the true education of my youth, introducing me to the joyous intricacies of what was then called *Dutch finance*—that new, uncharted world of notes and shares and annuities, of lotteries, bearer bonds, Refuses, and Puts—which was only then taking hold in and around the Royal Exchange in London. At no small expense to himself, Josh had sent to him at Exeter a commercial periodical, the *Collection for the Improvement of Husbandry and Trade*, published by a Mr. John Houghton, apothecary and coffee trader of London. Upon its twice-weekly arrival, my cousin and I would leave off our dull studies of figures or Greek to scrutinize this treasure-filled publication, poring especially over the Actions of joint-stock companies and their prices, until the pages wore thin between our fingers. The familiar names of these companies became a kind of incantation with us—*Hudson's Bay, Lustring, Blue Paper*—and each evening, as we sat in my father's parlour before a dappling fire, we would calculate and recalculate the value of our holdings. "Marry, William!" Josh might say. "The Derby I purchased last week at fifty-five pounds stands now at sixty-five and more. I warrant I have outdone every jobber in the City this day!" Of course, these wondrous gains (and our equally wondrous, though more infrequent, losses) were wholly of the imagination, for we two together had not a groat in the world. And yet the excitement of our manoeuvrings was hardly diminished by this fact. For Josh and I fancied ourselves among the New Men of England, in spirit if not yet in fact. We understood well the most important lesson of the time—namely, that the real wealth of Englishmen would henceforth derive not from the actual doing and making of *Things*, nor from the owning and exploiting of *Lands*, but rather from the buying and selling of *Prospects* and *Risks*.

Thus my eagerness upon arriving at Wapping, some scant few years after being introduced into these mysteries. What I had heretofore only read and talked about with my tutor was suddenly present before my very eyes. Nor was I alone in my excitement. All of London, it seemed, was in thrall to this new religion of finance. And why should it not be so? A century of strife and hardship—of civil war and plague, of fire and the threat of Popish treachery—was coming to an end. That old devil King James had shown his cloven foot and packed off to France, where just another double-dealing Catholic rogue would hardly be noticed. King William was upon the throne, and subject to a great Compromise that would henceforth keep the nation's finances safe from the meddling of overbearing monarchs. *Stability* and *Toleration* were the game now, leaving any man free to prosper by his wits—or else to perish by the lack of them. And there was little doubt in my own mind to which fate I was destined.

All of this, however, was still but hearsay to me on that September afternoon when first I arrived on my uncle's doorstep at Wapping. My portmanteau having been deposited (by a rather supercilious young footman) in my garret room at the top of the house, I was immediately conducted across the courtyard to the private offices of the warehouse. Here Mr. Gilbert Hawking, my uncle, sat deeply engaged in a bill of lading. This impressive figure—a severe, hatchet-faced gentleman who wore a chestnut periwig as large as a Dartmoor lamb—rose from behind his massive desk as I entered. "Nephew," said he, "I've not seen you these dozen years. You are quite changed, I see."

"And 'twould be a sorry thing indeed if it were otherwise, Uncle."

"Hrmph," said he, looking somewhat abashed. "I see your point, sir."

Fearing that I had offended him (for giving offence is, I own, a tendency in my behaviour), I quickly added, "But though I was not yet seven years old when last we met, when my dear mother was buried, I can say that you yourself have changed but little. Still the hale and prosperous gentleman of old, unless appearances deceive."

This seemed to mollify him. He shook his artificial locks in gruff satisfaction. "More prosperous than hale, I'm afraid, and not enough of either for my taste." He gestured toward a stool across from him. "Though one must recall that 'twas Capua that corrected Hannibal."

I stopped. "I do not understand you, sir."

"Oh, 'tis an *Expression*, merely an *Expression*. 'Tis meant to say that luxury will be the ruin of one. I trust you are familiar with Hannibal, and are aware that his star began to fall only after tasting the luxuries of Capua?"

"Indeed, I see," said I, not seeing at all, but taking the seat he offered.

After exchanging a few observations regarding the weather in Devonshire and the soundness of various family members, my uncle turned to the immediate business at hand. "Now," said he, patting the account books strewn across the desk before him, "as you are indeed the son of my dear deceased sister, I am well pleased to be in a position to do something for you." Here he removed a tortoiseshell snuff-box from his waistcoat, snapped open the lid, but then merely fingered the clasp in thought. "And yet I believe 'twould be doing you no service to molly-coddle you like some . . . some soft-cheeked niece. I expect toil and effort from you, sir. By which I mean that you must work for your supper, though it be served on your uncle's table."

"I would not have it otherwise, sir," I lied. Then, compounding the lie, "I am no stranger to hard work. And I warrant you will find me as eager a clerk—"

"*Under*-clerk," he interrupted me.

I gave a small bow of my head. "As eager an *under*-clerk as you will find anywhere."

"Very good," said he. "For 'tis only meet and right that you begin small. Granted, others who do not share your advantages must undergo a long apprenticeship before advancing further. But a young man of your family and education (incomplete though the latter may be) follows a different path." He peered up at me then. "Pray do not think yourself above the position of *under*-clerk, however. There is much for you to learn in that capacity. And you must not look to correct *Magnificat* before you learn *Te Deum*."

I narrowed my eyes in confusion. "Another *Expression*, sir?"

"Yes, yes," he said impatiently. "Meaning that you must gain experience and qualifications before you can advance to greater things. You see the sense of the adage?"

"Yes, Uncle."

"Good." He took his portion of snuff finally and grimaced. "You must remember, Nephew, that you are in London now, and in London a man must put himself upon his own legs; no one else will do it for him. 'Tis a city brimming with opportunities, for the man resourceful enough to take advantage of them."

"So I have heard it observed, Uncle. And it will be my goal to prove myself that kind of man."

"Having said that, however," he continued, not really heeding my answers, "I must also warn you that there are temptations to *Sin* and *Wickedness* at every turn in the metropolis. 'Tis all too easy to succumb. Thus you will do well to remember that, in Trade particularly, a good name is better than a golden girdle."

"Sir?"

He sighed. "Good name—surely you understand that. And golden girdle?"

I shook my head.

"By the Lord Harry, sir! Think of it as saying . . . oh, 'tis better to have a spotless reputation than an estate of forty thousand pounds, or the like."

"Ah, that is indeed good advice, Uncle."

He eyed me carefully, as if wondering within himself if I were an idiot. "Have you any money?" he enquired of me then.

"My father was good enough to send me off with a gift of fifty guineas, sir."

"Strange. In his letter he makes it out to be a hundred."

I gave a little cough. "I meant to say, sir, that I have but fifty remaining, my expenses *en route* being greater than anticipated."

He nodded—with vague approval, I thought—having perhaps settled to my advantage the question of my idiocy. "Then I will provide you with a little against your first year's earnings. Your clothes, if I may say so, are not of the London style. And you will find that a man is oft judged here by the quality of his breeches." He pulled a bell cord behind him. "You begin your *under*-clerkship in one week's time," said he. "In the meanwhile, you will have the names of a few merchants in the City who will welcome your custom as my nephew. Unless you wish to remain a clerk for the rest of your days, I would suggest a few fashionable coats; a frock, say; a number of waistcoats of silk; a half-dozen pairs of cloth and leather breeches; stockings, of course; a pair or two of passable buckled shoes, a few hats, and some fine ruffled shirts and neckcloths: also a dozen cambric handkerchiefs. Eventually, a new periwig or two, though that perhaps can wait. Oh, and a small sword, of course—the sharper the better—which you would do well to carry on your person at all times. Do not expect your current ready money, of *whatever* summe, to go as far as you expect in meeting these expenses."

The sneering footman entered the room again, and I understood that the interview was at an end.

"Welcome to London, Nephew," my uncle said then, abruptly, before turning back to his accounts.

❦

THIS WAS NOT, you may say, the warmest welcome ever received by a young man arriving in a strange household. And yet, despite all, I was not much discouraged by this somewhat brusque reception. For I had learned early in life that 'tis better to understand a man than be loved by him, the benefits and disadvantages accruing to oneself being more predictable in the former case. And though my uncle could not be said to overflow with *Bonhomie*, I had come to London in search of fortune, not family. And besides, I soon discovered that my uncle's household was not entirely devoid of readily affectionate natures. For there was employed there someone who, it would seem, took an immediate liking to me, though for what reason I cannot imagine.

I met this woman—the housekeeper of the place, Mrs. Popper—upon leaving my uncle's offices and making for my chamber to settle in. She stood in the passage before my door, scolding a young maid for some infraction concerning the state of my bed linens. As I approached, they both fell suddenly silent.

"Be off now, Mary," the older woman said, casting a wary eye on me.

"If you please, ma'am, and *sir*," said the girl—(By gad, she was a pretty thing!)—before curtseying and scuttling past me down the stair.

"You'll be Mr. Merrick now, I think," the woman said, folding her plump red hands upon her apron. She had a pleasant, owlish face and a *Corporeal Architecture*, so to speak, of such grandeur that it might have been the work of the famous Wren himself. "My name is

Popper, Mrs. Florence Popper. I am housekeeper and cook here. And if there's aught amiss in your arrangements, it's me you'll be seeing to correct it."

"Mrs. Popper, a pleasure to make your acquaintance," said I, bowing low in the cramped passage. "Though I must own that, judging by what I've seen thus far of the household, we may never speak again if it's only complaints I may bring to you."

She scowled. "You've a pretty tongue in you, I see. More's the pity. But I thank you for saying so. 'Tis not often I hear a compliment within these walls."

"*That*, Mrs. Popper, is something I shall endeavour to change without delay."

She clucked her tongue, though I could see that I had pleased her. "Is that the way the young blades speak in Exeter these days, sir? I would have doubted it."

"I flatter myself, Mrs. Popper, that I am not the average young blade from Exeter."

"Well," said she, "you'd do best to save that manner of speaking for the young ladies, where it might do you some good. Men are apt to find it mocking, and punish you for it." She gestured toward the door of my garret. "We've begun unpacking your portmanteau, though I thought you might wish to do it yourself. Some gentlemen, I know, are most particular about their clothing."

"Not I, for my uncle has just now informed me that I must toss out my country clothes and buy new, if I am to have any prospect of success in London. So your maids may be sure of having some Exeter waistcoats with which to polish the banisters."

"Did Mr. Hawking say that, truly?"

"He did. Though I must confess that at times I understand a Gypsy soothsayer more readily than I do my uncle."

At this she let out a stifled gasp of merriment, having herself, perhaps, been victim to my uncle's *Expressions*. "Be that as it may,

Mr. Merrick," said she, gathering up her skirts. "What matters most is what is said, not how 'tis said. And mind you, there's many a tippling-house filled with the ruins of men who underestimated your uncle and his like. You'd be well advised not to do likewise."

"Think you so?" I asked playfully.

Mrs. Popper regarded me with a chiding air. "I do, Mr. Merrick. I think you'll find there's more to him than meets the eye. Or the ear." She resettled her bonnet upon her head. "But now I've work to attend to, and I'm quite sure you have other things to do besides flattering old women, so I'll wish you good day, sir. Please ring if there's aught we've neglected, and I'll have Alfred or Mary see to it at once."

And at this the good woman turned—a manoeuvre of some logistical sophistication, given the close quarters—and unsteadily descended the stair.

⬥

THAT EVENING, as the sun lay low above the glistening waters of the Thames beyond my windows, Uncle Gilbert called me from my garret and bade me follow him across the courtyard to his warehouse. This building, he informed me, was where I was to serve as his *under-*clerk, until such time as I proved myself worthy of better things. The warehouse, a fine brick structure backing directly onto the wharves, was not idle even at this late hour, a heavy-laden argosy from abroad having arrived that very afternoon. Lightermen and dockers of every description—including a few formidable-looking *Blackamoors*—were relieving the ship of its cargo, which consisted of scores of casks and barrels filled, my uncle said, with the cheapest palatable vintage of Madeira he could find. Since this cargo would have to be reloaded onto barges to pass through the legal quays in the shallows upriver, there seemed a certain futility to this rush of activity. And yet the trade must have been profitable enough. For indeed, looking around myself then, I must confess to a certain amazement at the extent of my uncle's commercial interests. Though I'd known him to be a rich man, I had not, till now, comprehended quite how rich. But this one cargo alone seemed enough to bring him a huge profit, the like of which would keep a country squire in plate and carriages for some time.

He introduced me to several of the clerks about the place, as well as to one or two of his factors and partners, who hovered about the casks like mother guinea fowl fretting over their unhatched brood. He also presented to me one Angus McTeague, his overseer, directly under whom I was to serve. This McTeague was a broad-shouldered, shockingly red-faced man with a set of grey teeth as wild and broken as a Saxon ruin. He seemed a friendly-enough fellow, and appeared quite calm and reasonable while conversing with my uncle and myself. But nary a few seconds of civilized conversation would pass between us without his excusing himself suddenly to upbraid one of the passing dockers—and with a vehemence that would have brought blushes to the foulest-mouthed oyster-wife in Billingsgate. Still more remarkable was the fact that my uncle seemed deaf, or at least well-inured, to these outbursts, allowing each *Verbal Paroxysm* to pass unheeded. Thus did our conversation proceed in fits and starts: "I trust, sir," McTeague would say, "that you'll be wantin' Mr. Merrick here to assist . . . excuse me, sirs—*Heigh, thou scurvy gowk there! Look sharp, thou seething, pox-faced gubbin, lest I give thee such a taste of the rope's end as th'alt not soon forget!*—and, as I say, to assist in the monthly castin' of accounts as will answer the purpose of the Customs levy, should such be desired. . . ."

'Twas somewhat unsettling, I thought. Yet I was no fit judge of aught I saw just then, for it was all quite new to me, and I much fatigued from my four days' journey from Exeter. And though it was of considerable interest to me how my uncle ordered his business, I own that my attentions flagged at times. After all, my position in this warehouse was in my mind only temporary—a mere *Stopgap* until I could establish myself in the stockjobber's game. Thus, when after a time my uncle suggested retiring to the house for our evening meal, I was not unwilling to postpone my commercial education for another day.

I followed my uncle's bustling form back across the courtyard to the house. Throwing his hat upon the floor just inside the door, he led me directly to the wood-panelled parlour, where a lavish table had been set out for two. We took seats across from each other, while a pleasant coal fire smouldered in the chest-high hearth. The same disdainful footman (the Alfred of whom Mrs. Popper had spoken earlier) brought in a fine sizzling joint of beef and a capon pie, which, for the next quarter-hour, my uncle and I partook of avidly, washing it all down with a bottle of choice Canary. I own I had not dined in this manner for some time, if ever, and I found myself wondering if all meals in my uncle's house would be so sumptuous.

"So, Nephew," my uncle said after a little time, "what think you of all you've seen thus far? Can you be useful here, do you think?"

"Indeed, sir, I do. Frankly, I am overwhelmed. The warehouse, this house—it leaves me quite speechless. I think my mother would have been well pleased by her brother's success."

He made no secret of his gratification at this last observation. According to the family lore, my mother, his youngest sister, had been his favourite. " 'Tis true my business prospers, while that of many another does not." He took a sip of wine. "Times are yet difficult for some. Like Daniel Foe, a hosier of my acquaintance, who was declared a bankrupt some years ago—owing me a hundred pounds, I might add—though the man's a blockhead and hardly typical." He paused to top up his glass and my own. "But no, there is too much wealth in the city now for anyone with sense to go a-begging. Uncertainty abroad keeps merchant capital at home, where it must needs be put to use. So it makes its way to 'Change Alley, where many now find themselves enriched. You need only look at what is happening to the districts west of the city, in what they now call the *West End*. What once was open fields is now sprouting mansions and terraced houses like so many mushrooms, catering for gentry and wealthy tradesmen alike. Mark me, soon there will be but one continuous sea of brick and masonry from Whitechapel to Westminster and beyond."

"And yet, Uncle," I felt obliged to observe, "here in Wapping I see a few fine houses, but many more less-than-fine."

He made a disgusted wave of his hand. " 'Tis true, 'tis true. For though it can be said that a rising tide lifts all boats, a *Leaky Skiff* will scrape bottom no matter what the tide."

"I understand you perfectly, Uncle," I said, with no small relief.

"I'Faith, the eastern portion of the metropolis is becoming home to more than its share of leaky skiffs. I fear I am getting out none too soon."

"Getting out?"

"I have yet to mention to you, Nephew, that I will be moving house to this same *West End* before long. A residence is being completed for me even as we speak, in a place called the Red Lion Square, the work of Dr. Nicholas Barbon, the builder."

"I see," said I, feeling somewhat light-headed suddenly.

"Ah, I have given you a start. But you must not be alarmed, Nephew. You are as welcome to live under my new roof as under my old, though 'twould be a long journey each day to reach the warehouse. Then again, this house will lie empty, unless and until I convert it to another warehouse. . . ."

"Uncle! You don't mean that I—"

"I was thinking aloud, sir, that is all. We have yet to see what stuff you're made of. Just recall that I can always send you back to your father's house at once, should you give me any cause."

"I will give you no such cause, sir, I swear it!" said I, with genuine heat.

"Excellent," said he. "Then I trust we understand each other."

Waving away a persistent bluebottle, he pushed his chair back from the table and rang the bell. "You will excuse me now, I hope. There is some paperwork that must be attended to before the morning."

Accustomed to the more leisurely pace of meals at Exeter, I must have appeared taken aback by this abrupt end to our supper.

"Are you not finished, Nephew?" he asked.

"I suppose I am."

"So I thought," said he, standing. "For in London, only women and the clergy have time to linger over meals. For a man of business, there is no end to work, as you will soon discover. Good day, sir."

I watched him as he made briskly for the parlour door.

And thus did my first day in London end. After quickly consuming a few extra morsels of the excellent capon, I proceeded to my garret, shed my boots, and spread out upon the fine counterpane that lay atop the bed. And there, looking about myself at the modest chamber that Mrs. Popper had attempted to make cheerful (going so far, I noted, as to place a single Dutch tulip in a delftware flower block upon the windowsill), I could not but feel well pleased with my current circumstances. For I was in London, finally—my *Land of Opportunity*. And it had not escaped my notice that the household I joined that day was a prosperous one, or that my uncle seemed to lack for nothing whatsoever in the world—except, perhaps, an *Heir*.

CHAPTER II

⊙ I WAS BUT ONE OR TWO DAYS at Wapping when first I had opportunity to venture beyond the confines of the port into the greater world of London proper. This was a journey I undertook with some trepidation—as a Musselman must do the *Hadj* to Mecca or Medinah, after dreaming of the place with reverential awe for the greater part of his existence. For such was my sense of anticipation, having discussed the details of life within that square mile of geography with Josh, my tutor, during those years together under my father's roof. Now, however, it was time to give flesh to these schoolboy reveries. And so, although I had yet to replace my supposed bumpkin attire with that of a prosperous London card, I left my uncle's lodgings and steered my steps westward, toward that part of the City of London which served as the financial heart of the nation, and even—Amsterdam be pox't!—the world.

But first I had to find that heart, and this proved more of a task than I'd reckoned upon. For the parishes I traversed *en route* were a perfect bear garden of noise and confusion, such as made even Wapping seem placid as a Cornish churchyard. The narrow streets were rendered near impassable by the crush of tradesmen, housemaids, carriages, horsecarts, hackney coaches, and even, in one hellish alley, a drove of some several hundred gibbering turkeys bound for Leadenhall Market. But the worst obstacle of them all was the street vendors. These last filled the air with their cries and the tolling of their handbells, selling all manner of goods—from brooms and cherries to ballads, old clothing, vinegar, matches, skinned rabbits, and small coal. Oystermongers and curd-sellers thrust their wares under my nose (as did a daggle-tail whore or two), and though there appeared to be honest folk about, the majority seemed to belong to the *Canting Crew* in all its several tribes—that is to say, beggars, cutpurses, vagabonds, and gypsies. Not wishing to seem a country cullion among these knowing types, I adopted a face of unruffled *ennui* as I made my way through the ordure- and offal-choked streets. But whether I succeeded, I know not. For 'twas certain only that more than one fellow with the brand of villain in his looks did seem to regard me with a calculating interest, like a butcher assessing the prize hog at Bartholomew Fair.

'Twas with considerable relief, therefore, that I found myself at last at the confluence of Threadneedle Street, Cornhill, and Lombard Street, where—in the shadow of that clean and noble edifice the Royal Exchange—I stood at the end of 'Change Alley itself. And here did my breath all but leave me. For within, I knew—hidden away amid the winding rows of booksellers, barbers, and tippling houses—were the twin objects of my pilgrimage: namely, *Jonathan's* and *Garraway's*. It was these two coffee-houses that of late had served as London's centers of stockjobbing. These were, in other words, the veritable *Alpha* and *Omega* of the world I longed to be a part of.

Jonathan's it was I came upon first, just a few steps off Cornhill. Pushing my way past a group of leering hang-abouts in the doorway, I entered the crowded coffee-house—and instantly I felt myself at home. For across that busy room from wall to wall were *Men of Finance*—merchants, brokers, and jobbers, Frenchmen, Spaniards, and

Flemings, Jews, Dissenters, and churchmen High and Low—conducting the business of the kingdom. To one side, an auction seemed to be in progress; to the other, a few more private transactions. Here was a lottery-man with his tickets, there an eager-looking merchant peddling a bill of exchange for discount, and over there a wigless, coatless man chalking share prices upon a board for all to see. Men stood about in groups, smoking and murmuring among themselves over a dish of coffee; or else glancing at a *London Gazette* or one of the other journals and pamphlets available for hire from a table at the back. Choking on the fug that seemed to hang in the air like a linen drapery, I picked my way across the room, my intention being to buy me a dish of coffee and observe the goings-on. But try as I might, I could not catch the attention of the young vixen serving the brew. Others—perhaps those known to her—seemed to have little difficulty. They slapped their penny on the board and, in a trice, collected their dish and their pipe. But no amount of shouting or handwaving on my part seemed able to bring the jade to look in my direction. Finally, face red as much from vexation as exertion, I gave it up and turned my back to her.

I watched for some minutes, engrossed in the hum of business about me, before noticing a certain gentleman who appeared to be a focus of attention for many standing about the place. This man, dressed in curiously old-fashioned Puritan garb, sat at a table near the back of the coffee-house, eschewing both coffee and tobacco as he turned from one interlocutor to the next. After each transaction— for such they appeared to be—he would signal to a younger man who sat at his side, a sheaf of papers in his hand, which the latter would consult or scribble into with an eagerness that was most comical to watch. Here, I told myself—if ever I was sure of anything—was a stockjobber and his scrivener. And I did look upon them as a visitor to Virginia or Massachusetts must look upon his first *Red Indians*— with an excitement sharpened by the honing of many previous imaginings. For this was one of the *New Men* himself, one who created wealth from nothing—a magician, a sorcerer, a modern-day alchemist of the markets. And I had ten silver crowns in my purse, just waiting for the touch of the philosopher's stone that would turn them into ten—or a hundred—gold guineas.

I know not how long I watched him there, amid all the noise and bustle of the place. I bethought myself of Josh, still at home in Exeter, and of what he might say if at my side just then. Josh had envied me upon my leaving. "I do wish I could go with you, Will," he'd said to me. "By gad, we'd take the City of London by storm, the two of us together, if it could be so." But, alas, it could not be so, at least not for some years, until he could accumulate enough of my father's money to leave my father's house. In the meanwhile, though, I carried my cousin's teachings with me in my heart, though 'twas poor substitute for his actual company.

Finally, spurred by the image of Josh encouraging me from afar, I screwed my courage up, reset my coat upon my shoulders, and set off across the room toward the supposed jobber, intending to take my first plunge into the world of finance. Pushing through the crowd of men around him, I placed myself beside his chair and, in the best style as gleaned from Houghton's *Collection*, enquired of him, "How go the stocks, sir?"

It seemed a long, silent minute before he turned his eyes toward me. And when at last he did, there seemed nothing but amused contempt in his glance. "You spoke to me, sir?" he asked.

"I did, i'Faith. I enquired of you what shares you have to dispose of." Then, feeling somewhat less certain, I said, "I trust I have not mistook you for something you aren't. We find ourselves in Jonathan's, do we not?"

"We do," said he.

"And are you not the man to see if one would turn a penny in the way of stocks?"

"Is it a penny you have to offer, then?"

Abashed, I continued: "I will not chop logic with you, sir. I have money enough for a share of your likeliest prospect. And I warrant that one man's silver is as good as another's."

"Ah, but there you are wrong, sir. There you are quite wrong." And at this he signalled to a pair of bully-rooks at his elbow. Laughter broke out as they lifted me by the arm-pits and propelled me toward the entrance. Through the door and into the alley they carried me. After tossing me onto a pile of oyster shells, they proceeded to cuff and kick me, cursing me all the while. "Come again and we'll give ye such a chaw-buck as you'll not know yer ears from yer elbows," the taller one cried. Then he threw my hat upon my crumpled figure and the two of them stalked back into the coffee-house.

I lay there a good long while, taking inventory of my pains. They were not extreme, the beating being more of a warning than an attempt to do actual physical harm, but my humiliation was quite real. Passersby stepped over me, clucking their tongues or ignoring me altogether. But not one stopped to aid me in any way—until, that is, a young man, not five years older than myself, emerged from Jonathan's door and crouched there beside me.

"Are you injured?" he asked, gently brushing dust from the shoulders of my coat.

"I'm not a corpus yet," I answered, "unless wounded pride be fatal."

He laughed and then, grabbing my wrists, helped me to my pins. "You'll live then," said he, "though not for long, if you makes a man like Menderlinck your enemy." He was a handsome fellow, with hair and eyes as dark as sea coal, and very well dressed, though his speech seemed to indicate humble origins.

"Menderlinck?" I asked.

"The gent as just 'ad you cast out on yer arse, not to put too fine a point on't."

"So I assume I did wrong in approaching him as I did?"

"Well, you din't do right, as I think should be plain by the cockleshells in yer breeches." He turned more serious then. "Why, you're the young lad from Exeter, I think."

This gave me pause. Were my provincial origins so obvious to all in London? "Yes, in point of fact. I'm Will Merrick, newly arrived in this city. And you are . . . ?"

"Jonathan Petroni, though known to all as Jack. Y'don't recognize me, I see."

"I'm sorry. I can't say that I do."

"I do business with 'imself, yer uncle. You and me, we met t'other night, whilst you was lookin' about the premises, though we din't speak. With a cargo at the wharf, there ain't much time for the social graces."

"Well, we've time for them now," said I, giving him a bow. "I'm very glad to meet you again, though I can think of better circumstances for it. You find me wanting in dignity at the moment, I'm afraid."

"Oh, I don't care a pin's point for a man's dignity, so long as 'e's the right sort."

This seemed quite reasonable for a London man. I thought I might like this Jack Petroni.

" 'Ere, Mr. Merrick, would y'share a glass wi' me, unless you be otherwise engaged?"

"That's an offer I'll not refuse, so long as you agree to call me Will. Have you a place in mind?"

"I knows an ale-monger along the alley—'tis a regular 'ouse of call for me, y'might say—if you be game for't."

"Lead on," said I.

I followed him down the alley, knocking the dust from my hat as I went. In a very few minutes, we reached an establishment that, judging from its sign, bore the name Pig and Whistle. 'Twas a place of no magnificence, but enough to serve the purpose, I supposed.

We entered the busy tavern and besought ourselves a table. No sooner had we sat than a most attractive young woman approached us.

"You're before your time, Jack," said the lass. "Is the business of the alley so slow?"

"I've brought the business 'ere today. Maud, this is a special friend, Will Merrick."

"Special indeed," said she, giving me a wink. Then, to Jack: "What'll it be?"

"The usual, Maud. You likes ale, I take it, Will?"

"I do."

"Two tankards, then, and a pickled egg or two to pique the thirst."

She scurried away and reappeared almost at once with two tankards of tawny ale and a trencher of eggs of an alarming greenish colour. Jack cleared his throat and then lifted his tankard (from which, I noted, there hung a shred of cobweb). "May all be fish that comes to yer net," said he, and we drank. "Ale to yer taste, Will?" Jack asked me then.

"Indeed it is," said I, quite untruthfully. To my tongue, 'twas no better than the belch that Josh and I would drink of a Saturday night in Exeter.

Jack smiled, well pleased by my response. " 'Not for me these fine brews from Flanders. A good ol' English ale is just the same, says I, and not near so dear."

Wishing to move on before I made some comment I'd regret, I said, "So, Jack, you do business with my uncle?"

"A bit," said he. "I come that day to tout the shares of a venture I'm fortunate to represent."

"You're a stockjobber yourself, then?" I enquired of him, aghast.

"Faith, though I don't like the name, I'm that and more, much more. Jobber, broker, banker, man o' business—for the mouse that 'ath but one 'ole is quickly taken. 'Tis always wise, in other words, to play of several games, for then a loss in one or two be not fatal t'yer fortune." He winked. "But I think y'know this, Will, for 'tain't the business of Gilbert 'awking's clerk that betook ye to Jonathan's this day."

"No, I have an enduring fascination with the *Stocks*, and would fain make my fortune by the buying and selling, if 'twere possible."

"And why should it not be possible, 'specially for a man of, shall we say, your advantages? Law, Will, 'tis possible for anyone." He leaned forward over the table toward me. "Know you whence I come?"

"You mean where you were born?"

"I do."

I cast about for a delicate way of answering. His name was Italian in sound, but he spoke like no foreigner. "I cannot, that is to say, I . . ."

"G'wan, Will, 'tain't no secret I shows me colours with every spoken word. But I ain't ashamed. Me dad was a bone-boiler in the awfulest lane o' Spitalfields. I've no education to speak of, 'ceptin' what I give meself. But I've rose above the rag-and-tag, I 'ave, and can play the 'Changes now as well as any man, and better'n most, in me own small way."

This, of course, I had heard before—*viz*, that in the London of the '90s, a man could make his way on merit alone, be he a *Duke* or a *Dogsbody*. So I vowed then and there to mark this man's words. From Jack Petroni, I knew, I had much to learn, no matter how many bones his father might have boiled.

"So 'twas not for lack of breeding that I received such treatment just now?"

"Law, no, Will. For Menderlinck would sell shares to a three-legged bullock if its credit be good. Nay, 'twas merely a matter of not knowin' ye. Like many in the Alley, 'e's not one to do business unless 'e knows what-all 'e's dealin' with, or else you come represented by a broker known to 'im." Jack took a draught of ale and smacked his lips. "But it ain't the likes of Menderlinck you should be seekin' out, anyways. Once you've made yer fortune, 'e's a good man to know. But there's plenty o' ways to turn a penny in 'Change Alley besides the *Greater Fish*."

"The *Greater Fish*?" I asked.

"Aye, yer Bank shares, East India shares, and the like. The great chartered corporations, which is mainly what Menderlinck jobs in."

"How, then, to make a fortune if not by such . . . marine giants, if you will?"

Jack smiled. "Law, there's any number o' ways in times like these. The government funds is one, o'course. Or take the lotteries. It costs a man but a few crowns for a share in a ten-pound ticket, sure to pay a pound per annum for sixteen years, or, if 'e buys the winnin' ticket, a thousand per annum for the same period." Jack rubbed his hands together. "And then, o'course, there be the *Projects*."

"Oh yes, the projects," said I, with much enthusiasm.

"Ahh, you likes the projects, do ya?"

"I do," said I. But this was an understatement, for I had read at length about projects in the *Collection*. 'Twas Josh who had told me of the first great diving project—that of *Captain Phipps*, who raised thirty-two tons of silver from a sunken ship off Hispaniola. After subtracting his own generous portion and that of his men, there was still booty enough to pay each land-based partner in the project a bountiful dividend, enriching them beyond their every expectation. Being but a lad at the time, I was at first transfixed by the romance of diving itself, and spent many an afternoon dreaming of my own descent to the deeps in a clanging metal bell, the fish and sea spinach swirling about my boots as the decks of some long-forgotten galleon emerged from the murk below. I was to be like the mighty Phipps himself (this being before that first discouraging sea crossing of my youth). I imagined myself ranging the waters off Brazil or the Indies, battling privateers and renegade Frenchmen in defence of my treasure. Boy that I was, I still imagined that the real adventure of life was in the *Doing*, rather than in the *Selling* of what was done.

In any case, Phipps was but the first dive projector. For after his triumph there arose in London an uncommon passion for treasure-hunting. Seeing the returns to be made, every man was eager to make his own—not by venturing out onto the sea himself, but by subscribing to the effort of one who would. Thus did grow in the great metropolis a market for *Sea-Scavenging* like nothing ever seen before. "Do you trade, then, in the shares of diving projects?" I asked.

"Nay, not the dive projects, Will, for dives be an old fashion already. Nowadays, the Projects come more varied, y'might say. Step down Birchin Lane this very day and you can purchase shares of a project to make whalebone whips, say, or a *Sucking-Worm Engine*, or special 'orseshoes made from the finest India rubber, guaranteed to improve any nag's speed. There's a project for the manufacture of a new chicken feed that'll improve the taste and texture of the flesh, and one for a mechanical *Wig Curler*, and one for a wondrous cream to prevent wrinkles o' the face (true, 'tis made from the water of Abyssinian goats, but such need not be advertised)." He cackled loud. "Nay, 'tis a country full of *New Ideas*, Will, and for every new idea, good or bad, there be a *Project*."

My excitement at hearing this, as may be imagined, was keen. To deal in such ventures, and at a profit—'twas the very dream that had brought me here! "Marry, Jack, you've whet my appetite profoundly! 'Tis the most enticing thing I've heard in donkey's years!"

"Do y'mean it?" he asked.

"I do, i'Faith!"

He cast a long, appraising look upon me. "I think I knows a place where such enthusiasm might be welcomed. And rewarded." He signalled to Maud, the serving woman. "Tell me, Will, 'ave you an hour free? I've a business proposition to make ye."

"I can think of nothing I would rather hear," said I.

"Good."

Maud appeared at his elbow. "Leaving us so soon, Jack?"

"Business, Maud, business." He rose from the table. "Put this on the account, m'dear. And add the usual for y'self—and not a groat more, mind you."

"As if I'd cheat *you*, Jack," said she. "Very pleased to meet you, Will Merrick." Then, just as we were leaving, the saucebox added, meaningfully, "Feel free to make yourself an *Intimate* of this establishment. We've more on offer than what's scribbled on the chalkboard."

I regarded her, speechless, as she winked again and carried the tankards away.

Jack was outside in the alley when I caught him up. He had already encountered yet another person he knew, and what a sight she was—a splendidly turned-out young woman who wore a fine crimson moiré suit and a velvet emerald cloak, trimmed with point de Venise. She, too, was a handsome thing to look at, and it occurred to me—not for the first time since my arrival—that London was quite as rich in feminine beauty as it was in all things else. But this woman was altogether of a different class than Maud—with a fine bearing and deportment to match her fashionable, if unusual, attire. I fear I must have stared at her in dumb fascination, mouth agape, like a simple Arabian shepherd regarding the Queen of Sheba.

"Miss Fletcher," Jack oozed with somewhat distasteful obsequiousness (and a rather paltry attempt at a more highblown manner of speech), "allow me to present to you Mr. William Merrick. Mr. Merrick is newly arrived in London, 'aving come to live with 'is uncle, a man I think you know—Mr. Gilbert Hhh-awking?"

"Indeed, I am acquainted with your uncle, Mr. Merrick. Good afternoon to you."

"And to you, Miss Fletcher," said I, breathless at this vision before me.

"Miss Fletcher, if I may say so, does 'er part for the *Less Fortunate* of the City," Jack went on. "While us men concern ourselves only with increasin' our fortunes, we're blessed to 'ave ladies like Miss Fletcher to look after the poor souls as are left behind."

"You flatter me, Mr. Petroni," Miss Fletcher said, with obvious impatience. "This was undoubtedly your intention. But I'm afraid I must hurry on. The owner of this tavern has promised a Sunday dinner for those poor souls, as you call them. I am already behind time for my appointment with him."

"Then we'll not be keepin' you, Miss Fletcher," he said, lifting his hat.

She nodded once to me and—rolling her eyes in mock exasperation so that only I could see—made for the tavern, kicking aside a burst cabbage in her path with a surprising ferocity.

"A fine woman, that," Jack said thoughtfully.

I could not but agree, and made it a point to remember her name.

"A bit too . . . *brazen*, some would say," Jack added, contemplating the cabbage in the gutter. "But never mind that. Let's be off now. The hour's late."

"Where are we bound, then?" I enquired of him.

"Not far," said he. "Just follow me." And, pushing through the crowds to Cornhill again, he hailed a hackney coach.

CHAPTER 3

WE GOT INTO A TAXI on the corner of Wall Street and Broadway. Jack gave the driver an address on East 23rd Street and then sat back, giving me that appraising look again while a recorded greeting by Judd Hirsch welcomed me to New York and reminded me to buckle my seat belt for my own safety.

"So what's your business proposal?" I asked Jack.

"Hold on till we get there, Will. I got a whole dog-and-pony show for you up at my place." He loosened his tie, then pulled out a cell phone and started making short, enigmatic phone calls for the rest of the trip.

We got out in front of a nondescript apartment building on 23rd just off Lexington. As we stepped into the mirrored elevator, Jack continued talking on his cell phone—until the doors closed and the signal apparently faded. Sighing, he put the tiny instrument away, saying nothing more until we got off at the eighteenth floor and headed toward the end of the hallway.

"The cleaning lady comes tomorrow, so it might be a pit," Jack said, turning three keys in their locks. When he finally got the door open, I followed him into the apartment. An anemic-looking dog—a greyhound, the rib cage plainly visible under its glossy gray coat—pranced up to us, whimpering and sniffing at our legs. "It's too early for a walk, you stupid animal," Jack said fondly as he punched a code into the alarm console next to the door.

I looked around the apartment. It was anything but a pit—cream-leather couch and chairs, a few Turkish-looking rugs, and big windows looking out toward the East River. It wasn't the kind of Upper East Side luxury my Uncle Gilbert was planning for himself, perhaps, but still pretty nice for a twenty-five-year-old *paisan* from the Bronx.

"Take a load off," Jack said, shucking off his suit jacket and tossing it onto a chair. "What do you want? I got all kinds of scotch, bourbon, champagne, whatever."

"Actually, I'll take some champagne, if you'll join me. I feel like celebrating."

Jack nodded approvingly. "I like your attitude," he said, and headed toward the kitchen.

I stepped into the living room and sat down on one of the leather armchairs, facing a built-in mahogany bookshelf stuffed with the most comprehensive collection of *Star Wars* novelizations I'd ever seen. The greyhound hopped onto the couch and, breathing fast, stared at me with a reproachful look on its face.

I heard a pop from the kitchen, and then Jack came in with two tall flutes in one hand and a bottle of—this surprised me, though I suppose it shouldn't have, given the fact that he had taken me to a Shamrock Tavern downtown—one of those cheap Spanish "champagnes" in the other. He poured and then handed me a glass. "Down the hatch," he said, and we both drank.

"Isn't this where you're supposed to bring out the cocaine and the five-hundred-dollar ladies of the evening?" I asked, then instantly worried—my smart mouth again—that I might have offended him. But he just laughed.

"Nah, that self-destructive, conspicuous-consumption crap is ancient history. The '80s was about glamour; the '90s is about twenty-year-olds in their underwear at computers, making millions." He gazed at the rising bubbles in his glass before continuing. "Nothing should distract from business, is what *I* say. So I do what's necessary to keep up appearances—the suit, the apartment—but anything that doesn't show on the outside, I go bargain basement." He got up and retrieved a box from a sideboard. "You smoke cigars?"

I didn't—in fact, I'd never smoked anything except the obligatory Marlboros behind the garage during adolescence—and didn't really want to start now. "Not usually. Are they Cuban?" I asked, though I already knew the answer to that one.

"Yeah, right, at eight bucks a pop? Nah, the Cohibas I save for when I want to impress somebody, no offense. These I get at the newsstand next to the Duane Reade." He unwrapped two cigars, then handed one to me. As he lit it for me, the greyhound's look of disapproval seemed to intensify.

"Very nice," I lied, rolling the foul smoke around my tongue. Then I asked: "What's your dog's name?"

"Jonathan Swift."

"I beg your pardon?"

"Ah," he said, making a dismissive gesture with the cigar, "my old girlfriend gave him that name. An English major in college. She said it was ironic, seeing as he's a greyhound."

"I'm not sure 'ironic' is the right word—"

"Veronica was *her* name. Get this: She was ten times better-educated and better-looking than me, and *I* dumped *her*. Now *that's* ironic." He leaned forward and rolled a lozenge of ash into a square silver ashtray. "Listen, Will, let me ask you a question. You said back at the bar that you came to New York to work on Wall Street. How serious are you about that?"

"What do you mean?"

"I mean, you don't just decide to become an investment banker, then cruise into Goldman Sachs and start pulling down seven figures overnight. You understand, right, that it takes money to make money, and that you gotta earn small before you earn big?"

"You sound like my uncle. In my first conversation with him he told me I've got to 'learn box-step before I can watusi.' That's why he's starting me off as a glorified gofer, he says."

"Well, he's right, Will, he's absolutely on the money. As a businessman, your uncle knows his way around the block. He took a little wine business and built it into the biggest gourmet wholesaler in the city. Granted, he was a little slow to catch on to the whole Web thing, but he's tryin' to make up for lost time now. Thanks, in part, to me."

"To you?"

"Your uncle has a boatload of capital, but it's all dressed up and nowhere to go. I show him where to put it."

"You mean he's a venture capitalist now?"

"Not officially, no. He's more what we call an 'angel investor.' The wholesale business practically runs itself these days, so he's got his finger in some other shit, like everybody else these days." He took a long suck on the cigar and then shot a stream of smoke toward Jonathan Swift. "But I'll clue you in on all this later. Right now I want you to tell me a little something about yourself."

"Like what?"

"Like college, for instance. You go?"

Tough question to start with. "Well, yes. I went to Northwestern. For a year."

"Just a year? What happened?"

"I dropped out. Not because I was failing or anything like that. I just didn't feel that what I was learning was . . . well, relevant to anything important." I looked up at him. "Does that disqualify me?"

"You're kiddin' me, right? At my end of the game, a guy needs college the way a snake needs work boots." He cackled at his own turn of phrase, which he had clearly used many times before. "So come on. Keep it comin'—tell me about your family, your hometown, whatever."

"Well, I grew up in Indiana, just outside Bloomington. Big family—three brothers and two sisters. I'm right in the middle, younger than my brothers, older than my sisters."

"What's your father do?"

"He owns his own business. Merrick Construction Materials Inc."

"Successful?"

"Very successful, actually. At least he did well enough to join the local country club and send his children to private school."

"Annual revenues?"

"Of the business, you mean? I have no idea."

He nodded contemplatively, taking this in. "So why didn't you stay in Bloomington and work in Daddy's business?"

"My three brothers did exactly that, so I asked myself what would the prospects be for me, the fourth? Even if the company turned into the Microsoft of the construction materials industry, I could never hope to be anything more than VP in Charge of Stucco and Brickface, if you know what I mean."

"So your Uncle Gil offered you a job."

"Exactly. Not that I'm any more interested in selling wine and cheese than I am in selling bricks. But I figured it would at least get me to New York. Within striking distance of Wall Street."

Jack nodded. He took a pen out of his shirt pocket and wrote something on a pad in front of him. Feigning nonchalance, I squinted to see what he'd written, but it seemed to be in some kind of hieroglyphics. "So how'd you get interested in the stock market?" he asked then.

"My cousin Josh. He was the one who got me started, at least.

He lived with us when I was growing up. Talk about irony—the guy was always hard up for cash, but that didn't stop him from subscribing to the *Wall Street Journal,* which must have cost him . . . what? Four hundred dollars a year? He was also the first person I knew who went online. Used to get stock quotes from CompuServe, back when CompuServe was the online service of choice."

"And so you and Josh had Wall Street fantasies together?"

"I guess you could call it that. We followed the movement of specific stocks and corporate bonds, even though we didn't know much about the companies behind them. We'd come up with mock portfolios and compete against each other—you know, see who was first to make an imaginary million dollars? I won, just about every time."

Jack seemed satisfied with what he was hearing. "I had this feeling about you, the minute I saw you," he said. He leaned forward on the couch then and stubbed out his cigar. "You ever hear of Pembroke Horton?"

"Um, no, should I have?"

"No." He got up and pulled out a drawer in a little desk by the window. "Here, look these over," he said, tossing some brochures onto the coffee table. Then he walked over to the VCR and inserted a videotape.

The tape began with an MTV-style montage of scenes from industry and finance—factories humming, ships being unloaded, a motherboard assembly line, a biotech lab, the floor of the New York Stock Exchange, etc.—backed by a noisy soundtrack of shouting traders, planes taking off, various electronic chirps and beeps. Then a deep, Columbia School of Broadcasting voice intoned: "Pembroke Horton, Making the Future Doable." I sat back and put a pillow behind me, trying not to grimace. What followed was a slick, over-produced infomercial for the firm, outlining its various divisions—securities underwriting, IPOs, brokerage services, M&A—illustrated with more montages, this time of suits, boardrooms, trading floors, and plenty of charts, all of them trending upward. It ended with total silence and a black screen, followed by three words flashed in succession: Experience; Expertise; Service. Then, the company logo, and static.

Afterwards, as the tape was rewinding, Jack asked me, "Sound like someplace you could work?"

"Absolutely," I said, trying to be polite. "It sounds like a top-drawer outfit. Solid and respectable."

"Yeah, well, Street Lesson Number One—discount for a certain bullshit quotient in the promotional materials."

"You mean—"

"It's a legitimate investiment firm, but in terms of prestige, it's no Merrill Lynch or Salomon Smith Barney, let alone Goldman. But people go for the whole wingtip-and-Armani crap, so that's what you give 'em. But if they're lookin' for a banker or broker to take 'em to lunch at the Harvard Club, well, they got the wrong house."

"And you work for them?"

"Sort of yes, sort of no. I have dealings with one of the guys over there—Ted Witherspoon, the number two guy in their retail brokerage arm—and sometimes I send good people his way. He's got openings right now for broker trainees. You interested?"

I had really come to New York to be a trader rather than a broker, and Pembroke Horton didn't sound like the classiest outfit to work for, but I knew enough not to let this opportunity get away from me. It was a beginning, after all. "Definitely," I said.

"How will you swing it with your job at Hawkings?"

"I'll figure something out. I don't have to start there for another week or so."

"Yeah, well, don't burn any bridges, is my advice to you. Tell your uncle you can only work nights for him because you want to take a bookkeeping course or something. Then you can do both jobs at the same time. With this economy, you don't want to close off any way to make an extra buck, seein' as you can turn that buck into two or three more with no trouble at all."

"I'll find a way," I said.

"Good." He gave me a card with a Wall Street address on it. "I'll make the arrangements with Ted. You just show up here next Monday morning at eight-thirty and ask for Melissa. She'll take it from there."

⌘

I WAS LATE getting back to the brownstone on Charlton Street. My uncle stood in the living room as I came in, fussing with his gold watch and looking agitated. "Fifty-five minutes after dinnertime, Will," he said. My uncle wore disapproval like an overcoat, wrapping himself up in it with obvious pleasure. "I went ahead and ate without you. In this house, young man, we value punctuality."

"Sorry, Uncle Gil," I said. "Subway delay."

"New York subway trains break down. Factor it into your scheduling." He picked up a newspaper and shooed me away with it. "Go now. Florence has dinner in the oven for you. Eat it quickly and then get dressed."

"Dressed?"

"Yes, dressed." He looked me up and down with a bony finger on his lips. "I've had Florence bring up one of my old suits from the basement. It should be a decent fit, though you're probably thinner than I ever was."

I was confused. "But what am I getting dressed *for*?"

"For the *opera*, William," he said, as if speaking to a particularly obtuse child. "We're going to the opening of *Der Rosenkavalier* at the Met. Make sure you're ready by seven oh five." Then, muttering to himself, he left the room.

Mrs. Popper came in and asked, "Are you ready for your dinner?"

"I guess I am, Mrs. P. But this is the first I've heard about going to an opening. Does my uncle always take his new employees to the opera?"

Mrs. Popper wiped her dimpled red hands on her apron. "Humor him. He has his ways."

I quickly devoured what Mrs. Popper had prepared (spicy red snapper, cauliflower polonaise, and an Asian pear Waldorf salad—the woman was a gem) and then ran upstairs to my room. An impeccable dove-gray Hickey-Freeman suit, along with an off-white linen shirt and a Hermès silk tie, had been set out on my bedspread. I dressed quickly and was pleased to find the suit an almost perfect fit. Looking at myself in the full-length mirror was something of a revelation. The figure in the glass was unmistakably a New Yorker, and a New Yorker of some consequence. I put my hand to my ear, cellphonically, and said, "Four thousand shares of Cisco, at the market. And do it *now!*"

"Well, well," Mrs. Popper cooed when I arrived downstairs. She tugged at my collar and then reset the jacket more squarely on my shoulders. "Nobody would ever guess that this suit wasn't made for you."

"I feel like Eliza Doolittle in *My Fair Lady*," I said. "You think I look natural in clothes like this?"

"You will," she answered, as she pushed me toward the front room.

At 7:05 exactly, my uncle appeared, very dapper himself in a sober navy suit. He had a look at me. "It'll do, it'll do," he said, pulling my tie a little tighter. Then, grabbing a white silk scarf from the chair, he rushed out the front door, scarf ends flapping behind him.

We flagged a cab on Varick and got in. After enduring another message of welcome from another New York celebrity (someone named Joe Franklin this time, sounding as if he were speaking from inside a small tin box), my uncle asked, "Do you like opera, Will?"

I considered lying, but I'd been doing a little too much of that since coming to the city. So I just said, as unassumingly as possible, "Not really."

"Well," he said with a sigh, "neither do I. Nobody does, except maybe one or two gay people here and there, and they only *really* like Bizet and the Italians." He pulled the tickets out of his jacket pocket and checked them. "Tonight is Richard Strauss. *Fin de siècle* Germanic in spirit, which means it's going to be slow and lush and world-weary, unlike the current *fin de siècle*. By the way, falling asleep is acceptable—it implies hard work and a frantic schedule—but snoring is emphatically not."

I nodded. "Sleeping okay, snoring not. Check."

"And don't ever, *ever*, say anything about the performance. Still waters run deep, you know." Then, catching himself, he said, "In other words, you can't make a fool of yourself if you maintain a studious and suggestive silence."

"I *know* the meaning of 'still waters run deep,' Uncle Gil."

"I'm glad to hear it. I was beginning to wonder what kind of an education you got back in Indiana."

"I had an English teacher who considered himself a connoisseur of clichés."

He cleared his throat then, looking somewhat wounded. "I prefer to think of them as time-tested adages," he said crisply.

"Right, right," I said. Then, as a sop, I offered, "There's nothing new under the sun, anyway."

He ignored me. "In any case, we're not really going for the opera. We're going for the intermissions."

"For the intermissions?" I asked.

"Just stay close to me and try not to say anything Midwestern."

⸎

WE ARRIVED LATE AT Lincoln Center, having battled traffic all the way uptown. My uncle paid the fare and then led me up the stairs. I tried not to act the newly arrived yokel as we crossed the central plaza, but I have to say I was tempted to twirl around and toss an imaginary hat in the air à la Mary Tyler Moore. Lincoln Center—despite, or maybe because of, the passé moderne-cheesiness of its architecture—seemed to me like some kind of magnificent latter-day acropolis, the stark-white arcaded buildings rising like monoliths on three sides, the central fountain spewing exuberantly, and that early-evening cobalt sky stretching above. I stopped walking, momentarily breathless, to take it all in.

"Come on, William," my uncle said as he scurried toward the tall front windows of the Met.

Collecting myself, I followed him through the revolving glass doors into the lobby. Bells were ringing as people dressed in everything from tails to leather chaps buzzed around the ticket-takers. The interior was opulent in a kind of quaint velvety way. Everywhere I looked I saw money—money in the red plush walls and carpets, money in the artwork, money in the snowflake chandeliers that hung from the ceiling like frozen fireworks. But most of all, I saw money in the frenzied eyes of everyone there, even—or especially—my uncle.

We surrendered our tickets and were deposited at the edge of a kind of architectural vortex. In front of us was a central flight of steps leading down into the warm, dark, richly red interior. This was framed by two molded stairways that curved up on each side, meeting again above us at a black statue of a skinny seated woman. Maybe it was something about the design of the place, but I felt vague stirrings of sexual interest as we entered.

My uncle, though, seemed oblivious to all but his business acquaintances. He was waving and shaking hands all around as we headed inside: "Hello, hello, good to see you, let's talk at the break, call me Monday, e-mail me tonight, meet me for lunch on Wednesday," etc., etc.

"Do you know *everyone* here?" I asked.

"Everyone I want to know."

He led me down to the crowded orchestra level, and then into the theater itself. Here again I had to force myself not to be impressed. The space seemed vast to me. Five tiers of seats unfolded around us, all crimson and gold; and ahead of us stood the stage, towering, flamboyant, huge. When we finally reached our seats and sat down, I felt slightly dazed. "Can I ask how much these two seats cost?"

"You certainly may," he said, seeming pleased. "Given that this is a special performance—an opening, you know—I'd put the approximate retail value of these seats at three hundred dollars each."

"Each? You spent six hundred dollars to see this opera?"

"Worth every penny. And besides, it's tax-deductible. Did you see that bar as we came in? I made one of my best business connections there two years ago, while waiting for a glass of champagne. It was *Tosca*, as I recall. Puccini makes people very susceptible to persuasion."

The buzz of voices intensified when the lights went down. A rotund white man with a graying Afro came out to much applause, bowed once, and started the orchestra. The huge curtain rose to reveal the interior of some Age of Reason palazzo. Two women were lying in bed together. *Okay*, I thought, feeling another provocative pulse in my loins. *Let's see what* this *is all about.*

Any prurient dimension to my interest, however, quickly waned as the opera went on. And on. And on. After twenty minutes, I remembered what my uncle had said about falling asleep, but managed to amuse myself in the best way I knew how—by trying to calculate the box-office take of the production. I estimated the average ticket price, multiplied by the number of rows, and then by the number of seats per row. Against the resulting figure for gross receipts, I tried to calculate costs for overhead, scenery, star salaries, etc. The act was almost over before I gave up entirely. All I could conclude was that this production alone generated a level of economic activity exceeding that of a small Caribbean nation.

My uncle was on his feet before the lights were up for the first intermission. "Come on, William, we've got business to do."

He literally pushed me out the doors into the lobby. The noise was disorienting. Somebody handed me a glass of champagne, and in the space of the next ten minutes my uncle introduced me to no fewer than fifteen or twenty glad-handing businessmen in suits identical to his own. At their sides, some of them had bony wives in shoulderless gowns; others had somewhat younger, meatier girlfriends in somewhat shorter dresses; one had a fussily tonsured, narrow-hipped Asian boyfriend who grimaced in commiseration as we shook hands. It was all dazzling in its way, but somehow I had the feeling that I had entered a time warp and come out on the other side into a world that (the Asian boyfriend notwithstanding) had not changed fundamentally in decades. The people I met all seemed to be Old Economy titans—retailers, clothing manufacturers, owners of trucking companies. Where, I wondered, were the Silicon Alley gazillionaires? Apparently not doing business at the Met. They were probably networking at tiny rave clubs in the meatpacking district. Josh had once clipped a *Journal* article for me about a $338 million B2B merger that had been concocted at a club called Chop Shop on Gansevoort Street.

I was just starting to feel numb when my uncle pulled me aside. "There's someone here I particularly want you to meet," he shouted into my ear over the din. "He's starting a little company called Stevedore Technologies, along with some alumni engineers from Cisco, Akamai, and Juniper. I might want to invest, so look intelligent and keep your mouth closed." He grabbed my elbow and steered me across the lobby.

"Gil Hawking, good to see you," said the tanned and fit-looking thirtysomething man we zeroed in on. Unlike everyone else we'd met, he was dressed casually—no jacket, no tie, just an open-necked blue shirt and cream linen trousers. The outfit seemed to scream—and very self-consciously—Internet-Internet-Internet.

"Good to see you, too, Ben," my uncle said. "Enjoying the opera?"

"Actually just arrived. I could barely get away for this."

"I know the feeling." My uncle subtly but firmly moved me forward by the elbow. "Can I introduce my nephew? Will Merrick, Benjamin Fletcher. Will is joining the company next week."

We shook hands—a maneuver that revealed a subtle but obviously expensive watch on his wrist. "You're joining a good company, Will," he said. "But Gil's not giving you the old 'start as a subassistant' routine, is he?"

"As a matter of fact—" I began.

"Will has to prove himself," my uncle interrupted, "just as anyone else does in my company. I don't approve of nepotism."

"Well, I don't have such scruples," Fletcher said. "I've been trying to make my sister a Stevedore vice president for a while now, but she won't bite, no matter how many promises of stock options I throw at her feet." A young woman joined us then and handed Fletcher a glass of champagne. She wore heels and an impressive ivory one-strapped gown that revealed a pair of smooth, well-toned shoulders. When she turned toward us, I realized that this was none other than the woman Jack and I had met outside the bar on Wall Street a few hours earlier. And as dazzled as I'd been by her in her street clothes, the sight of Eliza Fletcher in an ivory one-strapped gown hit me like a straight-arm blow to the chest. "Eliza?" Ben was saying. "You remember Gilbert Hawking, don't you? And this is his nephew Will."

I wondered if she would acknowledge our previous encounter, but she came right out and said, "Oh, Will and I have already met. We ran into each other on Wall Street today."

My uncle seemed taken aback. "What were you doing on Wall Street?" he asked me.

"I didn't get a chance to tell you, Uncle Gil," I said. "I met your friend Jack Petroni there and he showed me around a little."

"Small world. Jack is the one who introduced Ben and me." He turned to Eliza. "And you were with Petroni as well, Eliza?"

"Not a chance," she replied.

"Eliza's on Wall Street a lot these days," Ben said. "She's starting up a kind of food bank, working with restaurants down there to feed the homeless. Tell them what it's called, Lizzie."

She rolled her eyes in exactly the same way she'd done that afternoon. "Want Among Plenty," she replied.

"That's where the extra millions go after the IPO. Got to give back to society and all that, right, Gil?"

"Yes, of course," my uncle said, with perfect insincerity. He turned then to Eliza. "I have to steal your brother away for a few minutes. Would you excuse us?"

The two of them moved away, praise God, leaving me alone with Eliza. She moved closer to me, and I caught a tantalizing whiff of some kind of scent that reminded me of green tea.

"Enjoying the opera?" I asked lamely.

"I hate opera. And so does my brother. We come here to please our father."

"Your father?"

"Joseph Fletcher? No reason you should recognize the name, really. He owns lots of radio and television stations, mainly in the South and Southwest, though he's trying to make inroads out here now."

"Is that the business they're discussing?" I asked, indicating Ben and Uncle Gil, who were in a huddle now near the water fountain.

"No, this is something else, something my brother is inventing, a networking equipment company. Trying to make his own mark, blah blah blah." I was about to utter some banal truism about the Old and New Economies when Eliza turned to me and added, "Listen, I really hate this whole networking scene. You want to go someplace and smoke a joint?"

I reran the mental tape of the last minute, wondering if I'd missed something. "Um, did I just hear you right? I mean, we just met."

"I'm not asking you to marry me."

"Well, God, I mean . . . okay, sure, yes."

Bells started ringing again, blanketing the many-tiered lobby with palpable disappointment. It was time for the next act to begin. "Too late," Eliza said. "Okay, there's another intermission later. Let's say we meet outside by the fountain. I know a quiet spot over at the Guggenheim Bandshell." Then she handed me her empty champagne glass and vanished.

"Come, William," my uncle said, waving me toward the doors. I ditched the champagne glasses and followed numbly. My uncle, meanwhile, seemed agitated. "It's frustrating," he muttered when we got back to our seats. "The man plays genial and forthcoming, but he won't budge an inch when he feels his interests are at risk." He looked over at me. "You and the sister get along?" he asked, but I was saved from answering by the sudden dimming of the lights.

I took in as little of the second act of *Rosenkavalier* as I did of the first. This time, though, it was thinking about Eliza that distracted me. I had no idea what to make of her offer. Had she been making fun of me, I wondered. Or was this just the way boy met girl at the Met? And was she implying that we would share more than just a joint? Clearly, my signal-reading abilities were not yet calibrated to New York, circa 1999. I decided that it would be best just to act as if this happened to me all the time back in Bloomington, and improvise as we went along.

When the lights went up for the second intermission, I leaned over to my uncle and told him I was going outside to get some fresh air. He scowled. "But we've got more people to meet."

"I *really* have to breathe," I said. Then, to underline the urgency of my need, I added, "Or else I might faint."

"Go ahead, go ahead," he said testily, as if I were a child telling his harried mother that he had to pee.

I was out of breath when I hit the chill air of the plaza. Shouldering my way through a phalanx of desperate smokers, I hurried toward the fountain, which somehow seemed less exuberant now after two acts of Strauss. I looked around for Eliza, but she didn't seem to be among the nighttime skateboarders or the Act III escapees heading toward the line of cabs on the street. Too early, I told myself. I was too eager. But the minutes passed. I circled the fountain once, twice, feeling like some obsolete radio satellite, looking for a signal from earth that no one was sending anymore.

Finally, it occurred to me that she could have meant us to meet at the bandshell itself, so I asked for directions and then sprinted across the plaza toward the little park to one side of the Met. I wove, linebacker-style, through the concrete tree planters to the shell-shaped structure at the far end. But she wasn't here either. Feeling crushed, I sat down on a bench and tried to head off my rising sense of humiliation. Was this some kind of game, I wondered—or an exquisite form of torture practiced on all newcomers to the city? I thought of what my uncle had said to me on my first day—"New York is full of temptations. Experience is knowing which ones are genuine promises and which are just scams."

My frustration keen, I got up from the bench and started running back toward the glowing lights of the Met.

Act III had already begun by the time I got back to my seat. Skewering me with a furious glance, Uncle Gil fumed but didn't say a word. I sat, sinking low in the seat, and wondered what I would tell him when he asked me where I'd been.

And so Act III passed, leaving even less impact on my psyche than did Acts I and II. Afterwards—after the hoots, the foot stamping, the ridiculous number of curtain calls—my uncle asked me, "Did you get your fill of fresh air? I was beginning to think you'd fallen down a manhole somewhere."

"I think I might still have some jet lag."

"There is exactly one hour difference between New York and Bloomington, Indiana," he intoned.

⤶

OF COURSE, WE RAN INTO ELIZA and her brother on the way out. As we oozed through the crush on the stairway, I caught her eye. "Hey, what happened?" I whispered, trying not to whine. "I was waiting outside at intermission."

"You were? That's so sweet. But I decided I was being too impulsive. We don't know each other well enough for that kind of thing."

"Well, there's a good way of changing that, isn't there?" I asked, desperate not to let this opportunity pass. "I mean, the not-knowing-each-other part?"

She seized my hand. "Okay. Let's go to dinner. You think your uncle can find his own way home?"

In point of fact he could, and actually seemed pleased to hear that Eliza and I were going out. Feeling relieved that I had redeemed myself in his eyes, I told him not to wait up for me. He winked and whispered, "See if you can get her to talk about her brother's electronic-switching thingie. He won't tell me anything unless I sign some nondisclosure agreement first, and I'm not ready to commit yet."

"I will," I said, though I had no idea what an electronic-switching thingie could be.

Eliza had already made a reservation on her cell phone and was now cab-hunting. She flagged one down, running out into the street to get ahead of the more timid souls who stood on the sidewalk with arms calmly raised. "Come on, Will, get over here!" she yelled back at me. I caught up and got in behind her. "Stellaluna on Park Avenue South," she told the driver.

I settled back against the seat and pulled at the knot in my tie. Fortunately, we weren't welcomed this time by any Gotham celebrity (my third cab ride in New York and already I was sick of those bright little recordings). But in the front seat, the driver was jabbering into his own cell phone, letting fly a torrent of language in which I recognized only the words "Global Crossing" and "Inktomi." I was about to attempt some conversation with Eliza, but then he hung up, as it were, and Eliza leaned forward to talk to him. "S.J. Padmanabhan," she said, reading his ID off the dashboard. "That's a Tamil name, right?"

He shot her a brilliant smile in the rearview. "You have been to Sri Lanka?"

"I was born in Colombo. My father had business there."

He shook his head at the unlikeliness of this. "I am from Jaffna. In the north."

"What brought you to New York?"

"Studies. I came for graduate work at NYU. Economics."

"What kind of economics in particular?"

They talked for the entire ride across town. I sat there in silence, wondering if I should feel jealous, or at least put-out. Wasn't she supposed to be paying attention to *me*? Already, my competitive-male hormones were kicking in—and it didn't help that when we finally got out at the restaurant, the two of them exchanged business cards. "How much do we owe you?" Eliza asked.

"Forget it. My treat." As he drove away he gave the horn a little valedictory toot.

"Come on, I'm starved," Eliza said, taking me by the hand and dragging me into the restaurant. Stellaluna, which apparently saw no reason to identify itself with anything as obvious as a sign, was an intimidating place. The dining room was all red, emphatically red—crimson walls, vermilion carpeting, cerise paper wall sconces, tomato-red upholstered chairs—and its clashiness was both clearly intentional and blatantly aggressive. A stiletto-thin black woman (slinky scarlet dress slit to her upper thighs) led us to our table and produced two palm-sized electronic devices on which the evening's menu was displayed, including, she informed us, hyperlinks for descriptions of each item, nutritional information, geographical origin of ingredients, chef bio, prices, and excerpts from reviews. I caught a glimpse of the first appetizer—in which the words "ostrich" and "Indonesian black nuts" were prominent—and decided to order whatever Eliza did.

"By the way," she said. "Forget what I said to you at intermission. I was just at my limit. Sometimes the whole New York power scene just gets to me, and I say things . . ."

"What if I don't *want* to forget it," I asked.

She eyed me for a moment with something like amusement in her expression. "Okay, don't forget it. Just don't make any assumptions based on it." She grabbed one of the twiglike breadsticks from the basket on the table and said, "So talk to me. Let's find out things about each other."

"Fine," I said. "We can start with Jack Petroni. How do you know him?"

She groaned. "Jack makes it his business to know everybody, even if they're not particularly interested in knowing *him*. I think he's angling to get in on my brother's IPO, if and when it happens. Like a lot of outer-borough broker boys, he's always got an eye on the main chance."

I decided not to tell her that this outer-borough broker boy had just gotten me a job. "So are you really setting up a Wall Street food bank?"

"Of course," she said. "But my real ambition is to open a chain of socially responsible restaurants. So I'm mainly there to study the tavern as a business model."

This surprised me. "A business model? The Shamrock Tavern? I would think you'd want to study someplace a little more fashionable. Like this place."

"That attitude, if you'll excuse me, is totally in-the-box." She leaned forward and flourished the breadstick at me. "Think about it. The Shamrock Tavern has been doing business on Wall Street since 1937. This place opened last month and will probably be closed within a year or two. It's so *courant* that it was passé the night it first opened its doors. But a dive like the Shamrock—well, it might not get me into *New York* magazine, but it can last forever. And that's what I'm after—a uniform revenue stream."

"Uniform revenue stream?"

"Exactly. And once you've got the organizational DNA, you can clone them. Get a half-dozen up and running and they can go forever, each doing its little part to beef up your bottom line. Naturally, you've got to have some Internet value-added—B2B efficiencies, mostly. But basically we're talking bricks-and-mortar here. Because bricks-and-mortar isn't going away, even if my brother seems to think so."

"But what will make them socially responsible?" I asked.

"You do a Ben and Jerry's," she said, warming to the topic. "You devote a certain cut of your gross to charity. It's perfect for this kind of social and economic climate. Everybody's rich, so they're feeling guilty, but they want to keep their money out there earning more. So they patronize a business like mine and get the moral bang without paying an extra buck."

I found this idea intriguing. It seemed so simple, and yet so ingenious—eliminate fashionability from the equation, add social responsibility, and the rest is cash flow. There seemed to be so many ways to make money in this town! "You need an investor? It sounds like something I want to get in on."

"You have any money?"

"Not yet. But I will."

"Talk to me when you have money." She stood up. "I've got to go to the loo. Can you order for me if the waiter comes? I'll take the house salad and a steak, preferably from a cow. And get us a nice bottle of wine."

I watched her cross that expanse of reds—admiring the confident feline swoop of her stride—until she had disappeared behind the rose-tinted glass doors. As I unfolded my napkin to wipe my streaming forehead, a waiter appeared at my elbow. "Hello, I'm Lars," he said. "If you have any questions about the menu, just touch the Help button at the top of the screen. Can I get you anything to drink?"

CHAPTER IV

I SPENT THE LAST SHILLINGS in my purse on a hackney coach to Wapping. This was an extravagance, of course, for the dinner with Eliza Fletcher at the Star and Moon proved to be no Cheapside bargain, despite the passing strangeness of the victuals on offer. And though my companion was doubtless mistress to a fortune the likes of which I could only aspire to, 'tis true now (and 'twill be true still, some three hundred years hence) that the man must pay the piper, though the woman call the tune.

I spied a candle in the front hall as I entered the house. Stepping into the room, I found my uncle snoring in a chair near the window, his wig sitting like a nestling cat upon his lap. "Sir?" said I, gently shaking him awake.

"Heigh, what's amiss?" said he, coming to. But then, seeing me, he appeared to recollect himself. He quickly clapped his wig upon his head. "Ah, Nephew. What's the hour? I seem to have nodded . . ."

" 'Tis late, though how late I cannot say."

"The clock across the room," said he, gesturing toward a large freestanding timepiece that had hitherto gone unremarked by me. A fine instrument it was, encased in rich mahogany, and boasting an extra hand to sweep the minutes—an innovation that had yet to reach the Merrick household in Exeter.

"It shows precisely ten past midnight, Uncle. I do apologize for disturbing you."

"Do not trouble your mind over that," said he, adjusting his wig. "I would fain hear of your evening, in any case. 'Twas a bit of fat, I thought, encountering young Fletcher and his sister at the theatre. I had wished to bring you acquainted with them, but had not hoped to do it so soon." His countenance darkened for a moment. "I thought it hardly discreet, however—you and Miss Fletcher going off to dine alone—and yet it seemed to disturb her brother but little."

"Miss Fletcher is quite a modern young woman, and certainly in no danger of compromising herself with me."

"Still, 'tis a kind of perversity, I say. Imagine an unmarried woman of family allowing herself to be seen at taverns and eating-houses all about the town. Some would say 'twas sure sign of a wanton nature."

"Sir!" I cried, not a little outraged in Miss Fletcher's behalf.

"I did not mean to cause offence, Nephew," said he, seeming to remark with satisfaction my protective attitude toward the young woman. "Perhaps I spoke in haste. I'm an old-fashioned sort in some respects, though the times be what they are. And though I don't approve, I won't measure others' corn by my own bushel. Besides," he added, "there's no denying the woman stands in the way of a fortune."

"Indeed." I cleared my throat. "Know you, sir, the extent of this fortune? I ask from curiosity alone."

"Of course you do," said he, tapping his angular nose. "She and her brother are Joseph Fletcher's only children. And though the estate must needs pass to the son, there's no end, I hear, to Fletcher's interests. I daresay he'll not hang all his bells on the one horse. Nay, the man who marries Eliza Fletcher marries five thousand a year, I'd wager, at the very least."

'Twas a summe of considerable consequence. "Her father must be a great man of business," I said, distracted.

"Such is his reputation. And his son, by all appearances, seeks to multiply the Fletcher fortune." My uncle took a small glass from the table and examined its dregs. "Speaking of which," said he, "I trust you were able to broach with Miss Fletcher the topic of her brother's business with me?"

"Regrettably no, sir. The topic came not naturally into our conversation, though I tried to raise it once or twice."

"Regrettable indeed. I would fain know more of his work. This new ship-unloading winch of his promises much. 'Twould be a boon to my own business and to that of many another in the kingdom. However, the man's close as a Kentish oyster, and said little of substance in my discussion with him. I had hoped you might learn more from the sister. But perhaps later, as your intimacy matures . . ."

"By gad, Uncle, you'll have me married off within a week of my arrival in London!"

Uncle Gilbert examined the glass in his bony fingers. "You have, I trust, no extant understanding with any young person in Exeter?"

"I do not. So you may scheme as you will, Uncle. My heart is yet unspoken for."

"Scheme I may," said he, smiling, "though not necessarily for your heart's sake."

"Do you not think that love is a prerequisite of marriage?"

"Indeed not. When you reach my age, I daresay you will find that love is like a cabbage—'twill grow most anywhere, if conditions be right, but it grows best in rich soil."

"Marry, sir, that's a sentiment worthy of Mr. Congreve himself!"

"I know naught of *Mr. Congreve*," said he, "but I do know something of *Life*. And certainly the likes of William Merrick could do far worse than Eliza Fletcher. Though the same, perhaps, could not be said in reverse."

"Ah, Uncle," said I, wondering just how much jest there was in this, "you have cut me to the quick. You think Miss Fletcher too good for a lowly *under*-clerk without material prospects?"

"It goes without saying. However, you *are* the nephew of Gilbert Hawking, which counts for something in this metropolis." He rose then to his feet. "But 'tis late. We'll have time enough to bandy words in the coming days. I am for bed." He took up his candle and used its flame to light another for me. "Breakfast tomorrow at nine. Pray do not be late."

"Tomorrow at nine," said I, taking the proffered candle. "Good night, Uncle."

"One more thing," he added then, as I turned to make my way upstairs. "Your business with Jack Petroni this afternoon. How came that to be?"

"We met in 'Change Alley, sir. He recognized me, having seen me with you at the warehouse on the day of my arrival."

"I see, I see. And what did you discuss?"

I thought it wise not to reveal the offer Jack had made me. "He merely explained to me something of the Alley's workings, sir. 'Tis of great interest to me, this business of buying and selling funds and shares. He seems quite the man there."

"Does he indeed? And a *Bumblebee* in a *Cow Turd* thinks himself a *King*." He went to the front door to assure himself I had locked it.

"But you yourself do business with him, sir."

"Yes I do. But I do business with many men I'd not sit at table with." Then, seeming to think better of his comment, he said, "Nay, 'twas unjust of me to speak so. Jack Petroni's a talented and ambitious young man, despite his background and his Italian heritage. And though I regard him in a tolerable good light, I would urge you to be careful. Commerce and finance—'tis an arcane world. Petroni is useful to me, and would perhaps be a worthwhile friend to you, but I can't say I fully trust his judgement. These young pups think, because they've earned a few guineas in the Alley, they understand the world. But there's never any substitute for the wisdom that comes with age."

"I'll remember that, sir."

"Oh, and by the by," my uncle went on, "will you be seeing Miss Fletcher again soon?"

I know not if I coloured then, but I felt some heat in my cheeks. "Indeed, sir, on Sunday. She has bid me come dine with her brother and herself."

He stroked his long chin in satisfaction. "You seem to make friends easily, Nephew," said he. "Well, I'll not discourage the connexion, certainly. But do look in on McTeague tomorrow—that is, if you find time between social engagements. Your schooling in the wine trade should not be left too long, since I still expect your under-clerkship to begin as stipulated on Thursday next."

"I will, sir." And with that I turned and, mind full of thoughts, mounted the creaking stair.

⌘

I BREAKFASTED ALONE next morning in the parlour—on bread and a delicious cold mutton, which Henry (the more agreeable of the household's two footmen) served up with some pottage. My uncle, it seemed, had had some early business to attend to, and so had eaten without me once again. All in all, I felt myself the worst sort of slug-gard, though it was barely half past nine on a Saturday morning.

Having thus fortified myself, I made my way across the court to the warehouse. Here I found McTeague fussing over the storage of a few mossy-looking barrels that contained I know not what. An intense odour of fish and spilt beer permeated the place, such that I was tempted to cover my nose with a handkerchief.

"Good morning, Mr. McTeague," said I in my halest voice.

He straightened up smartly and turned. "Good morning, Mr. Merrick, sir. How can I be of service, sir?"

"Look here, Mr. McTeague. 'Tis *I* who should be asking how *I* can be of service. I am, after all, to be your under-clerk."

"As you say, sir," said he, with undiminished complaisance.

I chose not to pursue the matter further. "Well," said I, "Mr. Hawking expressed a desire that you acquaint me with some of my future duties. So that I might begin at once to earn my keep, you might say."

"Certainly, sir. And where would ye like t'start?"

"I own I have no idea. Where *should* I start?"

"Wherever ye like, sir."

The man was exasperating. "Perhaps you can instruct me in the keeping of the account books," I suggested.

He looked so pained at this request—his face screwing up like that of a repentant sailor at the touch of the lash—that I demurred: "Unless, of course, you do not wish it."

" 'Tain't as if I don't wish it, sir, so much as 'tis Mr. Hawking bein' so *particular-like* about the castin' of his accounts—with the Customs and all—and I, havin' a good bit of knowledge in such matters . . ." He trailed off into silence.

"Very well," said I. "Then perhaps 'twould be best to start with the paying of wages to the men."

Here his grimace intensified. "Oh, sir," said he. "Wages, y'know. 'Tis a delicate business—handlin' the money. And the men, some of 'em, they'll lie through the teeth about what's due them, if you don't watch 'em careful-like, seein' as they'll know you're new. . . ."

"I understand," said I. "Then perhaps you can make me familiar with the scheduling of shipments, so that—"

"Oh, the ships, now, sir, there's a subtle job there. For if a schedule mistake be made, there's the Devil to pay—with a ship at anchor, say, and nary a man there to unload it. Or worse, a score of men standin' idly by, waitin' for a shipment to arrive. . . ."

I felt my resolve drain away. "Perhaps, then, I should just look about for a few days and see what I can learn on my own."

The relief was so plain upon McTeague's visage—he grinned from ear to ear, revealing the full glory of his broken dentition—that I could not but smile myself. "Now there's an idea, Mr. Merrick, sir. A look-about first is always best. For there's no learnin' like that through *Observation*." He touched the brim of his hat. "Now I'll be gettin' back to work, sir," said he, adding without conviction: "But feel free to ask of me any question at all, and I'll do m'best to enlighten you."

I saw the way it was. And so—after lurking about for a quarter-hour, kicking a few barrels and testing a few stowage lines—I slipped out of the warehouse and made haste back to the house.

I found Mrs. Popper upon the front stair. "Alfred has brought a letter for you, Mr. Merrick," said she. "From Exeter, unless I be mistaken."

"Exeter!" I exclaimed, much pleased. "From my sisters, I'll wager. Or else from my cousin Josh."

"'Tis none of my business, but I believe the hand to be masculine."

"Josh it is, then. Good old Josh!"

I hurried to my chamber, where the letter sat upon my side table, propped up against a candlestick. I shed my boots, hopped up on the bed, and—all patience gone—broke the seal. The letter was indeed in Josh's hand:

Will Merrick, you dishonourable dog, you [it read], *I trust you will not take it amiss if I chastise you roundly in this, my first letter to you, since whatever* Black Mood *I find myself in at present is entirely due to you—specifically, to your cruel and selfish removal from your father's house, which event has* left me doubly panged—first, in that your absence has robbed existence in these parts of all Spice and Savour, and second, that such a scoundrel as you should now be revelling in the countless delights of London—of London!—while others more deserving are left stranded, as it were, in this slough known as Despond, with nothing more rewarding to engage in than the teaching of Latin verbs to a pair of recalcitrant titterers (by which I mean your sisters Amy and Nell, if you cannot guess it), all the while thinking of the veritable Wagonloads of gold I could be harvesting in the Alley, if only I were there, in your place, rather than here, so apoplectic with Envy and Frustrated Ambition that I cannot even concoct a suitable conclusion to this infernal sentence. But let me not bore you with my Iliad of woes. How do you, dear Will? Have they crowned you King of Throgmorton Street yet? Or have you instead taken up with the whores and the maltworms of the City, passing your hours crawling along Fleet Ditch in search of a Nimgimmer and a remedy for French gout? More likely the latter, I'll warrant.

But you wish to hear news of home, no doubt. And I am happy to report that all is well here, famine and plague nowhere to be seen, and none of us yet forced to come upon the parish (although your correspondent may soon be driven to this extremity, inasmuch as your father seems disposed to cast me out once young Nell reaches her majority—for fear, methinks, that I have designs of the matrimonial variety upon her . . .). Your brothers do their best to convince all that they labour diligently in the brickworks, though for naught, as far as I can see. Jeremiah, as always, pursues his suit with Miss Skymartin—though, as always, she seems to have but one eye on him and t'other on the horizon, in search of some eligible *younger son of an earl or other. Meanwhile, the Misses Merrick pine for their favourite brother, and ask me to convey to you their love, since to do so themselves would mean to pick up pen and parchment, which*—Heav'n forfend!—*would no doubt strain their little minds and little fingers beyond endurance. They also wish me to inform you that they have received a little spaniel pup from their father, which they have named William in your honour, and which they say reminds them of you (perhaps because it makes water on the hall stairs whenever it senses its mistresses' disapproval).*

But I chronicle small beer—and you, of course, have fortunes to make, dragons to slay, empires to build, &c. &c. So I will sign off now and go beg a penny to speed this on its way. In the meanwhile, I shall look for your name in the next Collection—among the bankrupts.

Do take care of yourself, Will, and remember that the maxim is to Buy Cheap and Sell Dear, *and not the reverse (Pettering, I might add in this connexion, looks especially attractive right now). And do take the time, between triumphs in the City, to remember one who wishes you everything good, viz.*

Your cousin, your friend, and your servant
Joshua Richardson Dooling, Esq.

'Twas an excellent letter, I thought. And upon reading it a second time, I felt—for the first time since my arrival in the capital—a longing for that quiet life I had left behind—for the long walks Josh and I would take into the hills beyond Exeter, for the merry laughter of my younger sisters at their embroidery, for the little alehouse upon the River Exe that Josh and I ofttimes joked would be our own, once we made our fortunes (the aim, of course, was to make it into a bawdy house). I even wondered then if I had not done wrong in leaving behind all I knew—family, friends, and those who loved me—to come to this cold and ungodly place. . . .

But *tosh!*, 'twas only the maudlin sentimentality of an instant, a *Maggot* of the *Moment*. I *did* sorely miss those I had left behind, but the drama of the times was being played on the London stage, not in Exeter. And so I put the letter by and made myself three resolutions: first, to return the missive at my earliest convenience; second, to write as well to my dear Amy and Nell; and third (but not least), to see into the price of Pettering shares in the Alley. For though my good cousin was poor as Lazarus, he had yet a rich man's instincts.

❧

"NEPHEW!" THE VOICE THUNDERED—I knew not whence.

I stopped upon the stair, hat in hand. 'Twas as if the man had a *Second Sight*, and knew as soon as I did when I was setting out for some mischief or other. "Yes, Uncle," I responded.

He appeared below me from the parlour. "Ah, you are going out, I see. But your errand, whatever it is, must wait. I have the tailors here."

"The tailors, sir?"

"Yes, yes," he said impatiently. "By gad, man, we can't have you going abroad in those rags forever. Come along."

Sighing (for I had hoped to find Jack Petroni to enquire of him the price of Pettering shares), I followed my uncle into the parlour. Here were attending two men—one old, one near as young as me, yet both of a mincing disposition and finical manner of dress that in Exeter might have earned them bodily harm at the hands of the town's rougher element. The elder of the two—wearing a red wig of elaborate length and loft—held a measuring tape in his hands that snaked about his breeches and his shiny buckled shoes.

"Is this the young man, Sir Gilbert?" the elder enquired.

" 'Tis," my uncle answered. "And though I thank you for your 'Sir,' 'tis only King William, I believe, who has it in his power to elevate me so."

"Indeed," the tailor replied. Then, turning to have a look at me, he frowned prodigiously. "Oh dear," said he. "Oh dear, dear, dear. He has been out upon the streets like this, you say? In the City? Not just here in Wapping?"

"For something on five days," my uncle answered. "Is't so dire, then?"

"Oh dear, dear, dear," he repeated, and his young assistant did look upon me then with a glance of disapproval not unlike that of Jack Petroni's hound. "You've done well to bring me here, Mr. Hawking, for this is a task beyond the powers of any ordinary jacksnip. Look at him; the lad's thinner than Gonella's horse."

"You must add to his physical stature, then, as I must to his social," my uncle said.

"I'll do both, i'Faith, if you but give me cloth enough."

"I beg your pardon, gentlemen," said I, a little chagrined, "but I have been called 'well-made' by some. And, if I may say so, compared to this young gentleman"—and here I indicated the tailor's assistant, a scrawny blade—"I've the physique of a Turkish wrestler."

"Come, Will," my uncle said. "You need take no offence. I'm sure Mr. Barney here meant no slight."

"Indeed, young sir, I did not," the tailor declared with a simpering smile. "I meant only to describe for the gentleman the extent of the labours required."

This hardly mollified me, but I thought it wise to object no more.

"Would you remove your coat, sir? Babcock here will take your measurements." He handed the tape to his assistant and turned to Uncle Gilbert. "We'll have him looking fine as fivepence before long, Mr. Hawking."

"I'm sure you will, sir, though I reckon I'll be more than fivepence the poorer for't." My uncle laughed gruffly at his own witticism. Then, to me, he said, "You'll be glad to hear, Nephew, that Mr. Barney is tailor to many of the finer money'd men of the City. In a Barney's coat and breeches you'll pass in the Royal Exchange as well as any man."

"Does the young gentleman wish to cut a figure in the world of the 'Change?"

I was about to answer, but just then that popinjay Babcock, under pretence of assessing my collar size—and apparently in retaliation for my comment upon his stature—did choke me with the measuring tape. "Beg pardon, sir," he muttered, unconvincingly.

"Indeed," my uncle answered for me. " 'Twould seem so, for the lad is spending his off-hours touring 'Change Alley as a summer traveller does the Hebrides."

"I have a few pounds at liberty," said I. "I thought I might purchase some shares of this or that."

"Ah well, then you'd do best to speak to me, for a tailor to the *Money'd Interest* hears many a thing 'twixt the snip and the stitch. A word dropped here, a whisper there, can be turned to gold. In times like these, i'Faith, I earn more at the projects than I do at my trade."

"The projects!" said my uncle. "Is't wise for a tailor to venture into a realm about which he knows so little? 'Tis full of risk, is't not?"

"Only, sir, for one who buys the shares and keeps 'em. For him who buys and sells, and then—when prices fall, from rumour or from changing fashion—buys and sells again, there's naught but profit in it."

"Still," my uncle continued, "there are good projects and bad—many are of questionable value, to say the least."

"Ah, begging your pardon, sir, but it's not a project *per se* you're buying and selling. 'Tis naught but a piece of parchment. So, at least, say many of the gentlemen it is my honour to clothe. The average man, when he buys a share of, say, Martin's Miraculous Pig Feed, thinks he's bought a parcel of *Things*—pigs, patent, and all. But the money'd man knows he's bought but ink on paper. And if he plays it proper, he can buy when the prospects of divine-tasting pork are high and sell before the first chop comes to market."

" 'Tis pure folly!" my uncle protested. "For you act then as if the quality of the project itself were irrelevant! But any man who's bought a horse knows that a lame mare's a bad bargain, no matter what the price."

"But a mare's lameness is there for all to see. A project's value is but *Perception*. Marry, sir, I'd buy shares in a great *Flying Machine to the Moon*, should the money of London perceive it, at least for a day or two, as a worthy prospect."

But Uncle Gilbert would hear none of this. "Pugh," said he, " 'tis as bad as gambling. I don't like it."

"I see you don't, Mr. Hawking. But the *Proof* of the *Pudding*, as 'tis said, is in the *Eating*. Take my journeyman here." He gestured toward the little man. "Babcock, how much do I pay you?"

The named party came forward in all obsequiousness. "But ten shillings per week, sir, which there is some might say is donkey's wages for a skilled craftsman like myself."

"Indeed, 'tis said I'm the worst nip-farthing in the City," Mr. Barney said, giggling proudly. "And yet, Babcock, you are content as my journeyman, are you not?"

"More than content, sir."

"And how to explain this paradox?"

"Easily, sir. I keep in view the advantages of the tailor's post—the trim and ribbons, y'might say."

" 'Twould require a shipload of ribbons," my uncle observed, "to sweeten a salary of ten shillings per week!"

Mr. Barney flourished a hand and smiled. "So one might think, but though the young pup's salary is ten, his true wages be ten times ten."

"Dash my buttons, sir! You confound me with these arcane mathematicks!"

" 'Hardly arcane, sir. For the lad has made ten pound this fortnight alone on a well-turned bit of business in the Alley."

"Tush, sir, do you see green in my eye? A boy like this making ten pound? On what?"

"On *Information*, Mr. Hawking, sir. You see, a man being measured for his breeches is ofttimes instructing his broker as he stands. He that holds the tape cannot help but overhear. Be he apprentice, journeyman, or Master Tailor—'tis all equal. One plays the shadow of the man, buying what the gentleman is buying, and selling what he sells."

"Shadow indeed," my uncle said, "for 'tis no true man who merely makes himself an ape of his betters."

"That's as may be," Mr. Barney replied, taking no offence at all. "And yet, as I said, young Babcock here earns more as ape than as tailor. And the same may be said of his master."

"Damme, man, and an ape that rides in his own carriage is but an ape still," said Uncle Gil. "I prefer to earn my way by being *useful*, doing my part for the common weal."

("Truly," I nearly said then, "for where would England be today without a cask of rotgut Madeira in every tavern?"—but wisely thought the better of it.)

"Nay," my uncle went on, "I consider myself a man of the times—and as eager for a guinea as anyone else. But this shadow-play of yours I'll have no part in. I like to know what I buy and sell, and why I do it. Otherwise, 'tis a kind of witchcraft." He picked up his hat. "But I must go. As a man of business, I have some matters of substance to attend to. For no man ever slaked his thirst on the *Prospect* of a beaker of wine." Then, as he made for the door, he added, "When you are finished with the lad, Mr. Barney, do come see me in the warehouse and we shall discuss the particulars of cloth and leathers. I'll not have my nephew dressed in Kersey cloth."

"I understand, Mr. Hawking. Your servant," said the tailor with a bow.

When my uncle had gone, and I calculated that he was beyond earshot, I turned to Mr. Barney and said, "Sir, what you have said is of much interest to me. For though my uncle may think otherwise, I find the logic of your methods most convincing."

Mr. Barney nodded in gratitude. "I'm delighted to hear it. You will do well in the Alley, I think."

I remained mute for some minutes thereafter, whilst Messrs. Barney and Babcock completed their measurements of my person. But then, just as they were to leave, I asked, "I wonder, gentlemen, if you have heard any of your clients speak of Pettering shares in recent days?"

"Of Pettering!" Mr. Barney exclaimed. "Truly, there's been some whispering of Pettering, has there not, Babcock?"

"Aye, sir, there has. Much whispering."

"I see," said I. "And be they *Bulls* or *Bears*, as some now begin to call them, who do the whispering?"

The two exchanged a glance. "Upon my life, young sir, you have posed a question there. For distinguishing 'twixt the horn'd and the claw'd of the City is a matter of consequence, and not a task for just any Bacon. There are many who'd give their ears for such information as you ask for."

"I ask for naught that would cost you anything to give."

"True, but an empty hand is no lure for a hawk. Is't not said in every marketplace, No Penny, No Paternoster?"

"Mean you to imply that you would have me pay for the repetition of a few mere words?"

"Mere words they may be, and yet some words are as good as

pieces of eight. For instance, the word you request I might surrender for, shall we say, eight shillings?"

"The answer's a lemon, sir," said I, with indignation. "At eight shillings to repeat a word, you might babble at will in Covent Garden and outdo the Royal Mint!"

"As you wish." He signalled to his journeyman to continue packing up. Then, as he was leaving, he handed me a card. "By the by, this is my place of business, at the sign of the Fatted Calf. Should you ever wish to purchase a new frock or waistcoat—or even a particular word or two from those as it were on the inside—I can usually be found here. Good morrow, sir." And with that they left the parlour.

I held the card in my hand for some minutes, tempted to take it to the kitchen and toss it into Mrs. Popper's fire. But then I reasoned it would cost me nothing to keep it. And so I folded Mr. Barney's card and pressed it into my pocket. After all, a man whose assistant earns ten pounds in a fortnight might someday be worth listening to, even at eight shillings a word. For I was learning a valuable lesson of late— to wit, that nothing in this brave new age, no matter how insubstantial, did come to one but at a price.

CHAPTER V

∞ 'TWAS AT TWO O'CLOCK on Sunday afternoon that I found myself standing on the doorstep of Toliver House, the handsome brick pile in Arlington Street that served as the London home of Mr. Benjamin and Miss Eliza Fletcher. Its being a fine fresh day, I had walked the entire distance from Wapping—quite an exhausting journey, as it came out, but one that served to acquaint me with the part of London then being called the *West End*. As my uncle had asserted, the district was awash in new construction. Along every street were row upon row of excellent new residences, all of them seemingly designed to absorb as much of the city's excess capital as 'twas possible for brick and masonry to absorb.

Arlington Street itself, off Pickadilly, boasted a particularly fine assortment of houses. A few of them, indeed, were of such *Verticality* (reaching four storeys) that one could easily take each meal of the day at a different altitude above the street. I also suspected, judging from the quality of persons to be seen thereabouts, that I could toss a stone after church on a Sunday morning and be sure to hit at least a few earls—and even, if lucky, a duke or two.

My knock upon the door was answered by a footman. This man—

a callow-seeming caddice-garter, I thought—took my hat with the barely concealed distaste of someone being handed a week-old mackerel. Following his directions to the drawing-room, I found myself in a chamber of generous proportions and luxurious appointments, with fine damask draperies upon the windows, honey-coloured wainscotting, and a very fine chimney-piece of watercolours, depicting a tranquil Dutch scene of windmills and plump cattle. This last I examined with some interest, having heard that pictures of a certain kind could appreciate in value as swiftly as an East India bond. Wondering at this seeming absurdity (for could not anyone with a few pennies-worth of paint create a similar commodity?), I sat myself down and waited.

I was but five minutes in my chair when Miss Fletcher herself rushed into the room. She was looking uncommon handsome, dressed in a mantua of ruby velour trimmed with a fine Flanders lace, and she wore a fetching mole upon her cheek that I suspected had not been put there by Nature. "Mr. Merrick, what a pleasure to see you again," said she, sweeping toward me. I rose so smartly to meet her that—damn it all!—I sent my chair tumbling over on its side.

"Think nothing of it, Mr. Merrick," said she.

We both moved to right the chair again, and collided, such that I nearly put the poor lady on the floor.

"Hah, I am a clumsy oaf," said I in mortification. "Do excuse me, Miss Fletcher. You must think me a country rube of no breeding whatsoever."

"Breeding, Mr. Merrick, is a matter of the *Head*, not of the *Elbows*." She steadied herself and touched my hand. "And besides, I do not share this London prejudice against the country. As you may know, my brother and I are only recently come up to London ourselves, from Dorset. And though I'll not pretend indifference to the delicious pleasures of the town, I do sometimes yearn for the sweet air I left behind, and for the plain and honest company."

"As do I, as do I," I assured her.

"But see here, Mr. Merrick, have you any tobacco?"

This sudden gust did all but overturn my little barque. "I'Faith, I do not. Why d'you enquire?"

"Because I wish to smoke it, of course. Do I shock you? Are you like my brother, then, and think it unbecoming of a woman to smoke a pipe?"

"B'm'Faith, I suppose I do, though I know the customs of the world do alter. But alas, I have no tobacco."

"Oh fie!" said she. "Then I'll have to send that devil Jeremy as my agent. And he's not above taking his market penny for the service."

" 'Twould be my honour," said I, "to perform this service for you—at once, if you wish it."

"Another time, perhaps. For our dinner is very near prepared, and my brother awaits us within."

We adjourned then to a separate chamber used exclusively for dining. Here we found Benjamin Fletcher, standing over the large oak table, a sheaf of documents and drawings set out in front of him. I wondered if these might be plans for the unloading engine in which my uncle took such an avid interest. 'Twas whispered about the town, my uncle said, that Fletcher's winch might truly be a project of great merit, and that once he got a patent for't, the man stood in the way of a fortune—as would any partners he might take on to assist in bringing the shares to market.

"Hallo, there you are, then," Benjamin Fletcher said when he spied us. He quickly gathered up his documents, as if eager to keep them from my sight. "Good day to you, Mr. Merrick."

"And to you, sir." I gestured toward his documents. "Hard at the task, I see. Might these be plans for your great secret project?"

He jerked upright like a man startled by the crack of a whip. "You know about my winch, do you? But, of course, your uncle will have spoken of it." His body eased again. "I do beg your pardon, Mr. Merrick, if I am somewhat protective of my *Brain-Child*. But there are spies who would rob me of my thunder, so to speak, and pass the noise off as their own."

"I understand your fears," said I, much interested now, though not wishing to show it. "But today I come to steal not your papers, but merely a bit of your sister's company, which in any case I hold to be the greater treasure."

He seemed a bit surprised at this. "Handsomely said, was it not, Eliza?"

"Yes," said she. "Though it smells a bit of the lamp, I think. Did you prepare your flatteries beforehand, Mr. Merrick, so as to deliver them ready-made?"

Here I must have blushed a little, for I confess I did the night before prepare a few pretty things to say. And so I lied: "You do me an injustice, madam, for if I had me a script for this play, 'twould be better writ than that."

"Truly, then, I shall expect your *Billet-Doux* to be of the first quality. Assuming you will send me some?"

Damme, but this woman did play upon me as upon a harpsical! One more innuendo of that sort, I thought, and I should be her slave forever!

"Come, Sister," Mr. Fletcher said. "You go too far. And Mr. Merrick here hardly seems the billet-writing London beau. He is too much the man of sense for that. For I do hate the impudent fops this town affords, who spend more time admiring themselves in pier-glasses than aught else."

At this, to my relief, the dinner was brought in, ending conversation for the moment. And 'twas just as well, for a rare dinner it was—a fricassee of rabbits and chickens, a dish of roasted pigeons, mutton prepared in the French style, an onion pie, and a multitude of anchovies spread like fingers upon a kind of salver, which did please me especially well. All was served with an assortment of Bordeaux and Burgundy wines of excellent quality. So deep was my content—and so fervent my attention to the meal—that I fear I may have remained mute for some minutes, concentrating instead on the dismantling of my pigeon.

"I think, Brother," Miss Fletcher said at last, "that Mr. Merrick enjoys his dinner."

"B'm'Faith, 'tis the best I ever ate," said I.

"Indeed," she continued meaningfully, "he seems to relish it as much as you do your wine."

"My chef will be well pleased," Benjamin Fletcher intoned, ignoring his sister's barb. "He is an Englishman by birth, my chef—though he learned much of French cuisine when I brought him to the Continent during the recent war."

"You served King William in the present conflict?" I asked.

"I served King William, yes—and myself. 'Tis my firm belief that this Frenchman Louis must needs have his jacket laced, for no nation is safe if there be such a tyrant in the world. England now trades on all the seven seas, as you know, so that a wind in *Constantinople* can topple a tower in *Coventry*."

"Oh please, Mr. Merrick, do not send my brother down this path, for then we'll hear no end to it."

"Perhaps, Sister, Mr. Merrick takes more of an interest in the world than you yourself do."

"Well, I do not wish to earn Miss Fletcher's displeasure—" I began.

"*Natural Philosophy*, sir," her brother said then, interrupting me. "The sciences will be the making of England. Mark my words, Mr. Merrick. We stand on the threshold of a new era, when the discoveries of applied science will change the nature of trade and commerce in all its aspects."

(And here Miss Fletcher did press my foot with her own under the table, though I must confess I took a genuine interest in her brother's words.)

"We live in a time of great genius," Fletcher went on. "Newton, Hook, Wren—they have laid the groundwork, so to speak. Now we men of business must take the knowledge they have wrested from the realm of Nature and put it to use in the realm of Trade. 'Tis a kind of revolution. Already we see what may be called the *Connectedness of the World*. One can step down any street in the City this day and find the riches of Brazil, of Virginia, of Africa, in every shop window. 'Tis as if England had spread a great net or web o'er the earth, designed to snag its choicest offerings. And this is only the beginning. The sea journey that once took months will someday take weeks, and the overland coach trip of five days will soon take three or less. . . ."

And so did Benjamin Fletcher continue for some time in this vein. Consuming glass after glass of French wine, then Spanish brandy, and finally Oporto, he orated ever more warmly on the bright future of English commerce in the current age of *Invention* and *Discovery*. I sat enraptured—not only at his grand words, but likewise at the collusive glances of his sister, who to my delight did not absent herself after the meal in the customary fashion. And though her glances had something ironical in them, yet I could see that she shared something of her brother's excitement at being so near the heart of these great historical changes. For the feeling in that room was but a mirror of that throughout the city at this time—that the world was being remade even as we spoke, and that each and every one of us would be touched by these changes, e'en to the point of making us all rich.

"Know you, sir," Fletcher continued (well into his cups by now), "know you what an *Invention* like my winch can mean to the conduct of English trade? By my most recent calculations, I reckon 'twould make superfluous the labours of a score of lightermen for every cargo of every shipper in the kingdom! Nor are the efficiencies merely those of labour. I have discussed these matters with Mr. Edmund Halley, who is an acquaintance of mine, and he is quite in accord with me. Time, sir, is like money in the coming age, and with my winch at his disposal, a merchant can have the most capacious argosy unloaded and back upon the waves within a day."

"Benjamin," Miss Fletcher interjected then, "I think perhaps you say too much." In the last few minutes of her brother's oration, her expression had changed from one of indulgence to one of mounting alarum. "I fear you bore Mr. Merrick with these paeans to the current age."

"Nonsense, Eliza. Mr. Merrick here is our friend, and the possessor of a lively intellect that can appreciate such things as *Pneumaticks.*"

"*Pneumaticks?*" I said.

"Benjamin!" Eliza spoke sharply. "I must insist that you be more mindful of what you say. True, Mr. Merrick is our dear friend—to become, I hope, even dearer—and yet we must not burden him with the dreary details of your project."

"Perhaps you're right, Eliza," he said, seeming a bit abashed now.

"Upon my life," said I, "I think it impossible to be bored in such company as this!"

"That's as may be," Miss Fletcher went on. "But I myself grow dizzy with this talk of revolutions, and would fain speak of matters less . . . turbulent." She turned to me then, and with a heart-tugging glance that obliterated my interest in all else but herself, asked, "Will you be accompanying your uncle to the theatre again soon, Mr. Merrick?"

From there the conversation moved on to other matters. After the Oporto, we returned to the drawing-room, where Benjamin Fletcher opened a many-compartmented cabinet of fine mahogany wood and proceeded to discourse on his collection of curiosities—

most notable among them being the complete skeleton of a large Brazilian rodent, a lock of hair said to have come from the head of the poet Campion, and the dried testicle of an Asiatic yak. Having finally exhausted his store of talk for the afternoon—and alluding to some pressing work awaiting him elsewhere—he excused himself, grasped my hand, and made me promise to return for another visit.

After he had gone, Miss Fletcher invited me to sit. "Your brother," said I, taking the chair I had earlier upset, "has much of interest to say, notwithstanding your persistent twitting of him."

"Yes, do not misconstrue my feelings. I do recognize the value of his great vision of the future. And yet, as we discussed at our last dinner together, those with their eyes trained a mile ahead sometimes forget the road that must be travelled 'twixt here and there."

"Have you acquainted him with your project to create a series of charitable chophouses?"

"He would only scorn it if I did. He knows I have money from our father, and would fain have me invest it all in that mighty winch of his."

"You think it a bad prospect then?" I asked.

"On the contrary. If I know my brother, 'tis like to be the best prospect possible. And yet 'tis *his* project, not mine, and I prefer to ride my own horse, though another may gallop faster." She rearranged her petticoats (revealed to sight, as per the current fashion) before her. "Though, of course, if he truly needed my help, 'twould be his in a moment."

"I should think there'd be no end of money'd men eager for shares, if his winch be all it seems to be."

"Ah, but there's the rub. He refuses to divulge anything of his winch's workings, fearing—quite rightly, I think—that his ideas may be stolen. And there's few of the money'd men as will commit themselves unless he does. Even that little he revealed to you at dinner—

about which I trust you'll be discreet—is more than he has said to anyone else. Tomorrow, when his head clears, he'll chide himself for letting even that much slip from his lips."

"Pray put his mind at rest, then, for I'm not inclined to bruit it about the Alley."

"For that I thank you, Mr. Merrick. But enough of this. Surely there are topics beyond gears and pulleys that a man and a woman may discuss in London these days."

There were. And I was not at all averse to turning our conversation from matters of the head (and the pocket) to those of the heart. "Indeed, madam, for I have not yet commented upon the gracefulness of your attire this day, which does flatter your person most delightfully."

"Oh please, Mr. Merrick, I'd rather return to gears and pulleys, if the alternative be the advantageous effect of Flanders lace upon my bosom."

"Then you are unusual for your sex," said I, "for I have never known a woman yet who did not take an interest in her clothing."

"And *I* have never known a man who did not take a greater interest in what lies beneath that clothing. But neither topic is therefore fit for conversation."

I wiped my brow at this. "Then you have stymied me again, Miss Fletcher," said I, "for you forbid me every topic I broach."

"Perhaps, then, you should resort to *actions* rather than *words*."

I do not think I mistook this invitation, and yet I hesitated. Could this woman truly be as bold as all that? Having seen a few stage plays in my time, I knew the reputation of London women. But Miss Fletcher, by her own admission, was not of London. What's more, she was a woman of considerable breeding and station. I did not wish to overplay my hand, and so I sat there, as if paralyzed, fearing to offend.

A moment of most awkward silence passed, during which the sound of a lazy wasp beating itself against the windowpanes could be distinctly heard.

"And so, Mr. Merrick?" she asked then, as if prompting me.

"So?" said I. "B'm'Faith, Miss Fletcher, I own I don't know what it is you wish of me."

"Do you not? Do you not, Mr. Merrick?" She sighed then, and turned her pretty head aside. "Then you are not alone, sir. For here am I, surrounded by a city teeming with energy and creative genius, but in service of what? Of Projects and Engines, of winches and carriage wheels and new techniques for the manufacture of watered silk. Is there naught else to which the genius of men can be turned? Can there be no Engine for the more inventive conduct of love and courtship? Or is there insufficient profit in such a project for any man to think it worth the effort?"

"I, Miss F-fletcher," I stuttered, "I am one who thinks it worth every effort in the world!"

"I wonder," said she, glaring at me. But then her countenance softened. "I am an impatient woman, Mr. Merrick, and some would say an unreasonable one. I fancy ofttimes that I have been born into an age that is not my own."

And here Miss Fletcher rose from her place, her cheeks colouring. "I'm afraid, Mr. Merrick, that I feel somewhat indisposed of a sudden, and will have to beg your indulgence."

"Indisposed?"

Her dissatisfaction with me was quite obvious. "Yes, it is merely an undercooked sardine, perhaps, or else some other inadequate fish. Pray excuse me," she said, ringing the bell. "Jeremy will see you to the door. Good day, sir."

And then she was gone. Jeremy, the footman, was upon me with my hat. And before I knew quite what had happened, I was out the door and upon the paving stones of Arlington Street. Looking up at the windows of the place, I tried to marshal my spirits, but with little success. And so I finally turned away, wondering what on God's earth I had done wrong, and if anyone ever would understand the arcane workings of the feminine mind—be they *Pneumatical, Hydraulical*, or aught else besides.

⌘

THAT EVENING, after another long, though less hopeful, walk, I returned to the house in Wapping much fatigued. And as the *Great Lion* of the African plain does fall upon the unsuspecting *Antelope*, so did my uncle accost me at the door, a plate of pickled herring in his hand. " 'Tis you, Nephew," said he. "You have quite startled me!"

"As well you might say the tree startles the lightning that strikes it," said I, hand to my racing heart.

My uncle frowned. "Perhaps I *did* catch sight of you coming off the street," he admitted. "You are just arrived from Fletcher's, I think?"

"I am."

"And it was a pleasant dinner, then?"

"Most pleasant, yes."

He was gaping at me with sharp anticipation. I smelled the odour of herring on his breath. "And?" he asked.

"And most nutritious as well, given the variety of dishes."

My uncle made as if to box my ears. "Come, sir, you know what I'm after. Did Benjamin Fletcher speak to you of his winch project?"

"He did, and he did let slip a few details of its workings. But, alas, I am sworn to silence."

"Sworn to silence? *Sworn to silence?* Tush, scoundrel, empty the bag now. What said the man?"

" 'Tis all *Pneumaticks*, sir," said I (for though I wished to honour my vow to the lady, I am a practical man and 'twas my uncle, after all, who put the roof above my head).

"*Pneumaticks*?! Bless my soul, but it does sound wondrous strange to me."

"To me as well, Uncle. And yet Fletcher said his *Engine* would do the work of a dozen lightermen or more."

"Did he? A dozen or more? Well, we live in a time of great advances, I suppose."

"So said Mr. Fletcher, at some length," I replied. "He even mentioned several members of the Royal Society in that connexion, not least among them Newton himself."

"Newton! Did he say Newton was involved?"

"His reference was couched in more general terms. And yet he did say he had been in correspondence with Mr. Edmund Halley concerning the matter."

My uncle put down the plate of herring. "Well, Halley is no Newton, but he certainly has a fine understanding. And if Halley be party to this project, I'd not hesitate a moment to cast my penny in."

" 'Twould be worth enquiring, I warrant."

"Truly, if you could ascertain as much, 'twould mean much to me."

I smiled. "And so I would earn my keep before my very first day of *under*-clerking?"

"About your clerkship," my uncle went on. "I've spoken with McTeague on that score, and it seems your services in the warehouse may not be required after all. Indeed, I think you will be more valuable to me in another, perhaps more *informal*, capacity."

"And that would be?"

"As my *Instrument*. You may be aware that my old business proceeds apace, without much oversight from me. I have been looking about for other opportunities, Fletcher's winch among them. A lad like you—bright and alert—can be of use to me, serving as my eyes and ears in the City. Is this a position more commensurate with your abilities, d'you think?"

"Yes, yes, I do indeed, Uncle," said I. "For to be the *Instrument* of Gilbert Hawking would be a great honour."

"Excellent. Then your first duty will be to investigate this matter of Fletcher's winch. Talk to the jobbers in the Alley. Discover what you can and report it back to me. 'Twill not be easy, for most of that crew are cunning old birds, and old birds are not to be caught with chaff, you know." He eyed me then, verifying my comprehension of this last figure of speech. Satisfied, he continued, "In the meanwhile, my boy, let it be said that you've done me good service today. I am pleased. Very well pleased."

"Thank you, Uncle. I'm delighted to have pleased you."

"To the parlour, then," said he. "For I've a new vintage of Canary I'd like your opinion of. . . ."

Later that night, alone in my room at the top of the house, I tried to void my mind of my apparent failure with Eliza Fletcher. Instead, I spent the time preparing myself for my new position in the Alley— *viz*, as "apprentice broker and jobber" to Mr. Theodore Witherspoon—a position I was to assume the very next day. Jack Petroni had warned me that my duties for his associate might seem futile and unrewarding at first—I was to stand at the door of Jonathan's and attempt to steer all prospective share-buyers inside to Witherspoon's table—and yet I was eager, even enthusiastic, to begin. Drudgery, after all, was the inevitable price of learning. And besides, whatever knowledge I acquired as "apprentice broker" would serve me well as my uncle's "instrument," and *vice versa*. I did bethink myself that I should inform each of my employers of the other's newfound plans for me. But, ultimately, I decided to hold my tongue, until a better opportunity arose. For I suspected that my uncle would not look fair upon my partnership with Jack and his associates. And as for the double nature of my upcoming endeavours . . . well, if 'twas true that, as the tailor said, information was as good as cash—and more valuable for being little known—then I'd keep my secret at the *Bank* awhile, and see what *Rate of Interest* my small deposit might collect.

CHAPTER 6

⟨∞⟩ "GENTLEMEN, YOU ARE ABOUT to enter an absurd profession. In the next few weeks, you will be learning to perform a function that no one really needs nowadays and few people even want anymore, but for which you will eventually be paid an obscene amount of money: You are about to become stockbrokers at the end of the twentieth century."

It was showering hard outside. Big droplets of rain pelted the windows of the seventeenth-floor training room at Pembroke Horton Ltd., forming rivulets that crisscrossed on their journey to the bottom of the panes. From my seat at the back of the room, I could look straight into the offices of the building across William Street—as at a wall of television screens, each tuned to a different though equally boring cable channel. According to urban legend, there should have been at least one wild desktop lovemaking session going on over there, but I was having trouble finding it. All I could see was young men staring into computer screens, young men barking into telephone headsets, and one young man, in shirtsleeves and loosened tie, leaning back in his chair and squeezing drops into his eyes while a harried-looking Hispanic woman polished his wingtip shoes.

At the head of the room, Nicholson Pembroke, the eighty-three-year-old founder of the firm that bore his name, wiped his craggy nose with a handkerchief, stuffed it back into the little side pocket of his wheelchair, and continued:

"You may have read that we live in something called the Information Age. What this means to each of you is that in ten years, or perhaps five, the role you are about to learn is going to be nonexistent. Why? Because any knowledge, any guidance, any advice you may now offer a client—at a price—will be something he can obtain for himself—cost-free—if he just knows where to look. Access to the market? Perhaps that was something that, in my day, only a broker could provide. But those days are as nearly defunct as I am." He cackled softly at this last statement and then continued. "No, gentlemen, the value you add to the process of trading securities is rapidly approaching zero. To wit: You are training to become the operators of a ferry across the River Mammon—during the last few days before the opening of the River Mammon Bridge."

I looked around the training room. There were a dozen of us broker trainees in the room—eleven men and one woman—each seated at the kind of metal chair-*cum*-desk I hadn't seen since my days at Northwestern. Each of us had a notebook, various personal effects, and a paper cup of Starbucks coffee balanced on the desk attachment in front of us. We had been in that room for hours already. On our arrival, we had been met by a perky blond woman who had identified herself only as "Queen of the Cold Callers." The Queen, as we had no choice but to call her, had first kept us busy filling out applications, insurance forms, nondisclosure agreements, and various other documents of corporate indenture. After a bathroom break, she had shown us the same video I'd seen at Jack Petroni's place. Then she'd prepared us for the presentation she called "Mr. Pembroke's famous welcoming speech." That's what we were listening to now, in the half hour before we were to meet our training brokers.

Mr. Pembroke lifted a crooked finger and scratched his sunken temple. "Am I discouraging you, gentlemen, by implying that you are dinosaurs? If so, please cheer up. Why? Because you are going to be very rich dinosaurs. Because people—some people at least—still *think* they need you. Perhaps they haven't yet heard about the River Mammon Bridge, or perhaps they feel more comfortable in a sturdy boat with a real live skipper to hold their hand, or perhaps they don't even know that they *want* to cross the river until you offer them the ride, and then you're right there with the gangway down and the ferryboat all ready to board. In any case, it's not as if *nobody* needs you. For, you see, gentlemen, *we* need you, even if *they* do not. We here at Pembroke Horton have companies that want to go public; we have stock in our inventory that wants to be sold. That is what you will be doing for us. So you're not useless, you see. Just unnecessary, theoretically."

We must have looked disheartened, because he cackled again and said: "Did you come here expecting to enter a glamorous profession? If so, you're approximately a decade and a half too late. If it's glamour you want, join a dot-com or a biotech firm just going public. Retail brokers, I must inform you, are but the helpmeets of the New Economy. Silicon Alley, Silicon Valley; Austin and Boston; Northern Virginia and the I-270 Corridor in Maryland—*they* are the engines. You are the gas station attendants—in the age of the self-serve pump."

He coughed then—a long, clotted, phlegmy seizure that brought the Queen to her feet. Pembroke waved her away and, after a few long seconds, continued:

"So why are you here, gentlemen? Have you no self-respect? Perhaps. Or perhaps you understand that it will be some months, or even years, before the New Economy realizes that it can function without you. In the meantime, there is money to be made, and lots of it. Think of yourselves as the last coelacanths of Madagascar—fat, maladapted, but very much alive, despite all rational expectations. And when you become extinct, as you will before very long, rest assured that your extinction will be a well-financed one. For you will be rich, gentlemen. Very very rich." He looked around the room as if lost for a few seconds. "I think I'm finished now," he said. "Melissa?"

The Queen rose from her chair. "Thank you, thank you very much, Mr. Pembroke, for that frank and enlightening talk. Someone will wheel you away now."

Someone did, and when the old man was gone, the Queen turned to us and said, "Lady and gentlemen, don't think too much about what you just heard. Except for the very rich part." She cracked her knuckles and picked up the sheaf of our applications. "You will now be assigned to your training brokers and begin work."

She began calling out names. When she came to mine, she stopped and glanced around the room. "Which one of you cherubs is William Merrick?"

I raised my hand.

"Okay, Bill—"

"It's Will, actually," I said.

"I see." She made a note on my application. "Okay, Will. Actually, you're actually a special case. T.W. wants to see you—Ted Witherspoon, actually, in the almost-corner office. Go there now."

Amid stares of contemptuous respect, I gathered up my belongings and left the room. It took me a few minutes of searching, but I finally found Ted Witherspoon's office—as far from any corner as possible (the Queen had been speaking metaphorically, it seems), in the middle of a long corridor hung with enormous fake tapestries. I paused outside the door and pulled a few doughnut crumbs off my suit (I was wearing Uncle Gil's Hickey-Freeman again, until the new ones came from Barney's), then knocked and walked through the open door. A rotund, balding man was sitting in profile behind the desk near the window, staring down at his fingernails.

"Mr. Witherspoon?" I asked.

He looked over at me. "I hate you," he said. "I despise every molecule of your being."

"I beg your pardon?"

He held up a plump hand, and only then did I realize he was speaking into a headset phone. "In that case," he went on, "I love you. I'll put you down for the maximum. . . . Fine. . . . Hey, we've got a lot of history together. . . . Thanks. . . . Talk to you later, Dad." He pulled the tiny instrument from his ear, threw it on the desktop, and got to his feet. "You must be Will Merrick," he said, darting around the desk with surprising spryness to shake my hand. "Ted Witherspoon. Welcome to Pembroke Horton." He closed the door to his office. "Sit down, sit down," he said, pushing me into the chair in front of his desk. "I've heard a lot about you from Jack Petroni. Good man, Jack. He's sent me some of my best people. Says he has a good feeling about you."

"That's nice to hear," I said.

"Also says you're Gilbert Hawking's nephew, that right?"

"Yes, sir, it is."

"Outstanding. Your uncle's a first-rate businessman. Never met him myself, but I sure do like those Burgundies he imports." He reached down and felt the material of my lapel. "Good, very good stuff there," he said, light glinting off his sweat-moistened head. "But listen, Will, I've got something going down today and I can't spend much time, okay? I'll turn you over to my best broker in a minute, but I just wanted you to know that you're special, got that? You're not like those other kids out there, because you've got me behind you, understand? I'll protect you from the bullshit."

"I appreciate that, Mr. Witherspoon."

"But you've got to watch closely and you've got to listen, okay? The reason I have this office is I play the game a little different from the rest. You've probably heard a lot about this Big Swinging Dick crap, but forget that. Some guys out there still play the game that way, all testosterone and chutzpah, but that doesn't fly anymore, understand? Your market today is more subtle, your customer way savvier. You call up some Joe doesn't know you from Adam and say, "Joe, Joe, listen to me, I'm gonna make you rich with this stock, but you gotta buy today, don't ask your wife, don't ask your friends, buy now!"—Well, geez, he'll just laugh in your face. But that's the way a lot of these guys still operate—by the playbook circa 1986. That's why they're out there and I'm in here. You understand me, Will?"

"I think I do, Mr. Witherspoon, yes."

"Outstanding." He hit a button on his regular desk telephone and said, "Jeff? Stick your head in here a minute." Then he flopped down into his chair and poked a few keys on his computer.

A young, sandy-haired head poked in the door. "You rang, boss?"

"Jeff, Jeff, come in and meet Will Merrick. Today's his first day and I want you to take special care of him."

"He your new bitch, boss?"

"Yes, Jeff, he my new bitch." Mr. Witherspoon winked at me and said, "Jeff will take special care of you, won't you, Jeff?"

"I will, boss."

"Outstanding. Now go away."

Jeff grabbed me by the arm and pulled me out of the office. "Just what I need today," he muttered, "Ted's new bitch." He led me down the hall and into a big room crowded with desks and computers and phones, all networked by cables that snaked across the gray-carpeted floor. Scores of white-shirted young men, likewise interconnected by wires and cables, stood or sat around the room, lips moving. "Sit here," Jeff said, pushing me toward one of the lesser cogs in the network—a scarred metal desk with nothing but an old-style Touch-Tone telephone on it. "I'll be right back."

He returned in less than a minute with a stack of cards in his hands. "Welcome to the high-tech world of Wall Street," he said, putting the cards down on the desktop. "These are your lead cards—old fiber technology, yes, but you don't get the newer technology until you've been here a few weeks. And lead cards are still effective. Especially these. Most lead cards, they're shit—just the names of people who live in a zip code like 90210 or subscribe to *Business Week* or some other shit—but these leads are hot—*hot*! Where do I get these leads? Good question—and one that a lot of guys here would give a testicle for. But you don't need to know. All you need to know is they're the best leads money can't buy."

He picked up the top card and waved it at me. "Now, what do you do with these leads? Good question. You call 'em. Say whatever you have to say to get past their secretaries, their wives, their yoga instructors, whatever. Once you get the real guy on the horn, you don't talk to him. Repeat: You don't talk to him. You're not allowed to. You're a cold caller, not a human being. So you do one thing: You pass the guy on to one of my qualifiers—extensions 432 and 434. In other words, you get the guy physically on the phone, you transfer him, and that's all."

"That's all?"

"That's all."

Jack had implied as much in our talk the other day, but I guess I thought he'd been exaggerating.

"Okay, I can see you're discouraged," Jeff said. "And gee, Will, I feel your pain. You come to New York to be a hotshit stockbroker, not a telephone receptionist, but you know what? This is how it's done. Don't be a crybaby. Any questions?"

I couldn't think of any.

"Okay," he said. "Training over. Now get on the phone."

He walked away. For a few seconds, I just sat there and contemplated the crooked stack of cards in front of me. There was my day, staring me in the face—each card representing a minute of my life. So much for the glamour and excitement of working on Wall Street.

Sighing, I picked up the first card. Raymond Dortmunder, it read—listing a number with an area code I didn't recognize. For a second, I considered calling Josh in Bloomington to commiserate, but then I thought that somebody, maybe the Queen, might be listening in to all new trainees' calls. So I scooted my chair closer to the desk, pulled the phone toward me, and punched in the number on the card.

"Raymond Dortmunder's office."

"Yes, may I speak with Mr. Dortmunder, please?"

"Who's calling?"

"This is Will Merrick over at Pembroke Horton."

"Pembroke Horton *Brokerage?*"

"Yes."

(click)

Okay, strike one, I thought. I tossed the card aside and went to the next one: "Stephen Goldblatt's office."

"Yes, is he back yet?"

"Who is this, please?"

"It's Will Merrick."

"Will Merrick *of . . . ?*"

(pause) "It's a personal call."

"Concerning?"

"Concerning personal matters."

"Well, then, let me just take down your number—"

"Thanks, I'll just call back later."

(click)

Next card: "Todd Greenville's office."

"Hello there, this is Will Merrick, returning his call?"

"Are you sure? I place all of Mr. Greenville's outgoing calls, and your name doesn't seem familiar. Can you tell me what this is in reference to?"

"His investment portfolio. It's important."

"This is a cold call, isn't it."

"Uh . . ."

"Isn't it?"

"Well . . . yes."

(click)

Next card: "Securities and Exchange Commission. How can I direct your call?"

(click)

Next card: "Stanford Wall's office."

"Yeah, I just got cut off with him."

"I'm sorry. Let me put you through again, Mr. . . . ?"

"Merrick."

"Just a moment, Mr. Merrick."

(pause on hold)

The woman again: "Mr. Merrick?"

"Yes."

"Mr. Wall would like me to tell you that—well, this is what *he* said—if you call here again, your call won't be the only thing cut off."

It went on like that for the rest of the morning. I got maybe half a dozen people to stay on the line long enough to transfer them to a qualifier, and of those only one turned into a genuine lead. By twelve-thirty, intense demoralization was setting in. Here I was on Wall Street, I kept telling myself. Money was being made all around me— you could practically smell it—but I, William Tobias Merrick, couldn't even get a potential investor to stay on the phone with me.

Then, just as I was about to give up and go to lunch, my luck changed:

"Sonnenberg, Vaughn, and Carter."

"Yes, can you hold for William Merrick?"

"Well, sure, I suppose so."

(simulated phone forwarding noise)

"Ezra! You old dog! How the hell are ya?"

"I'm sorry, sir, this isn't Mr. Carter."

"Haw haw! Sorry about that, little lady. My guy said he had Ezra on the line. Tell him it's Will."

"Just a minute, sir."

(pause)

A gruff man's voice: "Who the hell is this?"

"Mr. Carter, can you hold for a second?"

"Yeah, right! I don't hold unless I know who this is!"

"I'm Will Merrick, sir. From Pembroke Horton Brokerage?"

"Jesus Christmas, a brokerage? (*Goddamn it, Jennifer! It's some guy from a brokerage!*)" I thought for sure he was going to hang up, but he came back on the line and said, "Okay, Will Merrick. What are you trying to sell me?"

"Well, that's why I have to transfer you. Technically, for reasons no one will explain to me, I can't try to sell you anything."

"I get it. You're new, right? Don't even have your Series 5?"

"Well, to be honest, this is my first day."

"Your first day! (*Goddamn it, Jennifer, this asshole got through to me on his first day!*) Not bad, young man, not bad." He laughed. "Took me days to get past anybody's secretary when I was in your shoes."

"You were a cold caller, sir?"

"Fuck yes. God, I remember my first day. You hate it, right? People treating you like shit?"

"Well, yes, sir, they are."

"I know exactly what it feels like. This was at Merrill, back in '73–'74."

"You were at Merrill Lynch, sir? That's my dream!"

"Yeah, well, keep dreaming. I'm talking about the days of stone tablets. Made a shitload of money there, eventually."

"Well, that's sort of what I'm hoping for, too."

"You do, huh? So what the hell you doing at Pembroke Horton?"

"This isn't a good place to make money?"

"Fuck no. This is the '90s, son. Listen to me: What are you, twenty-three, twenty-four years old?"

"Almost."

"You ever hear of a little thing called venture capital, boy? Fuck Wall Street! Fuck investment banks! You get yourself hooked up with some VC firm like us!"

"Like you?" I said. "Sonnenberg, Vaughn, and Carter is a VC firm?"

"Goddamn, son, you *are* green. Yeah, we're a VC firm, based down here in Austin. Lots going on here. You should get on a plane, boy. We could use hungry kids like you."

"I know I'd love that. But I just got here. And I've got family in New York."

"Fuck the family! Least you should do is sniff out something up there. Silicon Alley, in my fucking humble opinion, is terminally second-tier, but you got a couple good VCs up there. Whatever you do, though, get out of this brokering shit while you can."

"But how do I start? I mean, I'm totally new to all of this."

"*You* figure it out. But listen, what's your name again?"

"Will. Will Merrick."

"Listen, Will, let me do you a favor. Put me through to your owner."

"My owner?"

"Your broker—the guy making your life miserable."

"Actually, I'm supposed to transfer you to a qualifier first."

"Fuck the qualifier! Patch me into the broker. What's his name?"

Something told me I should skip Jeff and pass this man right on to Mr. Witherspoon. After all, didn't he say I was his bitch? "Ted Witherspoon," I said.

"Fine, get me Ted Witherspoon on the line. And you stay on, too."

I put Carter on hold and buzzed Mr. Witherspoon. "Sorry to disturb you, sir. It's Will Merrick."

"Will, okay, outstanding, what's the problem?"

"I've got somebody on the line who insists on speaking to you. Some VC."

"Some VC? What's it about?"

"I honestly don't know, sir. But his name is Ezra Carter."

"Ezra Carter! You know who that is, Will? Pass him through!"

I did.

"Ted Witherspoon speaking."

"Hiya, Ted. Ezra Carter here, from Sonnenberg, Vaughn, and me."

"So I heard. And your rep precedes you. Slam dunk on Permian Wireless last year, by the way."

"Thank you, Ted. *We* think it was a pretty good deal, too."

"So what can I do for Ezra Carter this fine day?"

"For me you can't do squat right now, Ted. But this kid you got—Merrick? He's good, resourceful—got past my girl Jennifer, and the woman's a pit bull usually. So listen, my friend, you be good to him, hear? You shouldn't be feeding him lead cards with VC phone numbers on them."

"You're right, Ezra, you're absolutely right. But you know about lead cards."

"Fuck lead cards! Now, Will, boy, you still there?"

"Yes sir."

"Okay, Will, I'm not normally this warm and fuzzy, but I like you. So here's the deal: You and Ted, if you get something good—I mean really good, no garbage IPOs or dead inventory crap—you give me a call and maybe we do some business. Okay? This kind of economy, I like to make friends if I can, you know what I mean? You got my number now, Will, and if you call again, I'll take the call—you hear that? *I'll take the call.* But it better be worth my while, you got me?"

"Yes sir, Mr. Carter."

"Fuck Mr. Carter! Call me Ezra, for God's sake. Okay, Ted, Will, pleasure talking with you."

(click)

"Uh, Will, you still there?"

"Yes, Mr. Witherspoon."

"What the hell was that, Will?"

"I have no idea. He insisted on speaking to you."

"You know that Ezra Carter is probably the biggest friggin' deal in Austin, don't you?"

"I didn't know that. He was on the card, so I called him."

"Jeez, you made friends with Ezra Carter on a cold call! How'd you do that, Will?"

"I really don't know. He just seemed to, I don't know, respond to my enthusiasm or something."

"Your enthusiasm about what?"

"About everything, I guess." I thought it might be wise to embroider here: "About the New Economy, the Internet, the whole thing. I was just talking about it yesterday with my friend Fletcher, who's got this amazing startup—"

"Your friend Fletcher?"

"Yes, Benjamin Fletcher?"

There was a long silence on the other end of the line. "You know Ben Fletcher, son of Joseph 'Fletcher Broadcasting' Fletcher?"

"Yes, and his sister Eliza. They're friends of my uncle."

"Your uncle Gilbert Hawking, of Hawkings Wholesaling."

"Right. He introduced Ben and me and we sort of hit it off. I was just there yesterday for dinner and he was telling me about his startup—Stevedore Technologies? Sounds really interesting."

Mr. Witherspoon laughed. "Unbelievable," he said. "You got some kind of gift, Will."

"Did I screw up there with Carter?" I asked.

"Hard to say. But in future, don't forward any calls to me, okay? Unless you get somebody like Ezra Carter on the line, they go to the qualifier first, then to Jeff."

"Absolutely, Mr. Witherspoon. I'll remember that."

"Outstanding." Then he said, "Listen, Will, question: Have you had lunch yet?"

"I was just about to get some."

"How about I buy you some lunch?"

"Sounds great, Mr. Witherspoon."

"Be at my office in ten minutes. And call me Ted, will you?"

(click)

Call him Ted, he said. I put down the phone, picked up my stack of lead cards, and dropped them into the trash.

He took me to the restaurant at the Regent Hotel. We sat on the outdoor balcony, at one of the prime tables overlooking Wall Street. A steady stream of office workers, brokers, and exchange employees, all with plastic IDs hanging from their necks, passed below, along with FedEx trucks, armored cars, security vans, and food carts selling everything from bagels to yakitori. The ambient noise from all of this traffic echoed along the pillared balcony, so that Ted and I practically had to shout at each other.

"So tell me, Will," Ted began, sawing at a bloody slab of porter-house, "how'd you like it this morning?"

I hesitated, unsure how to play this. "Honestly?"

"Hey, honesty is what this business is all about," he said.

I decided to take the chance. "Truth be told," I said, "I'm just not sure this is the route I want to go. I don't want to be a retail broker. I want to do deals. I think I'd be good at that—getting people together, making things happen. I want to be out there in the real action." I put down the heavy knife and fork. "I know cold-calling is the way everybody's supposed to start, and maybe I'm being really arrogant, but basically, I'd rather skip the scut-work stage and start playing the real game and making some money."

Ted looked at me for a long time. A long, long time. I started to get worried. Maybe I was trying to move too fast. Would the fact that I was already wimping out—after a single morning as a cold caller!—make him think I didn't have the right stuff for Wall Street?

Ted opened up a file he had brought along and pulled out what I recognized as my employment papers. With great ostentation, he ripped them up. I thought that was it—I was fired—but then he leaned forward and said, "Let's start over, Will. I made a few calls about you. I think I've heard enough to know I want you on my team, whatever your inexperience."

"On your team?"

"Something my own boss doesn't even know yet: I'm moving over to our underwriting department next week. Old Pembroke wants to put on a big push in the IPO area—we've been lagging behind there for years—and he wants me to be part of it. I need people to come with me, and I like what I see when I look at you. You're hungry—God, even Ezra Carter sensed that in two minutes on the phone—and you've got a way with people. So let's forget this broker training and put you on a different track. Sound good to you?"

"Are you kidding, Ted? IPOs? I'm there!"

"Okay, now here's the interesting part. I need a player on my team who isn't caught up in Pembroke Horton politics, a guy whose first loyalty is to me. So, if you do this thing, you'll be working for me, not Pembroke Horton. You'll be my off-the-books consultant. So *I'll* be paying your salary, not them, just so you know where I'm coming from."

This gave me pause, but I said, "Sounds fine."

"Now, I know you're thinking about your job with your uncle."

Actually, I wasn't, but I *was* surprised that he knew I was working for my uncle.

"Sure, Will, I know all about that—I talked to Jack, remember?—but here's the thing: I don't want you to stop working for Hawkings. You're in a good position there—Gilbert Hawking is about as connected as anybody in this town—and I think it wouldn't be a bad thing for you to learn what you can there—about the business, the gossip, the personalities. Pembroke will be on my tail to bring in new business, so anybody you can introduce me to—any friend of your uncle's—would be great."

"Like Ben Fletcher, for instance?"

"There you go," he said, shooting a finger at me. "Like Ben Fletcher, for instance. One of these days, he'll want to bring that Stevedore Technologies thing public. He'll need an investment bank to do that. So if, for instance, you convinced your friend Fletcher to come to Pembroke Horton . . . well, we'd all do very well—Fletcher, you, me, the firm, everybody." He put down his own knife and fork then. "Will, I won't lie to you: You can be really useful to me. In return, I can be really good to you. I can start you off at forty Gs a year—off the books and with no set hours, so you can keep working for your uncle—but think of that as just a percentage of your pay. We get some business together, there's bonus money, raises, whatever. And as I say, your hours can be flexible. Your main job will be to listen and learn, make friends, find out who's doing what, and help me in any way you can. Now don't say yes or no right now. Let's just sit here and enjoy our lunch. When we get back to the office, we can discuss it some more."

We did exactly that, though I have to say it was difficult for me to talk to Ted about anything else. I kept trying to calculate my position—$40,000 from Ted, off the books, plus the $30,000 my uncle was offering, also off the books, plus free room and board, plus whatever bonuses I'd earn from bringing business to Ted. I'd be making the equivalent of a six-figure salary my first year in New York!

After lunch, Ted paid the check and we walked back to Pembroke Horton. When we got upstairs, he steered me toward his office. "Just a few more words," he said as he shut the door behind us. "I'll send your regrets to personnel about the brokerage position. But first, I want to ask you one thing. What I said back at the restaurant, about me being good to you if you're good to me? You believe me on that?"

"Of course I do, Ted."

"You trust me one hundred and ten percent? And are you ready to give me some concrete proof of your trust?"

"You name it."

"Outstanding." He began caressing his tie like a pet. "Last week you told Jack that your dad had staked you a certain amount of money, am I right? When he sent you off to New York?"

"R-right," I said.

"How much you got?"

I considered being discreet—i.e., lying—the way I had with my uncle. But every instinct I had told me not to. "He wired fifteen thousand dollars to a checking account in my name."

"You have your checkbook with you right now?"

"Uh, yes."

"I want you to write me a check—to me personally, for fifteen thousand dollars."

"Well, let me think—"

"Will, Will, Will, this is your initiation. I got to know we trust each other completely. I'm telling you right now you won't regret it. You believe me?"

"Sure, but that's my entire—"

"I want you to write me that check right now, no questions asked. This is the one and only chance. Otherwise, we shake hands and you leave the building for good." He looked at his watch. "You got one minute."

I took the full minute. This was a game he was playing, obviously, but should I play along? I tried to do a quick risk assessment, but ended up going with my intuition. The man wanted to impress me. So I pulled out my checkbook and wrote him a check for $15,000.

He smiled as I ripped it out of the book and handed it to him. "Good," he said. "Wait here." And then he walked out of the office with my entire net worth.

Alone now, I reached back for the arms of the chair behind me and lowered myself into it. Already, I was being assailed by second thoughts. I had just given every penny I had in the world to a man I had met that morning. Talk to anyone in Bloomington, tell them you were going to New York, and you'd get more or less the same advice every time—watch your wallet. The city was full of conmen, they'd say. New York was the bull's-eye center for every ripoff ever invented in the history of mankind. If somebody comes up to you and tells you he just found a bag of money on the subway, and that he'll split it with you if you'll just help him deal with the situation, the smart thing to do is run the other way. No matter how foolproof it looks, you're going to lose money. These people live off rubes from the hinterlands, I was told. But I'd always dismissed the people who said this. I was too smart to get ripped off.

But now I had given $15,000 to a man who had just taken it out of the room—and who might never give it back.

I felt a drop of sweat ooze from my left armpit and trickle down my rib cage.

There was a telephone on the desk in front of me. I could call the bank right this instant and put a stop on the check. Check number 001—how humiliating!

I was just about to lunge toward the phone when Ted came back into the room. "Here you go," he said, handing me a piece of paper. "You just bought eight hundred and thirty-three shares of Rebus Telecommunications."

I looked down at the receipt in my hand. It was handwritten. "Rebus? What is it? What do they do?"

"You know, I'm not really clear on that myself. Something with fiber optics. We got the IPO set to go in"—he looked at his watch—"about thirty seconds. Want to come over here and watch?"

He sat down and started pecking at his computer keyboard. I got up and came around to his side of the desk. "The offering price—which is what you paid—is 18. Let's see how she pops in the after-market."

I stood behind him and stared at the computer screen. I had no idea what I was looking at. The screen was divided into several separate sections, two of them filled with columns of figures, a third depicting a bar graph, the last a line graph—all in red, green, and white. I remember thinking: Christmas colors.

"Here's the bids right here," he explained, pointing to a series of bars on the bar graph, standing tall in a line like the skyscrapers on Avenue of the Americas. The graphs were in motion. There were shifting bars, rising lines, numbers and letters flashing and scrolling all over the screen while the computer began to emit a series of odd little pings and chirps.

"What's happening?" I asked.

"Exactly what we knew would happen," he said. "Just watch."

I squinted at the four windows, having no idea where to focus. Pretty soon the screen began to swim before my eyes. "Is it going up?"

"Jeez, Will, read the goddamn screen! Of course it's going up!"

"So what's the price?"

"Watch this number." He pointed to the top figure on one of the columns in the upper right-hand window. It read 34.8125.

"Is that the price right now?" I asked.

"That *was* the price. But look at the goddamn bids!"

The number was now 38.125. Unless I was mistaken, I had just more than doubled my money. $15,000! "Can I sell now?" I asked.

"Whenever you say, Will. But look at the chart, damn it! Look at the bids and offers. This baby's set to run awhile."

But I couldn't look at the bids and offers. The only number I understood was the single morphing figure at the top of that one column. It was now 33.50. I had lost over $4,000 in the last fifteen seconds. "Sell! I want to sell!"

"I don't recommend it, Will. I honestly don't."

The price was back up to 36.125. "Do a limit order," I shouted, the heat in my face. "Sell at 40, all of it!"

"It's up to you, Will. But we don't have any substantial resistance until 41 and change."

"Okay, wait!" It was up to 39 even now, then 39.25 . . . 40.125 . . . 40.50. "How much higher?" I asked. "What do the bids and offers tell you?"

"It's getting a little sloppy now," he said.

40.125 . . . 39.875 . . . "Yes!" I shouted then. "Sell now. At the market."

"Sold!" he said, pointing to the latest price. "At 37 7/8."

"But you didn't do anything!" I said. "You didn't hit any keys! How did you sell?"

"That's because this was an unofficial transaction. The shares are in my name, in my personal account, and the way it works, I'm not allowed to sell for a certain period. It's a condition of buying at the initial offer price."

I felt as if a stone had fallen on my chest. "So, wait, this was all hypothetical?"

"No way. Let's just say I was your own private market maker." He opened a drawer and pulled out a ledger book and a small calculator. "Let's see: Eight hundred and thirty-three shares at 37.875 makes . . ." He scribbled in the ledger book, tore out a check, and handed it to me. It was made out to the order of William Merrick. For $31,550. "And no need to alert the IRS about those gains, since, like I said, this was sort of our own little transaction."

My hand was shaking as I folded up the check and stuffed it into my pocket.

"So now we understand each other, I think. You want the job?"

I couldn't speak, so I just nodded my head.

"Outstanding. And hey, don't think we get opportunities like Rebus Telecom every day. But we do on more days than you would think."

I remembered what he had said to me that morning—that he had something big coming down after lunch. I understood that I had been manipulated with expert skill and timing, but I didn't care about that. I was $16,500 richer than I was fifteen minutes ago, and this impressed me. Just as Ted knew it would.

"Now, my one requirement of you is that you keep our arrangement private. The best way for you to do your job is to tell nobody about it. I don't mean you have to lie or do anything dishonest, but I think you'll learn a lot more if you don't make a big thing out of the fact that you're working for me. Not with your uncle, not with Fletcher—nobody except Jack, who more or less works for me in the same capacity. You understand what I'm saying?"

"I do, Ted. You can rely on me."

"Good. Now, I think you might want to deposit that check and then go home and lay down a little. You look like you've been raped or something."

"You're right, Ted. I'll do exactly that."

I was about to leave when he called me back. "By the way, have a look now."

He pointed a chubby finger at his computer screen. Rebus was now at 44 even. "Should've listened to me," he said. "But you'll learn as you go along. Now go home and get some rest."

CHAPTER 7

To: *jdooling@boondocks.net*
From: *will2power@net2000.com*
Subject: *local boy makes good*

josh—
much as i hate to give you yet another excuse to whine (really,
j, how can you complain about bloomington when you have a
nice little puppy now to keep you company?)—anyway, much
as i hate to crush you, i nonetheless have to tell you . . . well,
how should i put this gently . . . READ MY WORDS,
DOOLING!!! I RULE THIS TOWN!!! well, 'rule' is maybe
an exaggeration, but yrs truly is definitely kicking some
major-league ass here. i've been here for less than a week, and
already i've LOST two jobs. sounds bad, right? but they were
terrible jobs, and instead i've stumbled into 2 amazing jobs.
one of them is with my uncle, who seems to have recognized
my genius right off the bat (no comments plz) and has spared
me the indignity of warehouse gofer-dom by taking me on as

his 'instrument,' by which i think he means 'industrial spy.'
turns out the old guy is a major player here—titan of local industry etc etc but also a kind of proto-vc besides. anyway, he's going to pay me to sniff around and find out what opportunities he should invest his money in.

   and the other job is equally bizarre. on friday i meet this guy—on wall st. yet—and it turns out he knows my uncle. we get to talking over a beer, during which conversation he too recognizes my incomparable genius, and before you can say risk arbitrageur he's offering me a job! turns out he headhunts for some midlevel investment firm (pembroke horton— ever hear of it?), and they've got a retail brokerage, sez he, and they can use some new trainees, sez he, and would i be interested? hell yes, i tell him, and so i started today, this morning, but it turns out the job is total scut work, but that's okay, because the guy i work for is moving over to the ipo dept anyway and he decides he wants to take me with him. it all seems a little dubious until we talk and i pick up that what he really sees in me is my connection to uncle gil, who knows all the movers and shakers in this town, and so this guy, who's from new jersey or something, seems to think I'm his ticket to the olde money of gotham, and so he makes me his 'off-the-books consultant' (by which i think he means 'financial spy'), and for a salary plus perks that could add up to something significant.

   seriously, j, this is all the god's honest truth and it should give you some idea what it's like here. THERE IS MONEY EVERYWHERE IN THIS TOWN!!! and all the rules about making it are changing by the hour, and nobody knows what they're doing but everybody's making money hand over fist (incl yrs truly, just this afternoon, but details later). you've heard all that stuff about the new wild west and the sheriff's out of town and everything is loose and improvisational? well, it's true—and guess who finds himself in the middle of it?

oh yeah, also I'm madly in love with this incredibly beautiful woman whose daddy apparently owns half the radio and tv stations in the southwest and whose brother is set to become the next larry ellison. (only problem—she thinks i'm a wimp with no imagination, but i'm working on it. . . .)

now i know you're going to think i invented all of this, but i swear to you that it's all 100% true, every word of it. my advice to you is to scrape together whatever money you can and GET OVER HERE! i'm serious—do whatever it takes. if i hear anything re: stock tips i'll let you know immediately, and you get on datek and buy when i say buy and sell when i say sell (because it looks as if i'll be in a position to know), and before the year's out you'll have your grad school loans paid off and you'll be on your way here with enough left over to start making the real money.

anyway, i should go now. rest assured that i am not on amphetamines or ecstasy but am giving you an accurate picture of the reality in this amazing time in this amazing place. more later, when i have a minute to breathe.

chrs, will

Someone knocked at the door of my room just as I clicked the send button. "Who is it?"

"Who else would it be?" Mrs. Popper said, her voice muffled by the door. "Your uncle wants you in his study."

"I'll be right there," I shouted back. I noticed then that an incoming e-mail had arrived when I sent the one to Josh, so I quickly opened it. It was from Jack Petroni:

To: <u>will2power@net2000.com</u>
From: <u>jackpetroni@zigzag.net</u>
Subject: Congratulations

Will—

I just heard the good news. I knew I was right about you. Ted thinks I'm a genius for finding you. And what's this about you making friends with Ben and Eliza Fletcher? You don't waste time do you, that's a nut I been trying to crack for months. I tip my hat to you. Anyway I want to say welcome aboard (because we have lots of business together, semiofficially, Ted and me, like he told you) and when can we have lunch or dinner or a couple beers again so we can talk about a few opportunities? I think you're gonna like this life Will. Call me.

—Jack

I moved the e-mail into my "answer" folder, then snapped shut the screen of my laptop, disconnected the telephone cord, and shoved the whole thing into the middle drawer of my desk.

I found Uncle Gil sitting in front of his own computer, frowning. He had the *Wall Street Journal*, *Fortune*, *Business Week*, and a half-dozen other publications spread out on the desktop beside him. "Do you ever trade stocks online, Will?" he asked, his eyes on the screen.

"Not really," I said. "E*TRADE tends to prefer customers who actually have money."

"Oh, poverty is no obstacle in today's market," he said. "With the way they push margin-buying these days, you don't need capital to make money, just the temporary use of someone else's capital." He pushed in the keyboard shelf and turned his swivel chair toward me. "But it's probably best that you save your money for a while before investing it. I don't pretend to understand this market. Nobody with any sense does. Six months ago, I had my broker start selling tech stocks short, and did nothing but lose money. Meanwhile, my holdings in good, solid, money-making companies have languished."

"I could tell from our conversation with the tailors that you weren't much for momentum investing."

"*Momentum investing*," he said with a look of distaste. "But I'm not stupid, Will, and the one rule I've always followed is 'Never fight the market.' So I've been doing a little speculative trading in the past few months—buying solid tech stocks when they're profoundly overpriced and then selling them again when they're ridiculously, outrageously, *obscenely* overpriced. Only to watch them go even higher." He waved toward his computer. "But it's expensive using a traditional broker. One of these days you'll have to teach me how to use this damned machine to buy stocks online. You know how to do it?"

"No problem. I have an imaginary portfolio that I follow online."

"Good," he said. "But that's not why I called you. I need you to go to the bank for me."

"Sure," I said. "For what?"

He picked a sourball from the candy dish on his desk and started crinkling the wrapper. "As you may know from working for your father, a business of any size needs a certain amount of cash on hand at all times . . ."

"You mean, like, for paying people off the books?"

He winced. "For contingencies, William, for contingencies." He threw the sourball back into the dish. "Until now, I've had McTeague handle it, but he's busy with other things, and I thought—blood being thicker than water in any case—this might be part of your new duties."

"My new duties as your instrument."

"Yes, as my instrument. It's not very much money—usually just five or ten thousand every week—so I'm not putting you in any great danger from street muggers. But you'll want to be careful all the same. For the occasional larger sums, a backpack of some sort might be prudent, since everyone your age seems to carry one."

"I've got something that would work."

"Good. I've already made the arrangements with my local branch of Chase, so they'll be expecting you. Here's my bank card and the withdrawal slip. It's the branch on Varick, just around the corner and a few blocks up."

I took the card and the slip, which was made out for $8,000.

"You'll need my personal indentification number, which is 6241." He squinted at me. "Just remember that I keep careful track of the balance in that account. I'll know if it's short."

"Uncle Gil! I'm your nephew!"

"Yes, and I wouldn't be the first person in history robbed blind by his own flesh and blood." I must have looked hurt, because he went on, "Come on, William, I don't distrust you. But you're young, and I don't want to find out in a month that you've been using the petty cash to wine and dine Eliza Fletcher at Balthazar, or wherever people go nowadays."

"Not even if it's to find out more about her brother's company?"

He tried to hide the smile. "We can arrange—informally—for certain of your entertainment expenses to be reimbursed," he said. "Provided they have a legitimate business purpose, of course."

"Of course." An image careened into my head suddenly, of me taking Eliza to some little-known gastronomic temple, in Tribeca, say—not one of the obvious, fashionable places, but an unpretentious, undiscovered gem, three weeks before it gets a three-star review in the *New York Times*. I'd order things that weren't listed on the menu—saffron-dusted quail, medallions of monkfish in lime-cilantro sauce, whatever—and all of it would be superb. "How did you ever find this place?" Eliza would say, savoring every forkful, dazzled by my wooing. . . .

Uncle Gil was staring at me. I snapped out of my reverie. "I'm sorry, Uncle Gil. What did you say?"

"I *said*, you remind me of your mother sometimes. She used to tease me, too. Though with considerably more charm. She used to say she could see through all of my little wiles."

"I won't even pretend to think that, Uncle Gil."

"You'd be wise not to. I've learned a thing or two since then. But go now. I need that cash before the end of business today."

I got my umbrella and headed out into the street. The rain was falling steadily now, pounding the taut nylon of the umbrella. Sheets of water, cobbled by the downpour, slid sideways along the street, disintegrating at the sewer openings into elegant gray cascades. I ran, splashing, to the corner, where glistening yellow cabs crept slowly along Varick, ignoring the frantic waving of pedestrians. I was already soaked, despite the umbrella. My sodden socks squished in my shoes at every step. I heard a rumble—thunder, maybe, or else the subway passing underground—and as I looked up, a gust of cold wind tore the umbrella from my hands. For a moment, it soared above the sidewalk, spinning wildly, and as I watched it, I felt a sudden, inexplicable wave of euphoria roaring through me. The umbrella dropped to the pavement and cartwheeled into the side of a parked truck, and I started to go after it, but then I thought, What the hell! It's just an umbrella. I could buy a new one for five dollars—three dollars if it stopped raining. This was New York! There would be money enough for a thousand umbrellas!

I started running again, plowing though puddles, feeling elated now, feeling invincible—until I stopped, out of breath, in front of the solid, stolid facade of the Chase Manhattan Bank.

❧

THE RAIN HAD LESSENED to but a drizzle when I emerged from the goldsmith's establishment some thirty minutes later. The man who served as my uncle's banker, a wizened Spanish Jew named Diego

Cardozo, had been forthcoming enough once he had examined—
with great care—my uncle's signed note, and now the purse full of
guineas lay heavy against my breast in the pocket of my damp man-
teau. Stepping from the doorway, I pulled at my hat brim and started
off toward home. The streets of Wapping were a sea of mud now,
veined by countless guggling channels of rainwater. Horses steamed
beside the stone warehouses. And there was my broken-ribbed umbrella, still wedged against the empty haywagon, like a great dead al-
batross.

I stopped and reassured myself of the sturdiness of my pockets.
On the left were my uncle's guineas; on the right were my own, so recently augmented by Theodore Witherspoon's remarkable feat of job-
bing. Together, they totalled more money than I'd ever held in my life.

I recalled then what my uncle had said just before sending me
off to his banker. "In the world of the Alley," said he, "one need not
have the capital itself to succeed, but merely the *Temporary Use* of
capital." And this made exceeding good sense to me, now that I
thought on it. 'Twas after all how bankers made their fortunes. This
Jew Cardozo had not the summe of all his clients' gold lying idle
within his coffers. Nay, he did but keep a portion at hand, for transactions such as the one just concluded; the remainder he lent out at
interest, or used for some other money-making prospects. And in
times like these, when all was growth and ferment, such prospects
were legion.

'Twas a revelation of a sort for me. For though I had hitherto understood all of this in principle, 'twas never clear to me in the fact till
now, as I stood on the streets of Wapping. For this, I realized, was
how the *New World* worked. In the *Old World*, wealth was land or
wealth was gold. But in the *New*, there was this other kind, this
shadow wealth—the temporary use of capital. 'Twas like a bull you
borrowed from a farmer to impregnate a dozen cows. The bull you

gave back to the farmer, but the tiny calf in each cow's womb was yours, there to grow and grow into a bull itself, who might live to sire a dozen more just like him.

I felt again that rush of high spirits in my chest. For, yes, I knew that Uncle Gilbert, my farmer, was sitting but a few hundred feet away, waiting for his bull. But until such time as I returned it to him, the animal was mine—and with it, or through it, all the world could perhaps be mine as well.

NOVEMBER

CAPITAL GAINS

CHAPTER VIII

⁓⁓ FOUR O' THE CLOCK on a frosty All Soul's morning is no time for any man to be abroad in the streets of Wapping, yet there was I, at the foot of Wapping Steps at just this time of night, beseeking myself a boat.

The choice of hour was not my own. At half past three, a lad in my employ, young Thomas Block, had wakened me with stones thrown smartly at my window panes. "Beggin' yer pardon, sir," said he when I opened the creaking casement. The boy stood below like a ghost in the milky moonlight. "She's just now come."

I needed no more alarum than this. Before long, I was dressed and letting myself out the front door of the house, wrapped in a woolen cloak against the chill. Thomas was there, his face red and chapped, the snot running down his upper lip.

"Where exactly?" I asked him in a whisper.

"Just off the steps."

I handed him a sixpence and hurried down the darkling street.

At Wapping Steps—the ship anchored midriver, just visible in the moonlight—I knocked up an oarsman sleeping in his bumboat.

"Deuce take ye," he growled, as cross as two sticks at being roused. "You'd best be a dream, whoever y'are."

"Come, Duffy, you'll think me a fine dream indeed—once I pay you thrice your normal fare."

"Oh, Will Merrick, is it?" He wiped his eyes with a ratty sleeve. "All right then. I know you'll make the journey worth my while. Where to?"

"That ship yonder," said I, stepping into his boat.

He peered out over the dark river. "The *Periwinkle*, ain't it? Back so soon from Plymouth?"

"You're well informed, I see."

"I knows every craft by sight that calls this river 'ome," said he, casting off the steps before adding: "Much good does it do me."

It required but a few minutes to reach the *Periwinkle*. She looked derelict in the night, wheezing and groaning in the current like a leviathan restless in its sleep, but I knew better. Her watch, having recognized my call, prepared the ladder and I clambered aboard. "Is the mate stirring?" I enquired of the grizzled sailor who met me at the deck rail.

"Expectin' you below, sir," said he.

I paid him and made my way belowdecks. Even at anchor in the Thames on a windless morning, the ship's lurchings were enough to queer my stomach as I ducked through to our meeting place. In near total darkness—and well-nigh choked by the air of the passage, which stank of seamen's linen long neglected—I tapped upon the door of the last cabin but one. Robert Tilden opened and let me enter.

"What news?" I asked, without preface. 'Twas candlelit within—the cabin a tiny space, with scarce room enough for the two of us. "Any word of the Carolina fleet?"

"None, sir," said he, shaking his head. Robert Tilden was a rough and pox-scarred man, but reliable as a sheepdog. "None before we left Plymouth."

I made a mental mark of this. Those Carolinas—a fleet of some thirteen sail of ships—were two months late to port. If they were sunk or captured or their cargoes lost, the price of raw cotton on the 'Change, already high, would soar.

"And what of the East Indiamen?"

"Now there's the news," said Tilden, his teeth gleaming in the candlelight. "Directly we weighed anchor this Friday last, we met the *Orion*, just making for the port—and looking much the worse for't. We hailed her, and, Law, quite a tale had she to tell. They'd met a storm, the Orions said, just north o' the Azores. Two of the fleet—the *Capricorn* and the *Firebird*, with all hands aboard—were lost, and two more had their cargoes spoilt. *Orion* herself just barely made the port, her foremasts split and staysails all in ribbons."

This was valuable intelligence indeed. That fleet—likewise overdue—held all the profits that the East India Company was like to see that season. "Is there aught else to report?"

"I should think that was enough," said he, somewhat indignant.

"Oh, 'tis, 'tis," I said, and handed him a small velvet purse. "I trust this will not be known ashore for some time?"

"Till noon at least, sir, for there's none can leave the ship till then."

"Good, very good," said I. "I'm in haste today, but come ashore tomorrow and I'll stand you a drink—a quartern of cold Nantz such as would make a parson dance."

He laughed. "You're as good as your word, sir. I know it well."

And then, with no more words than that, we parted.

Back at Wapping Steps, happy to walk again upon dry land, I paid the oarsman his inflated fee and hastened back to my uncle's house. I let myself in—quiet as a burglar—and crept up the stair, just as the good clock softly chimed the hour. In my room once more, I unlocked my portmanteau and retrieved from it a key—a key my uncle had vouchsafed me—and slipped it into my cloak. 'Twas early yet, but five o' the clock, and the Jew Cardozo would not stir till six. And so I sat on the edge of my bed, heart pounding, and did my accounting as I waited:

VAILS, &C.

Boy (Thos. Black)—6 d.

Oarsman (Duffy)—1 s. 6 d.

Periwinkle Watch (Mr. ?)—6 d.

Tilden—£2 10 s.

Running Summe—£2 12 s. 6 d.

Shortly before the clock struck six, I left my room again and descended the lightless stairway. Mrs. Popper was audible in the kitchen, starting on the day's baking, so I crept still more quiet than before and let myself out the front. The sky was streaked with a cobalt tinge of light as I ducked into an alley and turned my steps toward St. Catherine's. The streets were coming awake now. Carts were rattling toward the river, and the taverns already lively with lightermen and oarsmen downing the day's first pennyworth of warm ale. In a street off the former marsh, I stopped at a house I knew well by now and knocked. The ancient footman admitted me and conducted me without comment to the office of Diego Cardozo.

"Ah, Mr. Merrick," said he, with a dainty foreign music to his words. Cardozo was a man of middling size, with the long grey beard and plain clothes that bespoke his Israelite heritage. "You wake with the robins today. But is it not beforetime for Mr. Hawking's weekly cash?"

"Indeed, sir, but I am here upon a different errand. Mr. Hawking must needs have something from his strongbox."

"The strongbox? Again?" Cardozo's prodigious eyebrows rose as he stroked his whiskers with crooked, snuff-stained fingers. He seemed about to say more, but then stopped himself. Nodding, he reached below his enormous oaken desk and retrieved a ring of keys. "Follow me, Mr. Merrick," said he, rising stiffly from his chair. "You are quite aware of what to do by now, I think."

I was. I followed the stooped figure down the narrow stairs and into his fortified cellar. At the bottom, he struck two candles and lit the way down a passage lined with sturdy metal compartments, stacked three rows high. He stopped at the third iron door from the end. Selecting the proper key, he unlocked the door and, handing me the candles, took the heavy strongbox from within. " 'Tis always the greatest of the boxes," he observed, grunting with the effort, "that require frequent fetching." I followed him as he carried the box into a small closet at the end of the passage. "Cry out when you've done with your business," said he, taking one of the candles back from me. Then he stepped out of the closet and pulled the door shut behind him.

I emerged but a few minutes later and called his name. Muttering, the Jew descended the stair again. "You'll be the end of my poor knees, Mr. Merrick," said he, taking the strongbox from me and returning it to its secure locker. He slammed shut the door and locked it. "I must say, Gilbert Hawking never had so much business with me when McTeague was his agent."

"These are prosperous times, sir," I replied quickly, "and in prosperous times a man sees much of his banker."

The Jew squinted at me, his dark, watery eyes searching my face. "That's as may be," he said at last. "But next time I'll thank you to see your banker *after* he's broken his fast."

The precious packet stored safe within my cloak, I thanked the man. With a small bow, I turned and made my way out again to the street. And before another five minutes had passed, I had found myself a hackney coach and was on my way to the City.

⤜⤛⥫⤜⤛

"THE LAD SAID a gentleman awaited me," Jack Petroni said, coming up behind me in the church. "When 'e told me where, I knowed 'twas you, Will."

I turned and clasped his arm.

"You've news, I take it?" said he.

We stood in a quiet corner of St. Stephen Wallbrook. 'Twas a fine little church, I thought—one of the ubiquitous Wren's cleverer contrivances, with a comely dome said to be a model for the far greater one being erected at the new St. Paul's. But more important to me was its suitability as a place of secret rendezvous. For though it stood but a short walk from 'Change Alley, we weren't like to meet there anyone we knew.

"I've news of the kind we like best, Jack," said I, and proceeded to tell him of the East Indiamen's misfortune.

Jack clapped his hands in delight upon hearing this, drawing a daggery glance from the only other occupant of the church—a withered old crone a-praying across the way. Leaning closer to me, he whispered, "You 'ave the required document, then, to turn this intelligence to our advantage?"

I withdrew from my cloak the packet from my uncle's strongbox—a running cash note (payable to bearer, and thus as good as gold), which my uncle kept locked away at Cardozo's "for contingencies." Since the Jew had no knowledge of what was in my uncle's box, there would be no record of the note's removal—nor of its eventual return to the box later that day, if all went well. In the meanwhile, Jack could use the note as collateral to raise the cash we needed.

Smiling, Jack took from me the folded document and transferred

124

it to his own pocket. "All right, then," said he, "I can 'ave me boys in place within the hour. You knows what to do now, Will, I trust?"

"I do," said I.

"Then let's away." He clapped me heartily on the back then—making a noise that echoed in the vaulted space of Wren's little church. The old crone shot us another dagger. "Act well the rôle, me lad," Jack said, "and we'll 'ave done before the midday meal."

⌖

I ENTERED JONATHAN'S COFFEE-HOUSE at ten o'clock precisely. Slipping past the wall adorned with notices of ships to be sold, tutors to be hired, and "lost" documents to be reclaimed for a price, I approached my usual table near the back. Here I found my man, a jobber I'd previously had business with (for by now I was a familiar figure in Jonathan's, having represented my uncle—and myself—in many a transaction over the past months). "Mr. Bentley, sir," said I. "What price a *Refusal* on East India?"

The jobber eyed me carefully. A *Refusal* was a covenant to buy shares at a set price on a future date, and they were not bought or sold without a purpose. "Do you ask, sir, in Gilbert Hawking's behalf?"

"I ask, sir, but in whose behalf I will not say."

He paused, then gave a price I knew to be too high.

"Can you not do better than that, Mr. Bentley? 'Tis a bit dear, is't not?"

The jobber frowned. "What would you pay then?" he enquired.

I named a price, and he another, and we went on in this manner for some time, I making much noise over what was in actuality but a small purchase of covenants to buy shares. The effect, however, was noticeable about the room. The price of East India Refusals—hitherto beaten down by the uncertain fate of the company's fleet—crept up as it became known throughout the house that the nephew of Gilbert Hawking—that same Hawking whose sources of information around the world were rivaled by few—did seem to have some intelligence concerning East India that was worth buying on. Indeed, sellers of Refusals became buyers as I stood there, and the price grew ever dearer. Meanwhile, the price of East India *Puts*—each one a right to sell shares at a fixed price in the future and thus a bet *against* the company's good fortune—began to fall in contrary motion to the price of Refusals. Though I heard them not, I knew the rumours must be circulating—*old Hawking's nephew is buying East India; he must have good news of the fleet; the ships must be safely into port somewhere.* And so, having caused this dovecot flutter, I ordered a dish of coffee and watched as the trading soon reached a frenzied pace.

(And all the while, in the corners of the great room, Jack Petroni's agents did quietly buy up every East India Put on offer, and for an ever smaller price.)

The true intelligence reached Jonathan's at noon, but by then 'twas fiddler's news at best. Two gentlemen entered the house—well-known brokers for several of the East India directors—and began softly enquiring after the price of Puts. Though they affected airs of nonchalance, their actions spoke volumes. And once they commenced buying these same Puts (from Jack's agents, who had by then nearly *cornered the market*, as 'tis said), the news spread rapidly through the room. "The whole fleet's been sunk," I heard one gentleman whisper aloud, his information not entirely accurate, but right enough. "Their entire cargo's lost, I hear!"

And thus, as a great ship tacking in high wind does reverse course, swinging west when all was east before, so did the price of East India come about. Those newly over-dear Refusals plummeted in price, while Puts, so recently bought cheap, began climbing toward the skies. My work of pigeon-plucking done, I drained my dish and slipped out of the clamorous coffee-house. After disposing of my few now-worthless Refusals in the kennel ditch, I made my way through the streets of the City to the Regent—the topping chop-house at which Theodore Witherspoon had played my host on my first day in his employ. There I made short work of a joint of mutton before proceeding on to St. Stephen again. Jack was already there, standing in our appointed corner.

He danced a little jig at my approach. "There ye be, Will," said he, in merry pin now.

"Have we been successful, then?" I asked.

"As if you din't know. There's yer running cash note back, good as new. And 'ere"—he handed me a purse heavy with coinage—"is yer own portion o' the profits." He grinned broadly, his handsome face alight. "Like rollin' a drunken man, ain't it?"

"Truly," said I, taking the purse.

Arm in arm, we proceeded then along the side aisle to the front of the church. There—in the vestibule, where the stairs led down to the street—Jack stopped me.

"So, Will, as agreed, we say naught of this to our *Masters*?"

"I see no cause to speak of it to anyone, Jack."

"Good, good," said he. "For we do no 'arm to Theodore Witherspoon *or* Gilbert 'awking when we thus do ourselves some good. Ain't that right?"

" 'Tis so," said I, though wishing I were as certain of this as he.

"All right, then," he said, giving his heavy pockets a shake. "I'll be off now. Don't neglect to restore that note to your uncle's banker." Then he gave a little mock bow. "Your servant, sir."

"And yours, sir," said I, as I watched him bound down the stairs and skip away toward Threadneedle Street.

CHAPTER 9

∞ UNCLE GIL WAS PERCOLATING irritation when I got back to the house on Charlton Street late that afternoon. "Where have you *been*, William?" he snapped. "I've been trying your cell phone all day."

"I think the battery needs recharging. What's the problem?"

"That damned online brokerage you set me up with! I've been trying to connect all day, but it keeps saying my password is unrecognized."

"I'll check it out. You do know that passwords are case-sensitive, right?"

"Whatever the problem, just fix it. Your little disappearing act cost me money today."

"How so?"

"I had a tip, William, a tip. You know Bob Tilden, our Asia rep? He called in at noon with some information—something he heard about weather-related construction delays at two semiconductor plants in Taiwan. Said it could cause major inventory problems for the big chipmakers. So I tried to get online and short the dickens out of Intel, but I couldn't get into the account! I finally had to call my old broker, but by the time that old goat got moving, the news was out. Intel was already 'in the toilet,' as he so eloquently put it."

"Sorry about that," I said, as if I knew nothing about Bob Tilden and his breaking news from Asia. "Would you like me to check your password right now?"

"Another time; it's not so important," he said. "But I do wonder sometimes what I pay you for."

"It *is* a little unclear," I admitted, fingering in my pocket the check that Jack Petroni had given me in Trinity Church an hour earlier. "You never gave me the job description for the position of 'instrument.' "

"Yes, yes, very amusing," he said, looking disgruntled. "But I'll thank you to be a little more available to me in future. With the market overreacting to every piece of news, good or bad, there's money to be made on any little bit of advance intelligence you can get, if you act fast enough."

"I'll try to remember that."

"Good. And while we're on the topic of keeping your eyes open, you had a call from Ben Fletcher. Something about his changing tonight's restaurant reservation to eight o'clock?"

"Got it," I said.

"And do remember, will you, as you're hobnobbing with the Fletchers at my expense, that your main purpose of the evening is to keep an eye on my investment?"

After much agonizing, Uncle Gil had made a "small" investment of $200,000 in Stevedore Technologies, in what Ben had called a "country club round" of financing from wealthy individuals. This sum wasn't enough to get my uncle a seat on Stevedore's board, but it *was* enough to keep him interested, especially after I discovered (in my *ad hoc* attempt at due diligence) that many of the marquee names Ben kept dropping had indeed thrown money into the company. Even so, Uncle Gil was holding back on any further investment until Stevedore was further along on the development chain.

"I'll see if I can get him to say anything more specific. But you know Ben."

"Yes, I do," my uncle said. "I know him well enough to know that, like a lot of these current visionary entrepreneurs, he sometimes forgets that 'changing the face of communication and commerce' is a phrase, not a business plan. The technology sounds promising, and these analysts' white papers he's been feeding me are fine, but I'd like to see some plausible evidence that this company is going to turn a profit before my hundredth birthday."

"Profits, Uncle Gil? Isn't that a little old-fashioned of you?"

"I'm funny that way. You just make sure you get some useful information for me, all right?"

At this, he let me escape. I went upstairs to my room, took off my overcoat, and punched a number into my cell phone.

"What," barked the voice on the other end.

"Hi, Ted. It's Will."

"Will! I've been trying to reach you all day."

"I think my cell phone battery went dead."

"You're using it now, aren't you?"

I chose to ignore this. "Ted, listen, Ben has changed the time for tonight. It's eight o'clock."

"That's fine. It'll give me more time to get my act together. I want to run a few numbers before we meet."

"I thought we agreed this was going to be a social thing. You know, just get you two together to meet? I don't think Ben's ready to talk IPO yet."

"Relax, Will, I know the drill. I just want to do my homework, is all. The sister's coming, too, right?"

"That's the plan."

"Outstanding. It'll be like a double date. By the way, you see what happened with Cerebral today?"

Cerebral Pharmaceuticals was an IPO Ted had worked for Pembroke Horton two weeks before. "I haven't looked today."

"Up another twenty percent. Chip stocks got killed on some Taiwan news, so a lot of the money went over to biotechs."

"You're on a roll," I said, calculating this new gain. Ted had given me a *douceur* of one hundred shares at the IPO price of 12. The stock was now over 30.

"Hey," Ted replied, "if this dinner turns out all right, I might just have another bonus for you. See you there."

I tossed the phone onto the bed and went to the closet to choose some clothes. The restaurant Ben had picked—Yakuza—would probably be fairly dressy. But I had hopes of persuading Eliza to go out afterwards, just the two of us, and with Eliza that could mean anything from a drink at Petrossian to a game of foosball at some Lower East Side dive. Relations between us had been precarious ever since that dinner at her and her brother's Upper East Side apartment. Our romance, it seemed, was sometimes on, sometimes off. In fact, I was beginning to feel like one of those awful couples on television (Niles and Daphne, *Moonlighting*, that pair on the *Remington Steele* reruns, etc., etc.) whose relationships consisted entirely of *ad nauseam* iterations of sexually tense near-misses designed to keep us on the edge of our BarcaLoungers every week, waiting for the inevitable night they'd fall into bed together. But I was hoping that all of this would change tonight. Until now, I'd always felt a little intimidated by Eliza—not only physically and intellectually, but socially as well. (In this corner, a gorgeous, frighteningly intelligent businesswoman from a family whose net worth probably exceeds the GNP of Mauritania; and in the opposite corner, William Tobias Merrick, a kid from Bloomington four years her junior.) Frankly, she *still* scared me a little. But the past few months in New York had built up my confidence. I'd made some money, learned some ropes, bought some good clothes. I even had a decent haircut now (though it still pained me to pay $120 for a fifteen-minute razor cut by a ninety-eight-pound tattoo aficionado who went by the name of Kryzystov). I thought, in short, that I might finally be ready to take our relationship to the next level—though I wasn't exactly sure what that level would amount to.

After nearly ten minutes of dithering, I settled on the kind of clothes I knew Ben would be wearing—black cashmere polo shirt under charcoal-gray Jil Sander. Boring, but safe. I shaved, brushed my teeth, dressed, and looked at myself in the mirror. I frowned. Was this person in the glass someone who could woo Eliza Fletcher the way she deserved to be wooed?

There was a knock at my door. I opened and found my uncle standing in the hallway holding up a small piece of paper. "I've taken the liberty of jotting down a few questions—things you might just slip into the conversation when it seems natural."

I took the list from him. The first item was: "1: Describe the revenue-sharing model as stipulated in proposed alliances with Qwest Communications and AOL."

"Great," I said. "I should be able to segue into this somewhere between the discussions of current movies and last night's Knicks game."

He stared at me for a couple of beats before saying, "You're joking, of course. But I have confidence in your ability to pursue an agenda consistent with our interests while at the same time socializing with your new friends."

I folded his list and stuffed it into my breast pocket, right next to the similar list of conversation-steerers Ted Witherspoon had given me just the day before ("So, Ted, how did it go with the Cerebral Pharmaceuticals IPO?").

"I'll give you a full report tomorrow morning," I said, while my uncle started picking lint off the shoulders of my jacket.

❦

THE STREET ADDRESS Ben had given me for Yakuza landed me in front of an abandoned-looking former Nynex substation on Twelfth Avenue, a few blocks south of the ferry terminal to New Jersey. Wondering if I had somehow gotten the number wrong, I knocked on the unmarked gray-metal door. It was opened at once by a diminutive Japanese woman in an exquisite peach-colored kimono. As I stepped into the dimly lit foyer, she pointed at my shoes. I took them off—I knew enough to wear loafers and good socks, though it occurred to me that I'd forgotten to mention this to Ted on the phone—and stepped down onto the tatami. She donned a pair of white gloves and, looking subtly disgusted, carried my shoes into the next room.

When she returned, she beckoned me down a dark corridor. I followed, marveling at the utter silence of the place. We passed through a series of rice-paper shoji screens, leather-padded doors, and dim passageways so convoluted that I was sure the whole layout was designed to prevent any patron from catching a glimpse of any other patron on the way in or out. Finally, she slid open a screen into a private dining room. Inside, seated at a short-legged lacquer table, were Ben and Eliza Fletcher.

"Will," Ben said, rising to shake my hand. "Welcome. Come on in."

Eliza, conspicuously alluring in a black pajama-style jumpsuit, silently presented her cheek for me to kiss. It was warm, moist, and as firm and silken as a mozzarella skin.

"I hope you like kaiseki, Will," Ben went on, "because this place is something special. They usually don't let Westerners in here. And when they do, it's only on the recommendation of one of their regular members."

"So who vouched for us?" I asked.

"You know Tatsuro Nishikawa, chairman of Totura Electronics? I met him at Ron Insana's Christmas party last year. He took De Niro and me here after a poker game."

"Enough, Ben," Eliza said, pulling me down to sit beside her. "I'm sure Will is sufficiently impressed."

"I *am* impressed. You know Ron Insana?"

Ben was about to answer when the shoji screen slid open to reveal Ted Witherspoon. He must have come in a few seconds after I did, or else had taken a longer route through the shoji maze. "Ron Insana owes me twenty bucks," he said as he stepped into the room. "We shared a cab to Fort Lee one night, and he claimed he had a liquidity problem."

I struggled to my feet to make introductions. Then, as we were all sitting down again, Ted said, "I'll tell you one thing—this place is certainly out of the way. I think my cab driver thought I was going to some pansy whorehouse."

This seemed to stun everyone into silence. Eliza, the first to recover, clenched her jaw and said, "Actually, I think the pansy whorehouses, as you put it, are a little south of here. This is more of a crack-house area."

"Speaking of drugs," I said quickly, hoping to keep the evening from derailing even before it started, "Ted handled the Cerebral Pharmaceuticals IPO two weeks ago, didn't you, Ted?"

He—Mr. Subtlety himself—flashed me a can't-you-be-any-subtler look. "As a matter of fact, I did," he said. "But let's talk about that later. I could use a drink."

"That we can handle," Ben said. He reached for the little raku carafe on the table in front of him. "Do you like sake, Ted?"

"Love it, Ben," he answered, savoring the first names. "Can't get enough of it."

"Well, I bet you've never tasted anything like this we've got right here. A very special sake—Yamaga Tokubetsu Junmai."

"I know it well," Ted replied. I cringed, knowing that Ben would not let this pass unchallenged, and certain that Ted was about to go down in flames.

"You do?" Ben asked.

"One of my faves in the Junmai style. From Chiyonosono shuzo in the Kumamoto Prefecture, right?"

Ben's mouth opened then, but he seemed incapable of making a sound.

"Tell you the truth, though, I find it a little big-hipped and earthy. I prefer something in the Daiginjo style. You know Takasago's Ichiya Shizuku?"

Ben's state of flummox was only momentary. "Hey, if we're going that route," he said, "let's bump it up a notch. They've got a Tentaka Hinsho here that'll knock your socks off."

"Outstanding," Ted replied. "And I'd like to propose we follow it with something like the Chujonosono 100."

"An excellent choice," Ben said, his jaw tight. "But I think we can get the same high fragrance with better acidity if we go for the Kakunko from Sudo Honke."

"I don't know that one," Ted replied. I could see the tension in Ben's shoulders release. A palpable wave of relief seemed to expand from the table and lap the shoji screens. "So why don't I just let *you* decide. I can see you know more about it than I do."

Ben smiled, leaned back, and said, "I like a man who likes his sake."

"As do I, Ben, as do I," Ted crooned, and shot me a tiny grin.

Impressed—and appalled—by this demonstration of master salesmanship, I could only nod my head in tribute.

Fortunately, there were no choices to be made in the matter of menu—the chef had total discretion there—so the meal itself offered no opportunities for further alpha-male posturing. After a while, in fact, Ben and Ted seemed to get along brilliantly. They found they had interests in common besides premium sake—zydeco music, a seething hatred for Marc Andreessen—and soon were chatting away like old chums. This left me free to focus on Eliza, who seemed particularly warm toward me tonight. She wouldn't even taste a lot of the dishes we were eating (uni, she said, reminded her of a human tongue) and kept pushing them over to me to eat. This was fortunate, since although we went through a dozen courses, each was about the size of a quail egg (in fact, one of the courses *was* a quail egg, boiled in a mixture of seawater and rendered narwhal blubber, then drizzled with something our server refused to translate for us). Without Eliza's supplements, in fact, I would probably have finished the meal hungry.

"So you've made yourself scarce recently," I said, while Ben and Ted compared notes on rare live recordings of Boozoo Chavis.

"Have I? Maybe you haven't been looking hard enough."

I picked at some pickled radish, assessing this flirtation. I figured this might be an opportune time to give her the gift I'd found for her. I reached inside my jacket and took out a small box. "This is for you," I said, handing it over to her.

"What is it?"

"Just a little gift. I'm pretty sure you won't have anything like it."

Looking intrigued, she took the box and opened it. "Lightbulbs?" she asked, eyes sparking with amusement. "You're giving me earrings in the shape of lightbulbs?"

"Yeah, I thought you might like them. You get the reference, right? Lightbulbs, creative ideas? You know?"

"I've never seen earrings in the shape of lightbulbs," she said, poking at them the way a child pokes at a beetle in its palm.

"I didn't want to get you anything . . . obvious," I said, feeling uncomfortable now. It had seemed like a good idea when I was in the little boutique in SoHo. "Oh God, this is embarrassing, isn't it. Give them back." I reached across the table to grab the box, but Eliza snatched it away.

"No," she said. "I'm keeping them. I love them." She snapped shut the box. "And maybe they'll really work. Maybe they'll give me ideas. They've given me one already."

Given the close proximity of Ted and Ben, I decided not to pursue this line. "Uh, speaking of ideas," I said, wondering how red my face had become, "what about that one you told me about—the one for the socially responsible restaurant chain?"

"No, I'm off that. I had somebody look at the numbers and it didn't look too promising after all. Now I'm into something else." She leaned forward over the short-legged table, pushing aside her mug of green tea. "I've got this idea for a project—I'm calling it Prosperity High—to bring major corporations and public schools together into partnership agreements."

"Details, please," I said, enjoying her enthusiasm. Eliza got a certain look in her eye when she talked about one of her projects—passionate, even slightly fanatical. I loved the fact that she wasn't afraid to look foolish.

"The way it'll work is simple," she said, shifting into business-pitch mode. "A corporation donates a certain amount every year to an impoverished school system; the system, in turn, agrees to name their schools after the corporation's products. Sort of like what they're doing with sports arenas, only with a social agenda. So let's say Microsoft agrees to give three million a year to some poor school system in rural Washington State. They rename their schools Windows Elementary, Slate High, Internet Explorer Middle School, whatever. Microsoft gets good PR plus improved name recognition among future consumers; the schools get new buses, portable classrooms, computers, and extra teachers. My company gets a fee for bringing them together and administering the program."

"Okay," I said, "this time I want in. I've got some money now—not much, but enough for a minority interest or something."

"Hold on, cowboy," she said. "I'm not that far along yet. I'm still in the feasibility-testing stage."

"Is Eliza telling you about her new thing?" Ben asked, overhearing us.

"I say it's got legs," I said.

"I have my doubts," Ben said. "What would you call the sports teams? The Connection Wizards? The Active Desktops?"

"I hear you got a pretty interesting project yourself, Ben," Ted put in ham-handedly. "What exactly does Stevedore Technologies make?"

"We're designing a new-concept electronic switch for Internet routers. Fifty percent faster than anything out there."

"Fascinating," Ted oozed, seeming rehearsed. "How's that going?"

"Pretty well, actually. We just took on some extra engineers from Juniper. And right now I'm focusing on filling some management holes and developing partnership alliances."

Remembering my uncle, I asked, "What's going on with Qwest and AOL? I mean, revenue-sharing-wise?"

Ben gave me a funny look. "The lawyers are still haggling over that. Why do you ask?"

"Just curious."

"You thinking IPO yet?" asked Ted.

"Hey, these are still early days," Ben said, hands up. "We're not even up to third-round financing yet."

" 'Cause if you are," Ted barreled on, "I hope you'll consider switching from your current bankers to us at Pembroke Horton. Company like yours, we'd be willing to shave a little off our usual seven percent underwriting fee."

"Interesting. But we haven't even decided for sure that an IPO is the best liquidity event for us. We might look to be acquired, merge, whatever."

"In fact," Ted went on. "I have the authority to offer five percent if we have an agreement before the end of the month—four percent if you sign a letter of intent tonight. I've got one with me, in fact."

He pulled a wad of papers from the inside pocket of his jacket. So much for going slow, I thought. I wondered how Ben would react, but he surprised me. Laughing, he took the papers from Ted and said, "I'll have the lawyers look these over tonight. I assume I have until midnight."

"Tell you what—we have a signed letter of intent by the end of the week, the four percent deal still goes."

Eliza was stirring the soy sauce on her plate. "You don't believe in foreplay, do you, Mr. Witherspoon," she said.

Ted stuffed an octopus leg into his mouth and said, "Show me a man who does."

❧

THE DINNER BROKE UP at a little before midnight. As we were retrieving our shoes, Eliza put her hand on my arm to steady herself and whispered, "Would you be interested in a little after-dinner amusement?"

Possibilities flooded my mind, but I managed to say, "Sure."

Out on the street—vapors rising in the chill November air from an assortment of manhole covers, exhaust pipes, and our own mouths—we parted ways with Ben and Ted. They were both headed north, so we tucked them into a single cab. "What did you have in mind?" I asked.

She was hailing another cab for us. "We've both been hanging out with too many bankers," she said. "I need a little sociological entertainment. You ever been to a goth club?"

"A what club?"

"You'll find it interesting, I think. If you take it in the right spirit."
A cab pulled up at the curb. "We're not dressed right, so it'll cost us."

"Where we go?" the cabbie asked impatiently as we got in.

"To Bedlam." Eliza eyed my Jil Sander jacket. "Expect not to fit
in," she said.

CHAPTER X

⊘ A PENNY TO THE PORTER was the customary price of admission to the galleries of Bethlehem Royal Hospital—that great college of lunaticks known to all in London as Bedlam—but, given the hour, I allowed the poor man sixpence. A whiskered and toothless Cerberus, he examined the coin for clippage before unbolting the iron gate, muttering all the while over the lateness of our visit. Miss Fletcher, who was masked now to preserve at least the appearance of anonymity, seemed eager and somewhat impatient to enter. Her neck flushed a pretty rose, and she breathed fast and shallow, as a child does anticipating some deliciously frightening thing, like a ghost story.

I shared her sense of awed anticipation. Bedlam, which stood fully visible before us in the bright night, was a pile of such gloomy magnificence that it seemed more like a palace than an hospital for moone-calves. Entering beyond its barricade—fourteen feet high and crowned by two agonized stone figures of imposing size—was much like entering the country estate of Beelzebub himself, its grandness coloured by the unknown terrors that lay within.

We followed the porter's torch up the gravel path to the main entrance, which lay under a fabulous cupola, in turn topped by a weathercock in the shape of a flying dragon. "Wait there," the porter barked at us once inside the vestibule. He moved away then, taking the torch with him and leaving us in darkness.

Miss Fletcher took hold of my arm. Even here, at the entrance, the walls of the place echoed with the hollow cries of unseen inmates, and we could only marvel there in the blackness, listening. I cleared my throat to hide my discomfiture. Her hand upon my arm seemed to conduct a kind of *Electricity*. I felt my breath shorten, and other things lengthen. "You are certain you wish to go on?" I asked her.

She answered by squeezing my arm the harder. "Have you never been to such a place, Mr. Merrick?" she whispered.

"B'm'Faith, I have not."

"Then you have neglected one of London's more remarkable spectacles."

"Howso remarkable?"

"Remarkable in that here, like nowhere else in London, one may see mankind as it were naked, without the constraining garments of Convention and Custom and all else that keeps the behaviour of other men and women within narrow bounds."

"I'm not certain I understand you," said I.

"You must wait and see. And then, perhaps, you will understand."

After some minutes, the porter returned with a lantern. "You'll 'ave to find yer own way," said he. "Though I think, sir, you may prefer't that way?" He gave a phlegmy laugh and handed over the lantern before shuffling off into the darkness beyond.

"This way," Eliza Fletcher said, and pulled my arm. We ascended a broad stairway to the first storey, the lantern sending our shadows willy-nilly over walls and ceiling. At the top of the stairs we found a large room, which proved to be the source of the shouts and howlings that rebounded throughout the hospital. We stood at the door of this chamber, peering in through its window grating. A score or more of men ran about within, gesturing wildly in the shadowy light cast by a small fire in the hearth. 'Twas pure Chaos, in truth. A well-dressed man in a corner beat a mattress with a stick; two near-naked bearish men engaged in fisticuffs over possession of an excrement; two more shouted each into the other's face, the spittle flying as they debated matters of protocol (for one claimed to be Prince of the Air and the other Charles II); and one man skipped about the perimeter of the large room, reciting rhymes.

"Why, 'tis like Garroway's on a busy morning," said I.

The lady did grace this remark with a rather unladylike guffaw. "More than you would really wish to believe, perhaps," said she.

"But do they never sleep?" I asked. "This antic activity so late at night comes as a surprise to me."

" 'Tis the full moon, I warrant. For there is a kind of energy here, that only manic spirits at the full moon possess."

Just then the Skipping Man did come up to the door. "Heigh, thou," said he through the grating. "Give me a penny, sir, and I'll tell thee my secret."

"Thy secret?" said I. "How do I know 'tis worth the penny?"

He smiled a toothless grin, which seemed to release the odour of his rank breath. " 'Tis worth the penny to find out, is't not?"

Seeing the logic in this, I opened my purse and gave the man a coin.

"Ha," he said, plucking it from my fingers joyfully and skipping again in a little circle.

"Well, then, what is your secret?"

He leaned close to the grating once more. "Why, sir, 'tis that there's nary a difference 'twixt thy mouth-beard and thy wench's privy parts!"

"How now," said I, somewhat taken aback by this easy and unlooked-for vulgarity. "Mind your words, sir. To you this kind of talk is worth a penny?"

"Why not, sir? For 'tis what you paid, is't not? Halloo! Halloo!" He giggled again and skipped off across the room.

"I beg your pardon, Miss Fletcher," said I, "for that affront."

"I believe you have been sharped, Mr. Merrick. But no apology is necessary. Indeed, for all we know this intelligence he offered is not inaccurate. Further study would be required."

I knew not whose words were more shocking to me, the calf-brain's or my companion's. But before I could frame a response, Miss Fletcher had moved on down the passage. I could only follow, feeling that—despite the lantern in my hand—I was heading off into dark and unknowable territory.

We climbed another storey in the great house and found ourselves in a dim corridor, much quieter and darker than the one below. In the trembling light of the lantern, I could see a procession of doors down one side of the passage, each door pierced by a single barred window. At the first door we stopped and shone the light within. It fell upon a figure jumping up and down upon a bed of straw—a man, dressed in tattered shirt and breeches, his locks long, matted, and filthy. Upon coming aware of the light, he stopped his jumping, turned his unshaven face toward us, and growled like a beast. I could smell his stench from where I stood.

" 'Tis a lycanthrope," my companion whispered, her lips close to my ear as we both peered within.

I had heard tell of such *Wolf-Men*, yet had heretofore never encountered one. I could see now the chains encircling his ankles and wrists. "Is he really, then, by his own reckoning, a wolf?"

"So it would seem. Though the same could be said for many men, I suppose—in a more metaphorical sense."

We stood side by side and watched him awhile. With his eyes still upon us, he began to move from side to side upon the bed. His was a figure of some splendour, the musculature of his shoulders and arms thick and well-defined, so that it seemed to flow over his bones as he moved. He began murmuring quietly, riveting us to our place with his stare. Then he stopped, lay back against the straw, and proceeded to rub himself obscenely, his hips writhing, his noises becoming louder and throatier.

I pushed her from the door. "We must move on," I said.

"These scenes make you uncomfortable, Mr. Merrick?" she asked, as I led her down the passage toward the stairs.

"They do indeed, my lady, for I never know what will come next with these creatures."

"And that frightens you?" she enquired. "Not knowing what will come next?"

I sensed that I was being tested here, knocked upon like an organ pipe to hear if it were cracked. "It does not frighten me, precisely," said I. "But where there is risk, there is always some danger."

"Is risk, then, something for which you have an appetite only when it concerns shares and financial instruments?"

The dappling light of the lantern played upon her lovely face. I heard a rat scuttling in the shadows along the wall, and a distant cry of pain or despair. "I shall take my risk," said I, "in due course." And then I took her hand and led her down the passage.

After some further looking about, we moved into another portion of the house, where the milder crack-brains had liberty to move about freely. Here we found women in several apartments, some parading about saucily, some weeping and muttering and rocking on their knees in silent prayer. There were men here, too—though whether they were fellow inmates or visitors or the night watchers, I knew not. For it seemed that several of these men were engaged in amours with the ladies. A half-dozen couples we saw retreating into corners or side-rooms, arms entangled, whispering and petting and stroking. Miss Fletcher, grasping my arm again, steered me into a small apartment off the main gallery, hoping, perhaps, to escape this lewdness. But here we found another couple. They stood against the wall—the man, his shirtsleeves loose and breeches untied, moving against a blowsy wench with Scotch plaid petticoats asunder, her shawl slipping to reveal a smooth bare shoulder. I made as if to turn Miss Fletcher away, but she was immovable. "Mr. Merrick," she whispered, "now is the time for your risk-taking"—and it was lost from there. My hand plumbed her velvet neckline and I felt her taut, milky breast beneath my fingers. Desire clouded my head as she leaned against my chest, her breath warm and damp upon my cheek. Pulling away momentarily from her kisses, I deposited the lantern upon the ground and moved us into the shadows, her whalebone petticoats creaking under the pressure of my embrace. . . .

∼

I GAVE ANOTHER thruppence glove-money to the porter as we left. He returned payment with a knowing leer, as if aware of all that had just occurred within—as, in fact, he perhaps was.

Outside, amid the closed-up stalls that lined the edge of Moorfields, Miss Fletcher waited whilst I attempted to knock up a hackney coachman willing to conduct us to her lodgings in Arlington Street. 'Twas the matter of some few minutes to find one at such an hour, but eventually I succeeded. As I helped the lady into the privacy of the coach, she lowered the mask from her face. But though I searched those features for some hint as to her feelings about our late adventure, Miss Fletcher's countenance was unreadable.

Once we had settled ourselves within, she gave a quick sigh. "I own I leave that place with curiously mixed emotions. One would like to help the inmates who are wretched, and yet others seem quite happy withal."

"None happier than I, I warrant."

She smiled sadly. "I wonder," she said. Then, after a pause, she continued, "What we saw—and perhaps experienced—are the rude energies of life, ungoverned by reason or restraint. Did you not find our visit . . . invigorating, Mr. Merrick?"

"Indeed I did," said I. "And one aspect of the visit in particular."

"Quiet, now, I am in earnest. That which we saw is the raw stuff of existence—the unvarnished Essence, as it were, though untamed and largely wasted." Here she turned to me and asked, "Do you love mankind, Mr. Merrick?"

This inquiry did strike me as somewhat unusual. "I own I have not thought much on the topic. Of womankind, however, I know I am quite enamoured."

"You persist in bantering, and yet my question is quite serious. For individual men—and women, if you insist—I know you bear some love. But what are your feelings toward mankind itself?"

This was hardly the type of question I was accustomed to answering. Certainly, with the specimens of mankind just recently before our eyes, 'twould have been difficult to attest to any overarching love of the species. But I hated no man, so far as I knew. "I do not bear my fellow men any ill will, if such is what you ask."

"And yet you feel no qualms about cheating him in the Alley, if you can."

"Ah no, madam," said I. "For 'Change Alley is a marketplace, and in any marketplace the rule is *caveat emptor*. I cheat no one."

"Do you not? When you sell a man a share in, say, a project which you suspect may be a false hope, is this not cheating?"

"It is not, for the man I sell to can judge its prospects for himself."

"And if you know the project to be fraudulent?"

"Again, I say it falls upon the buyer to protect himself, not the seller to do it for him."

"And if it cause the buyer pain and hardship, once the sale is made and he finds himself having paid dear for a nothing?"

I felt annoyance gathering like bile within me. "Self-interest, my lady, is a natural impulse. I do not think a man can survive without it."

"I do not doubt but that he cannot," said she. "And prithee do not imagine I reproach you. I merely ask you the questions I ask myself."

"I daresay your case is quite different, Miss Fletcher, for works of charity—these schemes to feed and educate the poor—seem to be forever in your thoughts."

" 'Tis true I devote much of my energies to these schemes, as you call them. And yet I confess that the impulse behind them is more philosophical than heartfelt. Perhaps I am like the man who approves the land tax in principle, for the good it allows the nation to accomplish, but has no love of opening his purse to pay it."

"And yet few would pay the land tax if no one came round to collect. Your charity, on the other hand, is not coerced."

She seemed a bit surprised at this. "Would you neglect to pay a tax if there were no penalty for doing so?"

"I'Faith, madam, who wouldn't?"

She did study me long and hard then. "I see, then, that you are not so different from those poor lunaticks, Mr. Merrick, in at least one respect. You seem to exist in a state of innocent nature." With a gloved finger, she turned my face to hers and asked, "Is't, then, with your love as it is with your stockjobbing? Is't for sale to the highest bidder, and let the buyer beware?"

I own this did vex me. "Miss Merrick . . . Eliza . . . you cannot believe that!"

"Can I not?" she asked. Then, looking away, she said, "You are not a deep thinker, Mr. Merrick. You accept the rules and yet never question the game itself."

'Twas I who sighed now. "This is a reproach, no doubt, and yet I do not understand it."

" 'Tis no reproach, sir. I merely make the observation, with some regret."

For a moment we just sat in silence, rocked by the ungentle swaying of the coach. I knew not what to say to her. How, I wondered, had we come to this, considering what had passed between us not ten minutes before?

"Is there no one thing or one person," she asked then, "that you love above all others—for which you would sacrifice everything?"

I was about to pour out my answer, but she held up a hand to halt me. "You are about to profess undying love for me, for which protestation I have no patience at present. I ask you instead to look within yourself, with clear sight and pure heart, and ask the question of yourself, What is it means more to you than all else? What is your passion, sir? The thing that makes life worth the living?"

I did not hesitate. "I own I love life itself, and those, like my sisters and my cousin, who are dearest to me," said I.

This answer seemed to sadden her. "You do not understand me," she said. "I had thought you different from the others, your passions less conventional. But perhaps I was wrong." She turned away to open the tin shade on the coach window. "But, ah, here we are in Pickadilly already," she said, the sorrow thick in her voice.

The coach turned a corner and came to a stop before Toliver House. I took Eliza's hands into my own. "How shall I prove to you that this is no cupboard love I bear for you?" said I, with some heat. "What can I do or say?"

She pulled her hands away and gave me a kiss upon the cheek. "You have done enough this night," said she. "I am waxing melancholy again. It is in my nature, I think. I fear you must be patient with me." Then, brightening suddenly, she asked, "We shall see you again soon, I hope, Mr. Merrick?"

"B'm'Faith, I am at your service entirely. But will you not call me Will, even when we are alone?"

"I shall consider it," said she, gathering herself to exit the conveyance. I scurried out first and helped her step to the ground. Her little hand was warm in mine, and I felt moved to cover it with kisses.

"Mr. Merrick, sir?" The voice came from behind me. I turned to find a willowy young man with hair the colour of straw, standing before the steps of Toliver House. I recognized him as Ericsson, the dogsbody by which Theodore Witherspoon was wont to summon his underlings. "Fie!" I muttered, feeling the moment spoilt.

"I observe you have business to attend to, even at this hour," Eliza said. "Good night then, Mr. Merrick."

"Wait for me yonder," I said to Ericsson, then took Miss Fletcher aside. "Eliza," said I, "I do not understand in what way precisely you find me lacking. But I promise you I will do everything within my power to correct this . . . deficit, if only you'll allow it."

She put her hand to my cheek and stroked it gently. "We shall see, Will Merrick," she said, "for I still have my hopes." And here she removed from her garment the trinket I had given her earlier—that frivolous locket depicting a golden sun. She pressed it to her lips and smiled. "Good night to you," she said.

With regret heavy on my shoulders, I watched her turn and enter the house.

Ericsson was still attending at the coach door. "What is it, then?" I enquired, somewhat abruptly.

"He wants to see you."

"Now? At this hour?"

"He instructed me to await your arrival here and bid you come to him in Lombard Street, no matter what the hour."

I saw there was nothing for it. "So be it," I said, and climbed back into the hackney coach. The close space within still held the lady's scent—of tea and roses—and I gratefully breathed it in.

"Sir?" the coachman asked, looking behind at me.

"To Lombard Street," I said, wondering if I'd be allowed any sleep at all before the dawn.

CHAPTER 11

☉ WALL STREET ROARED AT 2 A.M. on that cold November night. A harsh wind scoured the gray facades up and down the street, and somewhere in the unseen alleys behind them, a trash-removal truck manhandled Dumpsters, their booms and screeches resounding in the darkness. Along the curbside in front of Federal Hall, a huge corpulent rat scuttled past the statue of George Washington, a Dove Bar wrapper fluttering in its teeth.

I passed a homeless person in the doorway of a dark coffee shop, sleeping under a pile of soiled blankets. Thinking of Eliza, I folded a dollar bill and slipped it under the heel of an old boot that stood on the lower step. A gravelly voice rose from the pile: "For another buck, I'll even say thank you."

"Deal," I said. I pulled another dollar from my wallet and stuffed it under the boot—but all it elicited from the mountain of rags was a hoarse, ragged laugh.

Rounding the corner onto William Street, I pushed through the glass entrance doors of Pembroke Horton. Awash in the sudden silence, I crossed the lobby and found Bob—the vastly overweight young night guard—listening to something classical on a battered clock radio.

"Sounds nice," I said, scribbling my name on the sign-in sheet. "What is it?"

He rolled his eyes as if my ignorance were not to be fathomed. "Henry Purcell?" he said. "'Dido's Lament' from *Dido and Aeneas*? Only the most famous piece of music *ever*?"

"I thought 'Stairway to Heaven' was the most famous piece of music ever."

Bob clutched at his chest. "Are you, like, trying to *kill* me, Mr. Merrick?"

"Have a good night," I said, and stepped onto the waiting elevator.

Ted was in his new office on the twenty-first floor, scowling at a Palm Pilot in his dimpled hand. "I hate this thing," he said, without looking up at me. "Everybody I know thinks it's the greatest thing since Jell-O, but I hate it."

"Anything I can help with?"

"My desktop's down and I don't want to talk to my wife, so I'm trying to send her an e-mail, telling her I'll be home late."

I looked at my watch. "It's almost two-fifteen in the morning."

"That's what I mean. I'm usually home by two." He tossed the PDA onto his desk. "But screw it; she's probably asleep anyway." He picked up a cruller from a napkin on his desk and took a bite. "How was the rest of your evening with Eliza? You get any?"

It took me a second to get my jaw muscles to work. "Excuse me?"

"Oh, forget it. I'm not really interested anyway. I was just asking to be polite." He gestured toward the seat across from him. "First of all," he said, "I want to thank you for putting together this shindig tonight. I thought it went brilliantly. You?"

"Y-yes. I think you made it pretty clear that you were eager to work with him. I just hope he goes for it."

"Oh, he'll go for it. The putzes he's got on board right now couldn't sell a Beanie Baby on eBay, let alone a public offering with this kind of potential."

"But he's not even sure he wants to do an IPO."

"He'll come around. We had a nice talk in the cab after we left you. Right now, Stevedore is eking by on Daddy Fletcher's money and contributions from a bunch of angels like your uncle. According to Ben, they haven't gone after real professional venture capital up to now because VCs demand too much control and would probably want to replace him as CEO with an experienced manager. He's right, of course. But given his burn rate, he's either got to do a couple quick VC rounds or else fast-track the IPO."

"But he doesn't even have a salable product yet."

"He's got a sexy idea and some sexy personnel—what more does he need? This is a cakewalk, a money magnet." Ted took another bite of the cruller, showering his necktie with falling crumbs. "Thing is," he went on then, mouth full, "even if we do IPO, we've gotta have some Sand Hill Road money involved. The Valley thinks we're clueless out here, so taking on board a nice little Mountain View firm helps our credibility with the market and gooses the valuation possibilities. I got somebody in mind who's ready to jump in at any time without making too many demands."

"But what if Ben says no?"

This set him off. "First of all, there's no way on earth Ben is saying no. Second of all, if Ben says no, you're in deep do-do, son. I don't pay you to bring me deals dead on arrival, am I right? You'll do whatever's necessary to convince Ben that IPO is the way to go and that I'm the man to make it happen. Do we understand each other?"

"Yes, Ted."

"Outstanding. So you want that little bonus I promised?"

Odd question. "Well," I said, "as you pointed out, it *did* seem to go well—"

"Because you got a choice here. I could give you five grand right now and you could go home and go to bed, or I could show you a way to turn that five into twenty by sunrise."

That got my attention. But I had been up since 4 a.m. the previous morning. How much money could any man expect to make in one day? "I don't know, Ted. I'm pretty beat."

"I got something for that, too." He took out his keys and unlocked the bottom drawer of his desk.

"What, are we going to do cocaine now?"

"Guess again," he said, rummaging in the drawer.

"Ecstasy?"

"Hell no. I want to keep you awake, not fuck you." He pulled a little plastic prescription container from the drawer and threw it across the desk at me.

I read the label. "Ritalin? I thought this was for adolescents with ADD."

"You know anybody in this business who *isn't* an adolescent with ADD?" he asked. "My kid takes it, but he sells me his extras for ten bucks a throw. Secret of my success. You can keep that bottle, by the way."

"Thanks," I said. I took one of the pills and washed it down with the dregs of a can of Diet Coke. "So where do we go to turn five thousand into twenty by sunrise?"

Ted grinned. "I like you, son," he said. He stood up and stretched. "Meet me downstairs in three minutes. I've got to pee and comb my hair."

Downstairs, Bob was still conducting his clock radio.

"The sound is a little tinny on that thing, don't you think?" I asked. Then, having nothing better to do than taunt him while Ted finished his toilette, I added, "Don't you think you could use a new one?"

Bob closed his eyes to savor one of Dido's more gorgeous phrases. "The radio is fine," he said.

"But that thing has got to be, what, fifteen years old? For fifty bucks, you could buy a nice little boombox with CD, cassette, and much better sound."

He paused in his conducting to take a bite from a half-eaten slice of greasy pizza. "I don't need a nice little boombox with CD, cassette, and much better sound," he said. "I have this."

Feeling expansive suddenly, thinking of my five-but-soon-to-be-twenty-thousand bonus, I said, "I'll buy that clock radio from you for fifty dollars. Then you can go out and buy yourself the nice little boombox."

"Not interested," he said.

"Come on, I'm trying to be nice here, Bob. Tell you what—I'll give you a hundred for the clock radio."

"It's not for sale."

"One fifty."

"Sorry."

This was mystifying. The little Panasonic had probably cost him twenty bucks. "Three hundred dollars, my final offer. You can buy one of those Bose radios and it'll sound like Carnegie Hall in here."

"Listen, Mr. Merrick," Bob said impatiently. "Are we done here? Because I'd really like to listen to this next part."

But I wasn't done. Maybe the Ritalin was kicking in, or maybe I was just feeling punchy from sleep deprivation, but before I could think better of it, I was leaning over his security counter and saying, "Bob, I will give you one thousand dollars for your clock radio. I'll write you a check right now, and I promise you it won't bounce. I give you one thousand dollars, Bob, and you give me your Panasonic clock radio. Do we have a deal?"

He held up a chubby hand. A wave of static suddenly surged and inundated the music. Cursing, Bob bent over and fiddled with the tuning dial until he had eliminated the interference.

"So?" I asked him. "Do we have a deal?"

Bob looked up at me with an expression of profound pity in his eyes. "Don't you have somewhere else to *be*, Mr. Merrick?"

Just then, the elevator chimed and Ted rushed out into the small lobby. "The radio cab should be out there already," he said.

"Good night, sirs," Bob sang out, his goatee glistening with oil, as we left.

I was still feeling shaken in the cab.

"What's the matter, Will? You look like you just saw the Antichrist."

"I think maybe I did. Or else I'm just feeling fried."

"The Ritalin will take care of that. But you'll be wide awake soon enough. There's nothing like making money to get the adrenaline flowing." Ted patted his pockets. The passing lights of Broadway strobed across the moist convexity of his forehead. "You having as good a time as I am?"

"You mean tonight?"

"I mean now, at this moment of history. Enjoy it, Will. We won't see anything like it again, at least not in *my* lifetime."

"Oh, the bull market."

"Bull market my ass! This is unprecedented, Will. Sui goddamn generis. Eighteen months ago, I thought we were redoing the mid-1980s—PC revolution and all that crap. A year ago, I thought maybe it was the '20s again, with electronics and networking instead of cars, radio, and airplanes. Six months later it looked like the Internet Railway Boom, then the biotech South Sea Scheme, then the optical

Tulip Bubble. But you know what? It's all of those things. Or maybe it's none of those things." He made a washing motion with his hands. "We're in new terrain here, Will. History is crap."

"I don't know anything about market history," I admitted.

"That's what I like about you. You're not held back by experience." He took a small bottle of nasal spray from his breast pocket and shot a spurt into each of his nostrils. Then he wiped his nose with a handkerchief and said: "All I know is, the guys thinking about history are making bupkus in this market."

"But didn't all those other boom times end with crashes?"

"Listen, son." He pointed the bottle of nasal spray at me. "Beware of drawing obvious morals. True stories never have obvious morals. Yes, of course, all those other boom times ended with crashes. But so what? You know what Donald Trump made during the '87 crash? Two hundred million dollars. True story—it was in the goddamn *New York Times.*" He patted me on the knee. "Thing you got to remember is that *nobody* knows how the hell the New Economy's supposed to work. It's all storytelling at this point— everybody's got a vision of the future, everybody's got their own *version* of the future, and it's just a matter of whose version looks convincing today. Ben Fletcher, for instance. Is he a visionary or is he a snake-oil salesman? Who the hell cares? As long as you're agile, it doesn't matter! A charlatan is a visionary whose idea bombs. You hear what I'm saying? Once upon a time, there was a little technology called Push. Enough said." He gave himself two more shots of nasal spray, put away the bottle, and spent the rest of the trip blowing his nose.

I looked out the window at the passing lights of Lower Broadway. Nothing out there—the sandwich shops, the discount drugstores, the clothing emporia specializing in designer knockoffs and odd-lot accessories—seemed to shout "Boom Time" to me. Did the bull market really make any difference to the people who streamed in and out of these places at lunchtime, the maintenance men and office secretaries, the hair stylists and construction workers? Did it really matter to any but a few thousand people in suits that Cerebral Pharmaceuticals doubled in value on its first day of trading? Or that Genesis Networking beat its totally fictitious quarterly revenue projections by a totally fictitious penny a share? If not, what was I doing here? What were any of us doing here, poring like medieval monks over our obscure texts—these balance sheets and analyst reports, these prospectuses and S-1 filings—looking for evidence of the coming of the next messiah? I looked over at Ted, who was now examining his nasal discharge in the folds of a paisley handkerchief. This was the man I had chosen as my mentor, my guide? *It's the Ritalin*, I told myself finally. *It's making you morose.* I fingered the little plastic bottle in my coat pocket and resolved to get rid of it as soon as I was out of Ted's sight.

After a few minutes, the radio cab stopped in front of a warehouse in Hell's Kitchen, not too far from the restaurant where we had met earlier that evening. Ted pulled himself out of the car and stood on the sidewalk for a few seconds, patting his pockets again. "So, feeling lucky?" he asked me when I joined him.

"Do I need to feel lucky?"

He pulled a chit of paper out of his pocket. "Not when you're with me," he said.

We walked over to the entrance and Ted pressed the intercom button. A male voice crackled over the speaker: "Is that Hunan Garden?"

Ted read aloud from the chit of paper: "One order of shrimp lo mein and five-treasure fried rice?"

The door buzzed and we entered a grimy, fluorescent-lit foyer. The elevator door was open. We stepped in and Ted pressed the button for the top floor.

"I'm going to quadruple my bonus by delivering someone his Chinese food?" I asked.

He ignored my faux-obtuseness. "You like boxing, Will? I mean, *real* boxing?"

"We're going to see a boxing match at two-thirty in the morning?" I asked. "You mean like an underground fight club? Is this legal?"

Ted laughed. "You crack me up, Will, you know that? You're a funny guy."

The elevator jolted to a stop and the doors slowly creaked open.

CHAPTER XII

BEFORE OUR ARRIVAL, I had supposed Theodore Witherspoon to be taking me to a gaming club. Some weeks before, I had accompanied Ben Fletcher to just such an establishment, and an impressive sight it had been—a large room filled end to end with deal- and baize-topped tables, each surrounded by a crowd of players. All were intent upon the toys of pipt ivory and painted pasteboard by which they won or lost great summes, their fortunes turning this way and that like weathercocks in an April wind. Fine ladies played at basset and ombre and comet, while Men of Fashion (among whom I recognized a young Tory hack famous for his pamphlets on the evils of gambling) pored over the hazard dice. At table after table, I saw coinage changing hands, the fabrication of which would have kept the Tower's mint busy for a fortnight.

Nor had that been my first introduction to such activities, for as a denizen of London's taverns and coffee-houses, I was no stranger to the City's passion for gambling. At Jonathan's and most other such establishments in the metropolis, men wagered on anything—the King's health, the ability of one man to down a pint of gin or another to balance a shilling on his nose, the likelihood of snow in Yorkshire by Twelfth Night. Indeed, 'twas said that one game buck at a tavern near Stoke Newington, floored by debt and his wife near bringing to-bed, did wager five pounds he could eat a live cat within the hour (though accounts differed on whether he succeeded or not, or what became of the cat).

But all of that was but a patch upon the spectacle I was to witness that night. For Theodore Witherspoon had brought me to no ordinary betting tavern or chocolate house for gamblers. He had brought me to Clerkenwell, to the infamous arena at Hockley-in-the-Hole.

The noise was near deafening as we entered the place, aswarm with the commoner forms of humanity in all their tawdry splendour. Bulb-nosed ostlers and their toothless hags, drunken soldiers and their trulls, members of the boiling trades—all pressed against the raised platform at the center of the arena, shouting and spitting and throwing peanuts and mouldy bread. Two men, stripped to the waist, stood upon the platform, having at each other with terrifying ferocity.

"This way to the galleries," Mr. Witherspoon cried into my ear above the din. He led me to a back stair, where he paid a few coins to the enormous keeper to let us up. Once having achieved the galleries—where persons of a somewhat more genteel sort sat in raised seats as at a play—we besought ourselves a free place. Just as we found room on the benches, one of the combatants on the platform triumphed over the other, sending him tumbling into the arms of the roaring multitude. For a moment, the din swelled even louder, as those who had wagered upon the victor cried cock and those who had backed the other cursed their luck.

Next to us, a red-faced and ill-mannered woman was engaged in berating her husband, presumably for failing to choose the winner.

Mr. Witherspoon leaned toward me. "I have your five-and-thirty pounds in this purse," said he. "Are you willing now to put it at risk? To win the horse or lose the saddle, as 'tis said?"

Knowing Theodore Witherspoon the man—and his taste for a certain type of *braggadocio*—I knew the way to play this card. "To be sure, sir," said I. "I am more than ready. I await your guidance."

This pleased him well. "Excellent," said he. "The next pair up shall be our surety."

The next contest did not begin for some minutes, giving the woman beside me opportunity to notice our presence. "Law," said she, in an entirely different tone from that she had used with her husband, "now you're a comely gent, ain't ye. 'Ow do ye do, young sir?"

"I am quite well, madam, I thank you. I trust you are the same."

"Oooh," she cooed, moving closer to me on the bench. "Better'n I was these few minutes past—now that *you're* 'ere."

I thought it best not to respond to this, but rather to affect an urgent interest in the doings of the clods and mullipuffs below.

"Do ye come 'ere often?" she enquired of me. She was careful of her language now, but her person exuded an odour that called into question the state of—or even the existence of—her underclothes.

"I'm afraid not," said I.

"Not even for the bull-baitin'?"

"Not even for the bull-baiting," I confirmed.

"Well, then, you've quite a treat comin'. Nothin' like the sight of a little blood to pique the *Manly Appetites*."

"Prithee, sir," her unfortunate husband said. "Don't mind the wench. She's in 'er cups quite good by now, and will say aught that comes to 'er mind."

The woman did strike him then, and with such force that I wondered if she might once have had a few turns in the ring herself.

Intercourse with my neighbours, however, was curtailed by the arrival of the next pair of combatants. A great roar went up as the two climbed onto the platform, for one of them was a midnight-black Moor with a physique of such size and apparent solidity that one might wonder whether he be man or mountain. His opponent, while no mere anatomy himself, was far from equal in stature to the other, though he deported himself with a confidence that, under the circumstances, would seem quite unwarranted.

The wagering began with much shouting and shilling-tossing. Mr. Witherspoon, I noted, rose from his place and entered into negotiations with a rough-seeming fellow who stood at one end of the gallery, serving only the finer quality among those present. He surrendered to Mr. Witherspoon a small piece of paper, which the latter folded away into his hatband. When he returned, he rubbed his hands together and said, " 'Tis done."

"My share as well?" I enquired.

"Aye, yours too, young Merrick."

"I daresay our money's on the Blackamoor?"

Mr. Witherspoon brayed like a donkey. "You receive no odds of four to one by backing the obvious choice!" said he.

I looked down again at the two pugilists preparing for their match. "There has been some arrangment, then?" I asked softly.

"Mean you an arrangement of the outcome? Nay, there is nothing of the kind. 'Tis a fair fight."

Farewell my five-and-thirty pounds, I thought. "The Moor cuts an imposing figure."

"That he does, that he does." My companion laughed again and clapped me on the back. "Come, sir, what's five-and-thirty pounds to men like us?"

I wiped my brow with my handkerchief, wishing to observe to him that five-and-thirty pounds was more money than I'd seen together in my first twenty years of life. But this was London, after all, and if I were to be the great man here, 'twould be best to act the part, no matter how painful.

Wishing to display my nonchalance with a jest, I said, "I trust you think Fletcher's winch project a safer bet?"

To my surprise, Theodore Witherspoon seemed to consider my

question seriously. " 'Tis difficult to say, for we don't know how many twenty-stone Blackamoors he'll have to vanquish ere he brings his winch to market. But I reckon the odds to be not so dissimilar as you think, though the rewards in Fletcher's case are like to be much greater. And even a Nine-Days-Wonder can be profitable for eight."

This answer gave me pause. "You have doubts, then, as to the prospects of Fletcher's project?"

A hand-bell was rung below, and the two men on the platform came at each other, fists before them.

"Watch the match, sir," Theodore Witherspoon said in answer to my question. "Watch the match."

I did—at least I attempted to watch, for the woman next to me did wax so animated during the subsequent event that I could scarce see a thing else but her sleeves and skirts. This member of what is sometimes called the "gentle" sex did jump about like a regular Indies baboon, gabbering and shouting and swinging her arms with such spleenful abandon that once or twice she all but knocked me to the floor. Meanwhile, below, the scene was no more tranquil. Scores of full-throated jackanapes pressed upon the edges of the platform, where the two pugilists were being pelted with onions, turnips, and potato skins enough to fill the stalls at Covent Garden.

But the fighting men seemed to heed naught of this Dutch concert. Their concentration upon each other was absolute. The Blackamoor, employing his greater reach and *avoirdupois* to good effect, let loose some mighty blows, but his opponent (who was called, judging from the cries of many in the stands, "Cobra" Jack Wolcott) moved about the platform with such agility that only a small proportion of the blows found their mark. Meanwhile, he peppered the giant with strikes of his own, none of them, alas, with any degree of force behind them.

Finally, by chance if not by art, the Blackamoor landed a bare-knuckled blow to Cobra Jack's face. Blood sprang from the Englishman's nose, spattering the spectators, who roared their approval. He staggered and fell to his knees, his arms up around his ears to shield his head, while the Blackamoor pummelled his shoulders. I thought sure 'twas the end of Cobra Jack right there, and imagined my five-and-thirty pounds dipping over the far horizon like one of my uncle's outbound argosies. But he was a tough bird, was Cobra Jack. Rising to his feet again, he pushed the sooty giant away and resumed his stance, gore streaming down his arms and chest.

And then—to my great surprise and the apparent delight of many in that place—Cobra Jack let drop his arms and stood up straight. He beckoned to his opponent tauntingly, as if inviting him to administer the *coup de grâce* without opposition. The Blackamoor, as puzzled as I, hesitated at his end of the platform. But finally, see-ing his opportunity, he approached, fists at the ready. He was just rearing back to deliver the final blow when Cobra Jack, moving with lightning quickness, swung about with his booted right leg and deliv-ered a swift but accurate kick to the Blackamoor's cod. The latter doubled over in astonishment and pain, at which Cobra Jack, taking one step forward, lifted his left knee to the Blackamoor's chin. A pro-nounced crack was audible even o'er the cries of the mob. The huge Moor fell to the platform with a mighty thunderclap, spitting out a sickening wad of broken teeth and bloody tongue.

Theodore Witherspoon and I—and all besides in the arena—were upon our feet then, cheering and shouting. He looked over at me. "Thus the name, sir!" he shouted. "He strikes like the cobra!"

But that was all I heard, for suddenly the mob below were climb-ing up onto the galleries and overrunning us. As I fought off the grop-ing hands of one such behind me (who, as it came out, was my garrulous female neighbour), I lost Mr. Witherspoon in the crowd. Fisticuffs to left and right, I resolved to make my escape, forcing my way back to and down the teeming stairs in such a way that my feet never seemed to touch a step. I reached the door (after climbing over a half-dozen Huguenot coystrils tearing at each other's throats) and hastened out into the cold night. After some difficulty, I finally found Mr. Witherspoon.

"Oh, there you are, Merrick. None the worse for wear, I hope?" He himself was looking a little disheveled, his coat torn at the sleeve, his stockings ripped, and his wig sitting crooked upon his head.

" 'Twould seem the outcome was somewhat controversial," said I, brushing bits of potato skin from my sleeves.

"Controversial, perhaps, but not in the least ambiguous. You shall have your winnings tomorrow—unless the man who took our wager does not survive this brouhaha." He stooped to tear off a buckle that hung from his shoe by a thread. "Not that the outcome was ever in doubt, to those in the know."

"But you said there was no collusion beforehand."

"Nor was there. But I'm not a man to throw a sprat without the odds of catching mackerel heavily in my favour. Advance intelligence, sir, is my meat. And I've seen this Cobra Jack in the ring before tonight."

"One would think his unique methodology would come to be known and thus lose its effectiveness."

"Aye, but he's new to London, y'see. I saw him fight in Norwich but six months past. Already, his stratagem was becoming known there. But Hockley-in-the-Hole was *Virgin Land* to his wiles, before tonight." He put an arm round my shoulder then. "But I'll not bet on him again, now his colours are known. For as I hope you know, Will, a *Deception* can work but once in any marketplace. Attempt it a second time at your peril." And here he did give me such a knowing look that I must needs wonder whether he knew of my morning's East India ruse at Jonathan's. "You may deceive a fool many times over, but a wise man only once. That's something to remember." He removed his arm and touched the brim of his hat. "Good night, sir," he said—and was gone in the crowd ere I could open my mouth to bid him likewise.

⚜

IT WAS ALREADY 4 A.M.—exactly twenty-four hours since I'd left the house for the first time the previous morning—when I finally got back to the brownstone on Charlton Street. I let myself in as quietly as I could and crept upstairs to my room. Ted's Ritalin notwithstanding, I could hardly crank up enough energy to brush my teeth. It had been a long day.

But a profitable one. I calculated the day's take in my head: Between my share of the morning's Intel trading and my incentive bonus for bringing Ted and Ben together (multiplied by our winning bet at the Hell's Kitchen boxing club), I had cleared almost $43,000. Not a bad day's work. Although there *had* been expenses. The tab at Bedlam alone had been over $800, including the two bottles of champagne and the various bribes it took to get us in, get us a VIP room, and get us out again. Of course, that was nothing compared to the stunning bill at Yakuza, which (thanks to the showcase sakes) had hit the low four figures. But Ted had picked up that check. Meanwhile, paying off Tilden for the Intel tip had set me back a chunk of money, putting the day's net at around $40,000—still my best day ever by far.

I booted up the laptop while I got undressed. It had been a mixed day on the Nasdaq, but I wanted to check how my holdings had done in after-hours trading. After the browser launched and the modem went through its bizarre static-and-Jew's-harp dance, I connected to my E*TRADE account and checked my portfolio. A volatile day: One of my major holdings—Verisign—had zoomed 18% in the after hours, but another—Agilent, my most heavily leveraged stock—had taken a

10% hit on a less-than-stellar revenue-growth number. I printed out the totals and added, by hand, the 40G take for today.

I frowned. My net worth was climbing toward $800,000. Not too long before, that sum would have seemed downright princely to me. After a few months in New York, though, I saw how little it was. To be in Eliza Fletcher's league—no matter what she said to the contrary—I'd have to be worth a lot more than that.

After disconnecting, I shut down the laptop. I felt strangely depressed suddenly. Things were moving fast, of course, but not fast enough. To get where I wanted to be, I was somehow going to have to be bolder, more aggressive, more daring.

I looked out my window toward Varick Street, the occasional cab or delivery van streaming past. New York was a rich city, and—despite my moment of doubt in the radio car with Ted—I knew it was getting richer by the minute. But there was only one word that meant anything here, one word around which all of this activity focused. You could practically hear it in the predawn rumble of traffic, in the shouts and shuffles on Wall Street, humming along a billion telephone wires and optical cables, in restaurants and clubs and real estate offices and gourmet groceries all over town. Leaning my forehead against the cold glass of the window, I whispered the word aloud: "More." I wanted *more*—to *do* more, to *have* more, to *be* more.

Eliza's words came back to me then, the ones she had said in the cab earlier that night: "You accept the rules but never question the game." I understood her better than I'd let on. But then again, she seemed to be playing a game herself. Tonight, just when I thought I had broken through, just when I'd had my first concrete proof of her attraction to me—those ecstatic five minutes in the VIP room at Bedlam—she had turned remote and philosophical again, pushing me away. Was this a clever way of making me want her more? It was something you did in any transaction—feign reluctance when you wanted something most. Like the boxer at the fight tonight: He seemed to be giving up, to be calling it all off, when in reality he was closing in for the kill.

Clearly, she was challenging me, spurring me on to greater acts of audacity and imagination. That's what muses did, after all. She was taking me on as her personal project—the Will Merrick Project for Turning Boys into Men.

I moved away from the window and started fiddling with the alarm function on my Palm Pilot. One thing I had learned in the past few months was that I was living in a time and place that did not reward caution. This wasn't a matter of winning or losing; in this city, it was a matter of winning fast enough, winning big enough. What would it take to get me all I wanted? More of more, less of less, and enough of this whole notion of enough. Maybe it was my lingering small-town caution and timidity that was holding me back. Maybe— to achieve what I wanted to achieve—I would have to become fear-less.

My energy giving out finally, I fell into bed and shoved the Palm Pilot under the pillow. In just a few more hours, I thought, the markets—and not just those on Wall Street—would be reopening. I wanted to be ready.

MARCH

PARTNERSHIP

AGREEMENTS

CHAPTER XIII

❧ "EVERYTHING I OBSERVE in London of late disgusts me."

Sir Reginald Hawking, my mother's eldest brother, examined his cup of chocolate with sleepy, scornful eyes. He licked his plump red lips and stifled a belch before continuing. "All is controlled by Foreigners, Jews, and Dissenters now," said he. "I scarcely recognize the place."

'Twas a bright forenoon in March, as we sat in the drawing-room of Uncle Gilbert's new house in the Red Lion Square. This fine abode, which had been home to us for some several weeks now, had proved a very modern and comfortable one—with logs and fagots rather than foul-smelling sea coal in the fireplaces, furniture of walnut and mahogany in place of the old oak, and a little *House of Office* on every storey, wherein a two-potted close-stool permitted easement away from prying eyes. We took meals in our own dining-room now, rather than on a gate-leg table in the parlour, as we had done at Wapping. And perhaps the most pleasant change of all: I was no longer relegated to a garret for sleep. My bedchamber in my uncle's new house was on the second storey, just beside his own, and was altogether larger and better-appointed than my previous quarters. One's stock in the household, it might be said, had risen.

Sir Reginald—in London for a short time, up from the family seat in Devonshire—sipped his chocolate disdainfully. He sat beside his wife, Lady Dorothea, a substantial female, who was as silent as her husband was garrulous, her face as grey as his was pink. Sitting there, they called to mind nothing so much as two great fat prawns, only one of which had been cooked.

" 'Tis all *Art* and *Tricks*—the work of these fanatick Whigs," Sir Reginald continued. "This Bank of theirs, design'd to let King William wage his war with France—it impoverishes all but themselves. They take in gold and give paper in its stead. Now there's a bargain!" Sighing, he wiped a smudge of ash from the lip of his cup. "And look who it is that benefits most—the so-called Money'd Interest. Jobbers and sharpers all. Disgusting."

My Uncle Gilbert, not wishing to contradict his elder brother but feeling perhaps obliged to defend a class of men on which his own interests were dependent, observed, " 'Tis true, Brother, that this Money'd Interest enriches itself, but I would argue that, in doing so, it enriches the nation as well. Do you not agree?"

"I do not," said Sir Reginald. "This excess of wealth, concentrated in the hands of men fresh from the dung-cart and the tanner's vat—'tis unnatural. And what is this wealth based upon? Shares and funds, paper and promises! All at the expense of the true wealth of the country—which is to say land, *my* land—which is taxed to death so that this Dutch usurper can make the world safe for tradesmen. I repeat: Disgusting."

"I agree, Brother, that many in London today derive too much wealth from activities of dubious utility. And yet one must not as it were discard the *Baby* with the *Bath Water*. There is much genuine innovation afoot in the land at present—new discoveries in the applied sciences that will change commercial life in untold ways—and without a market in shares and the like, these efforts would lack the capital necessary to come to fruition."

"*Innovation!* Even the word revolts me." Sir Reginald looked about the room, remarking its prodigious size and bright new furnishings. "But I understand your prejudice here, Gilbert. 'Twas *Innovation*, I suppose, that allowed a younger son to afford such a house in the Red Lion Square. I call it by another name—"

"Sir Reginald, dearest," his lady admonished him. "You will recall that we are guests in this house."

Her husband lifted his great hands as if in surrender. "True, I do not wish to disparage your achievements, Gilbert," he went on, in a somewhat mollifying tone. "And yet I cannot approve of this . . . *Commercialization* of everything. This preoccupation with getting and spending among the Middling Classes. Before long, I'll have one of these greedy upstart Projectors as my neighbour at Draymore Park."

I could not let this stand unchallenged. "And yet, sir," said I, breaking a long silence, "a greedy upstart Projector can labour as hard and thus be as deserving of a fine house as any man, can he not? As my tutor was wont to say, 'Greed may be a private *Vice*, but a public *Virtue*, so long as it is a spur to industry and ingenuity.'"

Sir Reginald turned his head slowly to gaze upon me as upon a cockroach that had begun to speak. "Your tutor?" he asked.

Feeling cowed by his imperious tone, I muttered, "Yes, sir. Mr. Joshua Dooling, my cousin from Galway. I think perhaps you have met him."

"An Irish tutor? Hrmph. 'Twould seem as improbable a creature as a Hindoo butcher, and just as contrary to Nature."

This response, combined with the look of disapproval from my younger uncle, silenced me at once.

"All I wish to say, Brother," Sir Reginald went on, ignoring me now, "is that you must needs be careful of your associates. He had best use a long spoon who sups with the Devil, and a longer still who would have business with the likes of these Money Men." Here he put down his cup of chocolate and rubbed his meaty hands together. "But enough of that. You must be wondering, Gilbert, what it is has brought us up to London at this time of the year."

"I am delighted to serve as host to you and Lady Dorothea at any time of year, and for whatever reason. But, indeed, your letter was somewhat dark on the matter of your purpose."

Sir Reginald gestured toward me with a sausagelike finger. "Perhaps our young nephew here has some other business to see to at present?" said he.

"If you wish it, Brother, young Will can leave the room. However, let me assure you that he is my trusted ally in all matters, whether they be of a personal or a business nature."

"So be it, so be it," said Sir Reginald. " 'Tis no great secret, after all. I have come to London, Brother, to consult with these same Money'd Men, much as I despise them, as to the mortgaging of the Devonshire estates and the liquidation of a few other assets."

I could see that this news did take my younger uncle somewhat by surprise. "I see," said he. "Though, frankly, I had no idea you found yourself in such straitened circumstances."

"Tush," Sir Reginald responded. "You need not gloat so, Brother. 'Tis not as bad as you hope. I merely find myself in need of the ready cash to fund certain . . . capital expenditures on the land."

"Capital expenditures?"

"It has come to my attention that the land surrounding Draymore Park may contain a good deal of coal. My intent is to mine the estate and thereby supplement the Rents, which have proven quite inadequate to meet our rising expenses." He made a broad gesture then, indicating the house around him. "Like you, Gilbert, we seek to improve the quality of our surroundings. So we intend to engage in a bit of *Innovation* ourselves."

" 'Tis a most forward-looking plan of action!" Uncle Gilbert exclaimed. "I approve of your resourcefulness, Brother. And yet, I trust you know that I would be more than willing to assist—"

"Thank you, Gilbert," Sir Reginald interrupted him, "but I do not find it necessary to indebt myself to my younger brother on such a trifling matter. I am told that any initial outlay will be recouped before very long. England's appetite for coal, I am assured, is inexhaustible."

"Indeed it is," said the other. "And I shall be happy to assist you in any way I can with the financial particulars."

"Thank you. Of that kind of assistance I *will* avail myself, your knowledge of these persons being superior, naturally, to my own. But there is no great hurry. The coal is going nowhere for the time being." He removed a thread from his coatsleeve and placed it in his empty cup. "We will have further discourse on this matter in due time. But for now, I see that Lady Dorothea is quite fatigued after our journey."

Uncle Gilbert jumped to his feet and pulled the bell. "Certainly, Brother. Mrs. Popper has prepared your rooms—which I trust you will find more comfortable than those I could provide at Wapping." Alfred appeared then in the doorway. "Alfred, Sir Reginald and Lady Dorothea will go to their chambers now. Please see that they are properly settled in and have everything they should require."

The ageing couple rose from their places and collected themselves slowly (for nothing to do with Sir Reginald and Lady Dorothea did but take some time). Then they bade us good-bye until mealtime and retired, trailing a smell of boiled cabbage behind them.

When they had been gone a few moments, Uncle Gilbert clapped his hands together. "Ha!" said he, "I see the spirit of the times has infected even that old Mumpsimus. And while I love my brother dearly, I confess I do relish seeing him involve himself in activities that, until recently, he would have considered beneath his dignity. As you have perhaps surmised, Will, Sir Reginald is not one to let his superior station in life go unremarked."

"I did note that he used the words 'tradesmen' and 'younger son' as if they were oaths."

"I'Faith, Old Money despises New. 'Twas always so and always will be. But mark my words, he'll not look askance at the New Money it requires to dig his coal." Here he removed his snuffbox from his pocket and, as was his wont, turned it this way and that in his fingers without opening it. "But while on this topic of New Money, Will, I've something else to discuss with you, concerning our friend Fletcher."

This change of subject did capture my full attention, for the matter of Fletcher was of surpassing interest to me just then. Some months earlier, Benjamin Fletcher (somewhat reluctantly, though at Theodore Witherspoon's insistence) had applied for a Royal Patent, prefatory to bringing his winch to the Alley as a joint-stock company. If all went well, shares were to begin being sold within a fortnight. In preparation for this event, I had begun selling all my holdings in other shares and instruments, in order to have as much cash in hand as possible. For my rôle in bringing the principals together, I was to be allowed to purchase as many shares as I desired, at substantial discount. Fletcher's winch, I had decided, could very well be the making of my fortune.

"What is it you wish to discuss, Uncle?" I asked.

Uncle Gilbert stepped to the door and quietly pulled it to. "I know that Theodore Witherspoon's plans for the joint-stock offering proceed apace," he began in a whisper. "Yet I have heard inklings of a certain lingering reluctance on Fletcher's part to proceed thusly in the matter. And as one who has built his own business up from nothing, I can understand his trepidation at the idea of subjecting his project to every whim of a market impatient for immediate gain. So I have been hatching a little plot of my own to propose him."

My heart beating faster suddenly, I said, "And what, sir, might this little plot be?"

"I propose that he allow Hawkings to purchase a controlling interest in his invention. In exchange for such consideration I shall guarantee him all reasonable freedom in the carrying out of his endeavours, so that he will be answerable to no mob of shareholders, but rather to one—and one who is in perfect sympathy with his aims and goals. What think you, Will?"

I own that these words did send a dreadful shudder through me. "You propose, then, what might be termed an *Amicable Acquisition* of the project?"

"I suppose it might be thus characterized," said he.

"But, Uncle," I said quickly, hoping to dissuade him if I could, "if I may be so bold, is Hawkings in a position to meet the price that Fletcher would surely ask for?"

" 'Twould be no easy task, certainly. And I'm quite sure that this Witherspoon creature would lead me the Devil's own dance before giving over on't. But as you know—quite as well as anyone, I think— my credit is quite sound in the City, and my friends many, so that acquiring the needed capital would not be out of the question. Admittedly, with the markets being as they are today, and the Publick's appetite for shares so ravenous, Fletcher doubtless could raise more through joint-stock than I could offer him. And yet, if I know the man, 'twould be worth much to him to bypass the hubbub of the Alley if he could. And there's no saying when the adoration of the market for projects like his might wane. I've lived long enough to know that 'Change Alley is a fickle friend—what it values today as gold may be dross tomorrow."

"I quite understand your point, Uncle, but . . . but . . . but what figure would you offer him?"

My uncle withdrew from his vest pocket a letter. " 'Tis all writ within, Will—the offer price as well as my terms, which I think all will agree are uncommon generous. I ask that you, as my Instrument, deliver it him at the earliest possible moment." And here he handed me the letter, which was sealed. "Ah, I see you are disappointed not to be privy to the details within. And yet I think it wise that this business remain between Fletcher and me, at least at this very early stage. 'Tis a delicate matter. Let us see what the man has to say, and then perhaps, if all goes well, you and I can have discourse regarding the particulars."

"As you wish it, sir," said I, though 'twas the last thing on earth I wished to do.

"Is there some difficulty, Will? You look somewhat taken aback."

"No, no," I assured him. "I will deliver your offer directly. For as it happens, I am engaged to meet with Miss Fletcher this very afternoon, and if her brother be there, both *Birds* may be slain with the single *Stone*."

My uncle smiled. "Ah yes, Miss Fletcher is a fine bird indeed. And yet, in this instance, 'twould seem to be the bird that slays the stone thrower, does it not?"

"If I understand you, Uncle, I can assure you that I am long since slain, as must be obvious to all."

"'Tis plain as the road to Dunstable, my boy. But what is less obvious is whether the mortality is mutual. How fares your pursuit of the lady?"

Here we were on safer ground, so I took a deep breath and said, "Honestly, Uncle, I know not. I am no authority on the fairer sex, and this example does seem more perplexing a case than most."

"Still," said he, "she hasn't rejected you yet. And your persistence must stand you in good stead. As must your association with a reputable trading house like Hawkings and myself."

"Indeed, sir," said I. "My position as your nephew may be my greatest asset with the lady."

"As it should be, my lad, as it should be."

I stole a glance at him. "If that be so," I pursued further, though with care, "some outward sign of your . . . fatherly affection for your nephew might improve his chances yet more with Miss Fletcher."

"What? What?" My uncle looked up suddenly at this, and I knew at once that I had played my hand too bold. "You are ambitious, sir," he said, in a tone that recalled our first stiff meetings some months before. "But there's a line 'twixt ambition and presumption. You would eat the calf in the cow's belly, I think, and I don't like it."

"I'm sorry, sir, I meant only—"

"I know exactly what you meant. You have proven yourself useful to me, and I own I feel a growing affection toward you. But you are not my son, Will, and I will caution you that such presumption will only put you in my bad books. Do you understand me?"

"Uncle, I do. And I am heartily sorry if I—"

"Let's hear no more of it, lad," said he, his countenance softening. "I know the way it is, being a young man come to London with naught but the burning desire to make his fortune. And certainly the temper of this curious age does little to discourage impatience. Still, this kind of thing does not become you, and I'll thank you to mind yourself and curb this . . . *Naked Appetite* in future." He dismissed me then with a wave of his hand. "But run along now and prepare yourself for your rendezvous with Miss Fletcher, for I'm sure you'll not wish to meet her in *that* cravat. And pray do not forget, in the throes of your passion, to present the letter to her brother. It *is* of some importance."

Feeling chastened by my uncle's words—and distinctly unsettled by this letter of his—I bade him good day and retired to my chamber. And since I had an hour free before having to set off to Arlington Street (for the journey was far shorter now that we had moved house to our more fashionable digs), I sat me down and took up pen and paper to write a letter to Josh Dooling, the contents of which I shall inscribe below:

Esteemed coz [I wrote],

If I am in fact, as you aver in your last of 21 February (very gratefully rec'd, by the by), the financial Purcell *to your old* John Blow—*which is to say, the Pupil who learnt his lessons so well as now to exceed in skill his Master*—*then I must tell you that this Purcell is one whose* Fairie Queene *still eludes him. 'Tis a source of much vexation to me. True, I do faithfully produce my share of* Odes *and* Anthems—*minor works (such as a recent £15 gain trading Lustring Refuses) which do serve to enrich me modestly*—*for as my relative is wont to remark,* Light Gains make a Heavy Purse. *But now I fear for what was to be my* Magnum Opus, *the bold stroke that would satisfy my ambitions and render me an object of envy among men and of attraction among women. As you know, I hoped this business of Fletcher and his Winch might present my opportunity, but now there is a difficulty there, for my dear uncle has just this moment revealed to me that he does hold Fletcher's Winch so dear as to assay an outright purchase of th'entire Project! And knowing what I do of Fletcher's ambivalence toward the notion of joint-stock*—*not to mention the recent turmoil in share prices in that place as well as in Birchin Lane (about which you have no doubt read in Houghton's* Collection*) I think Fletcher may in fact consider it seriously. But the question in all of this is: Would this new design of my uncle be destructive to my own interests, and if so, how do I remain loyal to him without spoiling my one best chance at attaining my goals?*

As you are aware, moreover, I have another great project on the anvil—*call it this Purcell's* Dido and Aeneas *(tho with a happier ending, I hope)—which is to say, the matter of Miss Fletcher. And this endeavour, too, has its despairing elements, for my standing with the lady seems to fluctuate like the value of a Hudson's Bay Put, up a guinea one day and down nineteen shillings the next. I find myself at a loss to know exactly what it is the lady desires of me at any moment, and whatever surmise I make is invariably the wrong one. Thus I speak prettily when she apparently wishes me to act boldly, and at other times give her bold actions when what she truly desires is pretty words. As one who must manage the vagaries of the distaff side on a daily basis, perhaps you can advise me here (for women's requirements of their tutors and their lovers cannot be so very different). What are the* Indicators, *so to speak, in the great* Market of Love? *When do I press my case forward without restraint, and when hold back to consolidate my hard-earned gains?*

And as if all of this were not distressing enough, now here are Lord and Lady Fishcake—viz, my mother's eldest brother, Sir Reginald, and his Silent Scourge—come to visit and fill these bright new rooms with the weight of their dark old disapproval. You will perhaps be interested (tho not much surprised) to know that Lord Fishcake hates all he sees about him, and informs us that England is gone to Hell *in a* Hand-Cart, *said hand-cart being carried jointly by the newly bereaved Sovereign and by Halifax, Paterson, and the other proponents of the New Finance. He thinks it scandalous that all the money now flows to "Jews, Dissenters, Sharpers, and Upstarts" (JDSU, for short), while the real "Producers and Growers" (P&G, if you will) are undervalued by all. As you can imagine, I do not relish the prospect of sitting at table with this Fount of Scorn thrice daily for the next fortnight or two, so I trust you will remember me in your prayers.*

But here I am droning on in the same plaintive tones of which I regularly accuse you. Your correspondent will therefore close on a less self-pitying note—with an offer that I hope will be most welcome to you. It has not escaped my notice that you turn thirty this Friday next. If you will allow me to play the Grand Man for just this once, I would like to make you a gift of £20, which I will keep on account for you here, and which I will dispose of in any way you see fit. Thus, if you wish me to purchase in your name a share of this or that, I am yours to command. If you fancy Derby, 'tis yours; likewise Sword-Blades or Salt Petre Bellamont. I shall even put the money to an Annuity if such be your desire (tho I'd rail you for timidity if you so chose). And pray do not thank me for this boon; it is only in my own behalf that I make you this gift. For the sooner your fortune be made, the sooner you can leave Exeter behind and join me here in London, where the only riches lacking are those which your presence would provide.

But I will close now before I grow any more maudlin. After all, I would not like you to think that you are in any way deserving of the great affection of

Your humble Cousin (and now Broker, I hope),

Wm. Tob. Merrick

Having finished thus pouring out my soul to my one true *confidant* in the world, I quickly put a seal to the letter, deposited it in the basket where Alfred would see it, and—after changing my cravat to something less objectionable—set out for the genteel environs of Pickadilly.

CHAPTER 14

⚭ WILLIAM AND MARY STROLLED gracefully up the sun-drenched Mall, their deportment impeccable, their breeding obvious, their noble bearing unruffled by the ruckus of the *hoi polloi* around them—until, that is, Mary spotted a squirrel in the distance and, breaking free of her restraint, bounded over the low fence and across the lawn after it, William behind her, their leashes snaking wildly at their heels.

"Shit!" Eliza said, and took off after them.

The two whippets chased their quarry up the curving stairs around the Central Park bandshell, treeing it finally on the wisteria trellis at the top. When we caught up with them, they had stationed themselves on either side of a baroquely twisted wisteria trunk. There they stood, trembling with concentration, their dainty front paws high on the vine. The squirrel cowered on one of the wooden cross-bars, just out of reach.

"Okay, you two," Eliza scolded, grabbing the leash ends and winding them around her left wrist. "That's enough of *that* nonsense."

"Doggy nature will out, I guess," I said lamely. "Even with inbred aristocrats like these two."

"They are *not* inbred," she replied as she pulled them away from the trellis. "They're just high-strung. The breeder warned me about this. When we get back to the apartment, I'll give them both some Valium."

William and Mary—named, Eliza said, for the college from which she'd received her B.A. in art history and economics—lost interest in the squirrel and began to sniff each other's butts.

"They really cost you four grand apiece?" I asked.

Eliza sighed. She was wearing black jeans, a light leather jacket, and a tight-fitting white T-shirt with three Chinese characters over the left breast. Her dark hair was pulled back into a neat ponytail, revealing the opulent curve of her cheekbones and the alabaster perfection of her long, lean neck. Somehow it seemed unfair to the rest of the world that I was the one strolling in Central Park beside this woman, on a brilliant, unseasonably warm Friday noon in March, with the snowdrops just rearing their white heads and the bare elms bristly with new buds.

Eliza was eyeing me. "Does that kind of thing really impress you?" she asked.

"You mean the fact that we're walking eight thousand dollars' worth of highly stylized dogflesh? Yes, it does impress me."

"You really are a lightweight, Merrick."

I shrugged. "It's easy to be unimpressed by money when you start adult life with a trust fund."

I didn't really mean the comment to sound as nasty as it did, and I could see it wounded her. "Okay," she said. "There's an argument to be made for that point."

"All I meant to say was, we're in different situations. Your whole life isn't at risk the way mine is right now. What if I don't make it out here? What happens to me? If I squander my opportunities here, I end up back in Bloomington, setting up shop as an investment adviser in some downtown strip mall."

She separated the two dogs with a well-placed thigh and started them back down the stairs to the Mall. "There are worse things that could happen to you," she said.

"Like what?"

"Like what? Like ending up at my little soup kitchen on Wall Street, that's what. Open your eyes, Will. It's a big city out here, and not everyone's wearing Prada."

This was not the way I wanted this conversation to go. She was already a few steps ahead of me, so I ran to catch up. I put a hand on her shoulder to stop her. "What is it with us, Eliza? What's wrong?"

"Who says something's wrong?" she said.

"That night at Bedlam, with what happened . . . well, I thought we were starting something."

"And didn't we start something?"

"Well, yeah, I guess. We go out together, have dinner, go to clubs. But it's been four or five months since that night, and we haven't really . . ."

"What—had sex again?"

Two old women on a nearby bench turned their heads toward us.

"Okay, yes," I said in a lower voice. "We haven't really had sex again."

She pursed her lips and pulled the leashes tighter around her wrist. "We were both a little out of control that night, Will. It was a strange place. Watching all those bizarre, Ecstasy-crazed people letting themselves go—we got caught up in the moment."

"Didn't you like it?" I asked.

"I liked it just fine, Will. That's not the point."

"Well, what *is* the point?"

She stopped walking and turned to face me, her face and shoulders speckled by the shadows of the giant elms stretching over us. "Would you marry me?" she asked.

It took me a moment to assimilate this, but I finally answered, "Yes."

"Okay." She started walking again, the dogs padding along in front of her.

"Wait. What does that mean—okay? 'Okay' as in let's get married?"

"No. 'Okay' as in okay, now I know. Will Merrick would be willing to marry me. I wasn't sure until now."

"And now you are," I said. "But do I get to ask you the same question?"

"No."

"That's not fair."

"Welcome to adult life, Will." She snapped her fingers at Mary—a sound of such crisp authority that every dog within earshot lifted its head. "Do not—I repeat, do *not*—eat old candy wrappers," Eliza scolded, stooping to rip the offending item from the whippet's narrow snout. If dogs can look sheepish, Mary did then. She glanced remorsefully toward William, but he seemed to be pretending not to know her.

"Then what do I do?" I asked. "How do we move this thing forward?"

"Oh God, now you sound like that troglodyte Ted Witherspoon. He's always saying that to my brother: 'Ben, how do we move this thing forward?' Are you looking for a merger here, one share of Fletcher for each share of Merrick?"

"At the moment, to be honest, I'm considering a hostile takeover."

"Mmm, I like the sound of that," she said. "But it would take more junk bonds than *you* could float, baby."

"Eliza, *please*."

"Okay, okay," she said. "Come over here with me." She led me toward one of the benches. We sat, and the dogs sat obediently at our feet, striking the noble poses of the ceramic dogs you see in tacky furniture stores. "I admit I've had some hesitation here," she began. "Some uncertainty."

All right, I thought, *here it comes.* "Because of who I am?"

She seemed legitimately confused. "Meaning?"

"Meaning that I'm just not . . ." I cast around for a way of saying what I'd been feeling for months now. "I'm not from the same world you are."

She stared at me with a look of incredulity on her face. "You mean that you're not *rich?*"

"Exactly."

She turned away. "You really are an asshole sometimes, Will."

"So that's honestly not it?" I asked.

"No, Will, that's honestly not it. It's the fact that you could even think that that's it that's honestly it."

I didn't know how to even start unpacking that last statement. She had clearly misunderstood me. Obviously, it wasn't just the money as money I was talking about. But like it or not, money was the marker, the symbol of a greater distinction. People tried to deny it all the time, but there was a connection between worth and worthiness, and it was there no matter what pious and sentimentalized lip service was paid to denying it. The rich *were* different. The class system was *not* dead, even in March of 2000. Poverty, in my experience, was virtuous only in books.

"I don't know," I said finally. "There are times I feel like one of your charity causes—that you're interested in me the same way you're interested in those rural schools you want to supply with computer equipment."

"That is a crock, Will. A total crock." For a brief second I thought she might start to cry. I looked over at the pigeons strutting along the pavement down the Mall, looking as fat and smug as small-town mayors. "You know what it is that interests me about you, Will? You show signs—sometimes, at least—of spirit."

"Spirit?"

She seemed embarrassed suddenly. "Oh, never mind."

"No, no," I insisted. "Being praised—I like this. Please continue."

She took a breath and looked over toward the bandshell. "It's just that I'm usually surrounded by people who take themselves so seriously. People like my brother, frankly—very important people who spend twenty hours a day changing the world by revolutionizing the way we get sports scores or buy dog food."

"So you like me because I'm not important," I said.

"Don't be obtuse." She looked over at me with an assessing eye. "You show sparks of life," she said. "Occasionally. Like those earrings you gave me. Who else would have given me something so childish? The guys I usually date would've given me something serious from Tiffany or from some exclusive private jeweler who caters only to the cognoscenti."

"Okay, so I'm not important and I'm childish. No wonder you consider me such a catch!"

She frowned. Then an idea seemed to occur to her. "You really want to move this thing forward?" she asked. "Tell you what: Next Friday I'm flying down to San Antonio to see my parents for a few days. Want to come?"

Next Friday—the weekend before the IPO, assuming it happened. How could I possibly leave town? "What about my job?" I said.

"You have a job? Could've fooled me."

No, I told myself. This was important. At least get this one right. "I'm sure my uncle will give me a couple days off. Give me the details and I'll buy myself a ticket."

"Never mind that. You don't need a ticket to fly on my father's corporate jet."

"His corporate jet?"

"Oh, will you stop being impressed by shit like that? It's embarrassing." She got up from the bench. "Come to my place around noon on Friday and we'll ride over to Teterboro together. Bring golf clubs, if you have them." She noticed my hesitation. "Isn't that what you want? A sign of serious intent? You'll get to meet everyone—my father, my mother, my fiancé."

"Your what?"

She put a finger under my jaw and gently pushed it closed. "Don't be too worried. It's something our fathers would like to see happen, but neither Laurence nor I take it very seriously. Besides, I think Laurence might be gay." She looked at her watch. "Aren't you supposed to meet Ben at the office at one? You'd better head down there. He hates it when people are late."

I got up and took her arm. "So we've made up now, right? We're okay, you and me?"

She gave me a quick kiss on the cheek and pushed me in the direction of Fifth Avenue. "Don't be late," she said. Then, turning away again, she called, "William! Mary! Heel!"

⧖

THE OFFICES OF STEVEDORE TECHNOLOGIES were on two floors of a filthy cast-iron building on the corner of Broadway and 20th Street. The tiny elevator, its walls muffled with gray quilted matting that made it seem awfully like a padded cell, emitted alarming creaks and crackles as it rose, but it did successfully deposit me on the fifth floor, give or take six inches. I climbed out and found myself in front of a pair of glass doors. Peering inside, I could see a semicircular receptionist's desk and the blurry intersecting planes of numerous glass-brick walls. There was no one sitting at the desk, so I pressed the bell and waited.

Five minutes and much bell-ringing later, a debonair-looking barefoot Indian man appeared and opened the door. "Oh," he said. He looked disappointed. "I guess you're not the guy from Domino's."

"I'm here to see Ben Fletcher."

"Hey Ben!" he shouted down the hallway. "You expecting somebody?"

Ben appeared out of an office at the end of the hall, eating an ice-cream sandwich. "Oh good," he said, and headed toward us. He transferred the sandwich to his left hand and extended his right toward me. "Good to see you, Will." I shook his sticky hand. "Have you introduced yourself to Sunil? Sunil Ghota, our chief technology officer, this is my friend Will Merrick, who works for Gilbert Hawking."

Sunil and I shook hands while Ben finished the last bite of his ice cream. "First time here, right, Will? Let me show you around. I'm sure you won't mind signing a nondisclosure document beforehand, okay? Sunil, we have one of those lying around?"

Sunil (who had the longest toenails I'd ever seen) went around the back of the receptionist's desk and produced a clipboard.

"It's just a formality," Ben said, passing the clipboard to me. Clamped to it was a two-page document, which I read through quickly. It asserted that the signee promises, on pain of criminal prosecution and/or civil litigation, not to reveal to anyone anything he sees, hears, reads, or smells (*smells*?) on the premises.

I signed both pages with the attached ballpoint. "Not that I'd understand anything I saw, heard, read, or smelled here," I said.

"Ha, ha!" Ben laughed, without conviction. "We'll just notarize that now." Sunil took a notary's seal from the desk drawer, impressed both pages, and witnessed them with his signature. "Good," Ben said, watching Sunil put the documents into a drawer and lock it. Then he looked up at me and grinned. "Now we can have a look around."

He led me down the gray hallway into a largish gray room filled with about two dozen chest-high cubicles. The room was absolutely silent except for the hum of the fluorescents overhead and an occasional burst of keyboarding from one or another quarter of the room. Hovering in the air were the faint smells of coffee, microwave popcorn, and the body odor of a variety of people who had apparently not gone home to shower in some time.

"This is command central," Ben said. He gestured proudly at the cubicles. "Where the future is being invented, as we speak."

I looked around the room. From where I stood, I could see the inside of three cubicles. All three contained skinny young men—two Chinese, one black, all three wearing white oxford shirts—staring at computer screens. "This is it?" I asked, disappointed. "Where are the irreverent nonconformists with tattoos and multiple body piercings? Shouldn't there be some long-haired guys in Phish T-shirts in here, shooting each other with water pistols?"

Ben grimaced. "Don't believe the PPP."

"The PPP?"

"Popular Press Propaganda. You know, the TV-movie version. We all work too hard to get into any of that nonsense. I run a disciplined organization here."

As he spoke, a paper airplane sailed over one of the cubicle walls. It struck Ben in the left temple and tumbled to the floor. "Okay," he said, "maybe some of what I just said is bullshit. But just remember that, in the New Economy, nothing is ever typical."

"I'll remember that," I said.

"Listen," he said then, pulling me toward the exit as an entire squadron of paper airplanes converged on us, "you want a Snapple or something?"

We got our drinks from a refrigerator in the makeshift lunchroom and headed toward Ben's office. "I hope you don't mind," Ben said, "but I've asked Ted to be here to discuss whatever proposal you have to make."

"That's fine," I said. Actually, I had notified Ted myself, since I was still on his payroll as well as my uncle's. It wasn't easy being the servant of two masters.

"Will, Will, Will," Ted said, struggling up from one of the chairs across from Ben's slate-and-tubular-steel desk. He was trying to affect composure, but the ragged worry was apparent around his squinting eyes. "Long time no speak. I hear old Gil has a proposal to run by us."

I took the letter out of my jacket pocket. "Basically," I said, "Gil knows you have some issues with a public offering, so he's proposing a buyout, giving you all the independence you need, assuming you adhere to a reasonable deliverables schedule." I shot a glance at Ted. Not wanting to sound like I was selling the deal, I added, "Which, of course, is a big if. Deliverables, I mean. It might be difficult meeting his terms."

"Let me see." Ben took the letter, opened it, and scanned it. "A very attractive offer, I'll give him that much."

"May I?" Ted plucked the letter from Ben's hand. After finding the information he wanted, he said, "It's not nearly as much as you'd get in the open market, Ben."

"I don't know about that. The IPO market's been getting a little dicey lately."

"With an IPO you'd still own over fifty percent of your own company."

"With a deal like this, I'd own a substantial stake in a larger company—one with actual revenues to bridge us over the dry spells. And think of the synergies."

"The S-1 is filed with the SEC," Ted wheedled, sounding a little desperate now. "Everything's set to go. It's a little late to back out now. I'm not sure it would even be possible."

"It would be possible, Ted." Ben turned back to me. "Will, tell your uncle we're not rejecting his offer out of hand. I'll have the lawyers look over the letter, and we'll see."

"We got a *lot* to talk about," Ted said. "Go away now, Will, so Ben and I can talk."

I made my good-byes and got out of there as quickly as I could. Once out on the street again, I headed for the little bodega on Tenth Avenue where Ted and I had arranged a postmortem rendezvous. I wondered what he would say to me. Things were getting complicated now. If Ted's interests and my uncles' were to come into direct conflict, I'd have to execute some cunning maneuvers to stay clear of the collateral damage. And I couldn't help feeling that if I brought enough resourcefulness to bear on the situation—enough of that creative imagination that Eliza was always talking about—I'd still be able to come through it all with everything I wanted: my financial coup, my uncle's favor, and, of course, Eliza herself. But it was not going to be easy.

With all of this in mind, I turned into the entrance of Casa Cubana. Ted claimed it was one of the safest places in Manhattan to discuss business, and, once inside, I could see his point. The place was quiet and totally off the radar of anybody Ted might care about. The only other customers at that time of day were a muttering eighty-year-old Karl Marx look-alike and a middle-aged Nynex lineman who divided his attention between the blaring TV over the counter and the waitress's tight jeans behind it.

I used the cell phone to call my uncle and reported the results of my visit on his answering machine. ("They'll get back to you. To us, I mean.") Then I ordered some food and sat back to wait.

I was well into a plate of incinerated chicken when Ted walked in, his dark suit rumpled and his round face slick with sweat. He yelled something incomprehensible to the waitress and flopped down into the seat across from me.

"You speak Spanish," I said.

"Yeah. I also own this place. Amazing the tax write-offs you can get running a dive like this." He mopped his shiny forehead with a napkin. "But we've got to powwow. This offer from your uncle sucks big-time."

"Sucks for Ben, you mean?"

"No, sucks for you and me!" He threw the napkin onto the table and cleared his throat. "It goes without saying, of course, that the client's best interests are my only consideration. But there's no way this acquisition does us any good."

"I would think you'd get credit if you took the deal to Pembroke Horton's M-and-A people."

"We need the IPO, Will! That's where I live now, and I just had two dot-coms go sissy on us because they think the market's too 'uncertain.' Christ, you want certain, buy a U.S. savings bond, am I right? But with IPO we've got a foolproof routine—go out at a high level, ladder the aftermarket, everybody makes money."

"I know that," I said. "And I want the IPO as much as you do, obviously. But what can we do? Ben seemed pretty receptive to the idea of an acquisition."

"He says he's worried about dealing with the expectations of shareholders. 'Ben,' I tell him, 'shareholders are born to be handled, I can do that for you. These days they don't need to see profits and prudent management; they need to see their CEO making funny with the Brain and the Kahuna on CNBC. I can do *that* for you, too.'" He grabbed another napkin from the dispenser. "I shared a cab to New Jersey with Ron Insana once, did I ever tell you that?"

"You mentioned it."

The waitress delivered his plate then—Spanish sausage dripping with melted cheese. He took a few greasy forkfuls before saying,

"Smart guy, is Ben, but he could use a little more in the iron-balls department."

Something occurred to me then—my stroke of imagination. "This is probably crazy," I said, "but what if my uncle's company acquired Stevedore and then took the combined entity public? That way, you'd get an acquisition *and* an IPO."

Ted stopped chewing. He stared at me over a hovering forkful of sausage. "Crazy is right. You think Gil would even consider that?"

"I could ask."

"It seems far-fetched," Ted said after a moment. He sat back in his chair and loosened his belt. "The market doesn't like it when New Economy marries Old. Look at what happened to AOL after the Time Warner thing. And Hawkings-Stevedore is kind of a weird fit. These things need a clean story, something to make it look like the combination makes sense."

"Hawkings Online," I said. Uncle Gil's online gourmet shop had been up and running for several months now, though without much fanfare. Despite the fact that it was a halfhearted effort on my uncle's part—"How can I *not* have an online store?" he would say—the thing was hemorrhaging money at an impressive rate. "It at least makes a story, right? Old Economy stalwart wants to go Internet, so it makes an Internet infrastructure play?"

Ted considered this for a few seconds. "I don't like it," he said after a moment. "But, hell, I don't have to like it. These days you throw anything and everything against the wall and just see what sticks. The question is, can you sell it to old Gil—not only the idea of IPO, but the idea of IPOing with me and Pembroke Horton?"

"Piece of cake," I said.

⊂⊃

"NO! ABSOLUTELY NOT!" Uncle Gil said. We were closeted in his floor office at the Hawkings warehouse in Tribeca. On the other side of the streaky glass partition, front loaders were moving back and forth, piled high with cases of cheap Gorgonzola. "I'm sorry, Will, I know you admire this Witherspoon fellow—and he seems to have earned the confidence of Ben Fletcher somehow or other—but if I ever took Hawkings public, with or without Stevedore, I'd go with Hampton Rucker at Goldman Sachs, my old roommate from Harvard. Not that I'd ever do it anyway. I have no objection to making money as an investor in this insane market, but I'm not about to send the company I've spent my entire life building out into an overbought market that seems to punish people for actually making money!"

"But if people are willing to pay a high price for something right now, why not take advantage of that fact while you can?" I thought of Bob, the night security guard at Pembroke Horton, and his literally priceless clock radio. "If the market is foolish enough to overpay for everything at this particular moment, why not cash in?"

"Because, Nephew, I don't care to do business in Cloud Cuckoo Land," he said. "In the current climate, I'd be paying far too much to acquire control of Stevedore as it is. But I happen to believe in Ben Fletcher and his infernal switching technology. I actually do think that Ben and people like him are building the infrastructure of the twenty-first-century economy—if people like Ted Witherspoon don't ruin them first."

"Ted likes to say that the shark and the pilot fish need each other."

"Yes, I suppose that's how all parasites comfort themselves."

"All investment bankers are parasites?"

"Of course not. Hampton Rucker at Goldman Sachs is not a parasite. It's these hysterics who would have us believe that everything is different this time, that P/E ratios are irrelevant, that there's no way to go but up. History teaches a different moral."

"Ted also says you should beware of drawing obvious morals from history."

"Interesting perspective. And if Ted Witherspoon dipped a sparrow's head in white paint and told you it was a bald eagle, would you believe him?" He pressed a button on his phone console. "But this discussion is over. Right now I need you to put something in my safe deposit box before the weekend. You have exactly twenty-five minutes before the bank closes." He brought a small metal briefcase out from under his desk. "I feel it's only fair to tell you that the contents are of considerable value."

I took the briefcase from him. It was surprisingly heavy. "It's a good thing you have one of the biggest boxes in the vault," I said.

"Oh, it will fit, Will, don't worry about that." There was a knock at the door, and one of the company's security guards walked in. "Davidson here will walk discreetly behind you, just as a precaution."

"Is he armed?" I asked, impressed.

"Let's just say he's prepared."

"Nothing to worry about," Davidson said. "Like Mr. Hawking says, I'm just a precaution."

"If you prefer, Will, I could have McTeague do it, but it's getting late . . ."

"No, no, I'm sure nobody's going to rob me between here and Varick Street. It's just that we've never had to resort to these 'precautions' before."

"You've never carried this much money before, Will." He looked at his watch. "You'd better start now."

I hoisted the briefcase and left the office, Davidson on my heels. Once outside on the street, he let an ample distance grow between us, but even so, I felt self-conscious. What could be in this briefcase, I wondered. If it had something to do with Hawkings business, Uncle Gil would surely have told me what it was. But I had never even seen this briefcase before.

I—we—reached the bank without incident. Davidson waited on the sidewalk while I went through the glass doors and applied at the desk to gain access to the vault. The bank officer in charge—Diego Cardozo—knew me by sight, but still went through the usual formality of checking my signature against the card. We entered the vault together, stuck our keys into the Hawkings box, and opened it. "Will you be needing one of the rooms today, Mr. Merrick?" Cardozo asked.

I was about to tell him no, that I would just slide the briefcase into the box, but my curiosity was piqued. "I will," I said. "If you wouldn't mind."

He carried the box for me to one of the privacy booths. "Just call when you're ready," he said, closing the door behind me.

I lifted the briefcase to the small desk and tried the latches. Locked, alas, though this was no surprise. But then I noticed the initials engraved on the metal near the handle: "RH." Apparently this was my Uncle Reg's briefcase. I retrieved my Palm Pilot from my jacket pocket and called up the contacts database. Uncle Reg's birthday was April 14 (I was a good nephew—always sent a card), and I knew he was going to be seventy this year. I tried several variations of his birthdate on the combination dials. 4-1-4-3 elicited the satisfying click I was looking for. Three cheers for unimaginative old technophobes, I said to myself as I snapped open the latches. Then I saw what made the case so heavy. Inside were numerous rolls of gold Krugerrands taped together between layers of soft packing foam. Also inside were some property deeds. And a felt bag. Which I opened. And in which I found, nestled within its soft folds, the proverbial diamond as big as the Ritz.

I held the stone up to the bulb of the little green-shaded lamp on the table. It glistened dramatically, shattering the light into a hundred glints and sparks. An impressive hunk of rock, I thought, slipping it back into its bag. Apparently all of this—the deeds, the gold, the diamond—was what Uncle Reg planned to use as collateral to fund his property development scheme. The old man was apparently going for the Big Score, like everybody else. And although there was no way I could safely use this stash for my own purposes—the deeds were nonnegotiable, of course, and the diamond too valuable and too noticeable—it certainly was interesting to know that Reginald Hawking was even wealthier than his brother. I wondered if Uncle Gil, or anyone else for that matter, realized quite how rich the old man was.

Feeling a slight buzz from being in close proximity to so much lucre, I returned the contents to the briefcase, closed it, latched it, and spun the combination dials back to their original setting. Then I lifted the whole case into the gray-metal safe deposit box and closed its lid. I took a deep breath and, steadying myself, called out, "Mr. Cardozo? I'm ready now."

CHAPTER XV

⊘ NOONTIME MONDAY FOUND the City of London abuzz with an intensity of jobbery such as was unusual even for that time of unprecedented exchange. Rumours of a great success concerning Admiral Russell's fleet near Cádiz had propelled the price of Bank and sundry government funds higher, and shares of a new project in Birchin Lane—the Company for the Reduction and Refinement of Sea Coal to One-Fourth Its Weight and Volume—were finding scores of eager buyers on their first day of offer. Having come that morning to Edward Lloyd's coffee-house in Lombard Street in order to purchase Assurances relating to my uncle's latest cargo from Leghorn, I was as it were in the thick of things. The tokens of Extravagance seemed everywhere in abundance, from the ever-growing headdresses of fashionable young ladies to the ever-finer carriages of their prospering husbands. Indeed, it seemed to me quite clear that if wealth were a river, then 'twas a river in flood that day, running o'er its banks and rushing this way and that through the streets, carrying all who stood in its path.

But I had busines of my own to conduct in the Alley as well. For if the joint-stock offering of Fletcher's winch went forward (and

Theodore Witherspoon seemed certain that it would, despite what he called my uncle's "misguided interference"), I must needs be prepared. Thus I spent an hour at Garroway's converting paper to gold—selling my Royal Africa Refuses, my discounted Tontines, my Derby and my Cuthbert Dykes, and, yea, even my beloved Hampstead Aqueducts, for cold hard Cash (and all at advantageous prices, too, shares having risen with the general optimism of the day). 'Twas against my nature, of course, to render so much of my wealth idle, even temporarily. But I did comfort myself with the thought that 'twould be a mere few days until I could convert it all to shares of Fletcher Winch. For as I wrote my cousin, 'twas no time to be timid. I must put aside all my fears and go forward, at least until some better solution occurred to me. For this was to be—this *had* to be—my masterwork, the *Great Leap* that would lift my fortune to the stars. Assuming all went well. Assuming Theodore Witherspoon's genius did not fail me.

Having concluded my business in the City, I proceeded by hackney coach to the house in the Red Lion Square. My uncle had already betook himself to the warehouse at Wapping, but Mrs. Popper was there, engaged in conversation with a master woodworker whom my uncle wished to engage for the rebuilding of the kitchen and dining-room. "Given the current demand for my services," I overheard the woodworker say, " 'twould be possible come Michaelmas, but not a day sooner, unless there be a Cancellation of Contract."

"I beg your pardon," said I, looking in on them. "Were there any letters, Mrs. Popper?"

"No letters, no, but a man came from Mr. Petroni, and said that gentleman would meet you as planned at the Blackfriars steps at two o' the clock."

"And are my elder uncle and aunt at home?"

"They've gone to Mr. Bloomingdale's establishment in Pickadilly, to purchase plate."

"Very good," said I. I took an apple from the bowl on Mrs. Popper's table and climbed the stairs to my bedchamber.

'Twas near half past one by now, leaving me but little time to change my clothing and make my way to Blackfriars. Jack was to instruct me that afternoon in shooting game, in preparation for my journey with Miss Fletcher to her family's great country house. There was an appropriate venue for such activity, he said, at Spring-Gardens, and so we'd find a boat at Blackfriars to carry us across the river to Vauxhall. 'Twould be no easy task for poor Jack, I thought, for my shooting skills were rudimentary, to say the least. But teach me Jack would try, so that I might avoid embarrassment in the fields and forests of Dorset.

The scene at Blackfriars—where Jack did meet me with a bag of fowling pieces strapped over his shoulder—was alive with activity at this hour. The river was thick with all manner of barges and wherries, and as Jack and I made our way to the steps, we were all but assaulted by the entreaties of a parcel of watermen, some of whom went so far as to pluck at our sleeves and jostle our wigs for attention. "Oars! Will you 'ave any Oars, sir?" went the general cry (which I, like many a newcomer to London, had misapprehended the first time I heard it, thinking something quite other than a boat on offer). I allowed Jack to negotiate the particulars with the most forceful of the applicants, and before long we were aboard a sturdy painted wherry, bound upriver for Vauxhall. Our oarsman, a Bible-backed ancient (though as strong as a young bullock, it seemed), proved just as vehement on the water as on the shore, keeping up a steady torrent of abuse against his fellow watermen:

"How now, thou son of a whore," said he to a confederate, whose craft was full from stem to stern with ladies of a certain age. "How came thee by that cargo of tun-bellied bawds? Bound for Spring-Gardens, I warrant, to stuff their one end with roasted fowls and t'other with raw sausages!"

"Avaunt, Rascal!" said one of the ladies, the eldest, who seemed responsible for the pack.

"What pious Fish-Fag is this?" he responded, with gusto. "Heigh, Madam Harlot, stop thy flappin' blowhole, for thy Word-Farts foul my air! Best save thy ire for the crab-lice that do call thy *Fur-Purse* home!"

At this vulgarity the woman was so astounded that she could say no more.

"Such Poetry," said I to Jack. "Have you ever heard the like? I think even great Dryden could learn from this fellow."

Overhearing me, the waterman did turn and ask, in a very different tone of voice: "A literary man, are you, sir?"

"B'm'Faith, I'm not," said I. "Unless the rhyme and metre of the markets be literature. And if that's so, then yes, you have the veritable Shadwell and Wycherly of 'Change Alley as your passengers."

"Stockjobbers!" he exclaimed.

"Nay, sir. Nor Brokers neither, though we are acquainted with many such."

The waterman spat then into the river. "Brokers," said he with disgust. "A Broker is a Black-leg and a Jobber is his Whore."

"I would think it t'other way round, actually," said I. "But hear, old Charon, how come you to have such scorn for these gentlemen?"

Our oarsman pushed a few hard strokes before saying: "Me four brothers and me, we give one o' these sharpers all we had in the world to buy us a share o' Pettering—them what makes the Water Engine."

"By gad, Jack! Do you hear? Even watermen take an interest now in the Stocks!"

"'Tis remarkable," Jack confirmed.

"But see here," I went on to the oarsman, "I own a bit of Pettering myself, and thus know it has not done poorly of late. What, then, is your complaint?"

The man's eyes widened in anger. "He said we'd double our

money in six months' time, and we've not made more than ten shillings in the pound, the scabrous cur!"

"Adod, Jack! The fellow carps of a fifty *Per Cent* gain in half a year!"

"He said we'd double," the waterman repeated.

"Well, this *is* a sign of greed. I should think you'd be grateful to the man. Instead you make as if he sold you gall and wormwood."

The oarsman spat again—letting fly a great gob of spittle that sailed away on the surface of the river. "I knows a night-soil man what earned triple his stake in Convex Lights," said he.

There was no reply I could make to this absurdity—though I did wonder for a moment why I had not bought this Convex Lights myself. And in any event, we were now approaching the shore at Vauxhall. So I merely tried to ease the man's bile with a bit of false comfort—"You must focus your mind on the gains you've made, my good man, and forget the gains you haven't"—whereupon he spat in the river once more. And as we disembarked, I whispered to Jack, "Should this make us uneasy—that e'en such *Riff-Raff* as this owns joint-stock?"

" 'Tis ominous, t'be sure," said he. "For when maggots do feast upon a fatted lamb, 'tis time the wolves moved on to other prey."

And at this we entered the New Spring-Gardens. It's being a Monday in March, and the weather not so fair, this pleasure ground did seem to want custom. Those walkways which of a summer Sunday are filled with all manner of company—young couples diverting their children, old men feeding the birds, rude young gallants pursuing unaccompanied ladies—were bleak and lonesome now, the retreat of a few idle ruffians who stared as we passed as if assessing the opportunity to do us harm. Jack made his way, I following, to a corner of the gardens remote from the central area, where some man of enterprise had set up what he named a *Shooter's Gallery*, the like of which I'd never seen before. Little targets of tin, cut in the form of partridges, grouse, and rabbits, were scattered out in a wooded area through which ran several winding paths. The design of the place was such that one might fancy himself on a country estate far from town, shooting game with the Lord of the Manor. And though it was an amusement merely, 'twas a new and unusual one—yet another Innovation of those heady days—and for me 'twould serve well as my education in game shooting.

At the booth we paid the proprietor, whose eagerness to take our coins bespoke the scarcity of ready marksmen before us. Then Jack unslung the bag from his shoulder and removed the two fowling pieces from within. "I'll instruct ye quick-like 'ow she's loaded," Jack said. "Then we'll try our luck in the wood."

This he did—though my clumsiness with the shot and powder put him somewhat out of countenance with me. "By gad, Will, if I didn't know better I'd say you play the ape wi'me."

"Alas no, Jack. I am quite in earnest. I've always had ten thumbs in matters such as this."

"That much is plain," said he. "'Tis fortunate you've a better way with the ladies than you do with a musket."

"Miss Fletcher might maintain otherwise," I said ruefully, brushing the powder from my hands.

Our fowling pieces loaded finally, we set off on the path into the wood. No sooner did we round the first curve in the path than we saw, off in the brush, a little tin hare. "Quick now, Will. There 'e is!"

I looked at my companion, struck by his enthusiasm. "It's not as if he'll run off," I observed.

"Y' must make *as if* 'twas real," he exclaimed, with some exasperation.

To oblige him, I raised the fowling piece to my shoulder, aimed at the hare, and fired. Several feet to the left of the metallic creature, a stone jumped into the air. "I shot wide," said I.

"Y' did," he confirmed. Then he lifted his own piece and fired.

There was a mighty "Ping!" and the hare, which seemed to be attached to a base by a hinge of some sort, fell over. "That's 'ow she's done," said Jack, looking well pleased.

It continued thus for some time. We would spy a tin quail suspended from an elm; I'd fire at it and miss; Jack would likewise fire but hit. Thus 'twas "Crack! Crack! Ping! . . . Crack! Crack! Ping!" all the while. I tried my best to marshal all of my concentration on the game, but without success. And so, after a good half hour of this disheartening activity, Jack and I fell into discourse on matters of business.

"So, is Fletcher's mind known yet as to yer uncle's offer?" Jack asked.

"Not yet, but I do know that of late he makes lengthy lamentations on the subject of raising money. He wants capital to give flesh to his Brain-Child, says he, but he despises the effort required to achieve that capital. Oft has he remarked the time he spends with bankers and brokers that could be better spent with those creating his winch."

" 'Tis bad for us if 'e sells to 'awkings," Jack observed.

"Indeed, I know that well. For my uncle has made it plain that he'd never bring the shares to market if he bought the project. So if he succeeds, he'll have the winch, and Benjamin Fletcher the money to create it, but we'll have naught to show for any of it."

We were on a narrow path now, in a deep wood overgrown with oaks. Gloom overtaking us, Jack and I walked along in silence for a moment. " 'Tis pity," Jack said then, "there's no other suitor for the prize—one with a long stocking who might buy and then permit us to bring the project to the Alley."

"Indeed," said I. "But 'twould require a considerable fortune to exceed my uncle's offer, which is said to be generous to a fault." I stopped then in my tracks, so sudden that Jack, who walked behind me down the path, did run up against my buttocks. "Hallo, then," said I. "I've an idea."

"You near 'ad a barrel up yer arse as well, if y' don't mind me sayin' so," he observed. "But what's this idea?"

"'Twould require a cunning hand at the tiller," said I, trying not to think too hard on the possible consequences of my grand idea. "And yet it might just be possible."

"What? What?" asked Jack.

I turned to him. "I think I know where that long stocking might be found," said I. "But we must return to the City directly." Then I thrust the fowling piece into Jack's hands and started back at a run toward the Spring-Garden's front gate.

CHAPTER 16

⏾ "HE'S NOT COMING," I said as I poured my fourth cup of coffee since lunch.

"He'll come, Will," Ted assured me. "After your description of him, I feel I know the man. He'll come."

We were in Ted's office at Pembroke Horton. I was pacing; Jack sat at the large-screen computer, preparing the PowerPoint presentation; Ted was leaning back in his chair behind his desk, his stubby hands locked behind his head. It was two-fifteen. Our guest was fifteen minutes late.

"I think maybe I misjudged him," I said. "He's old, conservative, out of touch. He's probably a government bond kind of guy."

"He likes money, Will. Besides, you've seen me in action. I'm great at this. I'll convince him."

"Ted's right," Jack said. "He is pretty great at this." He clicked the computer mouse a few times and said, "Okay, I got that one graphic to work again."

"See? It'll all be fine."

"If he comes."

Ted said: "He'll come."

Just then, as if to prove Ted right, his desk phone let out a little chirrup. Ted pounced on it. "Speak," he said. Then: "Okay, bring him in." He hung up and beamed at me. "It's showtime!"

Ted's secretary appeared at the door then and announced my uncle, Reginald Hawking.

"Mr. Hawking! I'm Ted Witherspoon. How the hell are you?"

Uncle Reg, looking distinctly uneasy, stepped into the office and took Ted's offered hand. "I'm doing quite well, thank you," he said, looking around the room like a prairie dog entering an aviary.

"Outstanding. Now let me introduce Jack Petroni, one of my associates. And your nephew you know, of course. Please have a seat. Anything I can get for you? Coffee, tea, a sports drink? Mary's got something here with echinacea and ginkgo biloba—good for whatever ails you."

"I'm fine, Mr. Witherspoon. I don't think I'll be staying long. I'm here only at my nephew's insistence." He gave me a look that would melt lead. "He assures me it will be worth my while."

"It will be, Mr. Hawking, it will be."

Uncle Reg lowered himself warily into the seat, eyeing the balancing metal bicyclist, the five-ball pendulum, and the other gewgaws that Ted kept on his desk. "My nephew tells me that you have a 'surefire' business opportunity to tell me about, Mr. Witherspoon. Is that correct?"

"It is, Reg—may I call you Reg? But first sit back and let me tell you a little something about what I do, Reg."

"I believe I'm familiar with the basics of investment banking, Mr. Witherspoon," my uncle said.

"Ah, but I'm not your ordinary investment banker, Reg. I do something a little different. To put it in a layman's nutshell: I invent wealth."

My uncle cleared his throat in a way that telegraphed extreme skepticism.

"Okay, okay," Ted added quickly, "lots of people 'create' wealth. But let me tell you how I—how we here at Pembroke IPO—*invent* it: We do it by compressing time. We look at companies—new companies, exciting companies, companies that are going to kick the twenty-first century's ass—and we make it possible for them and their backers to turn twenty, thirty, or even fifty years of potential earnings into current value. We telescope the future, you might say. Or how about this for the metaphor? We sell the chicken while it's still an egg. Where the rest of the world might look at a company and see twenty geeks and an idea, we see the next Cisco. And we *sell* it as the next Cisco. To people who want to *believe* it's the next Cisco. Just watch now. Jack?"

While I dimmed the lights, Jack clicked the mouse on his computer. The large screen facing my uncle sprang to life.

The presentation began with a cheesy countdown—a staticky retro number 20 on the screen, followed by 19 . . . 18—that familiar test-pattern descent—17 . . . 16—focusing the mind—15 . . . 14— lulling the expectations—13 . . . 12—but then a change—10 . . . 7. . .4 . . . 1 . . . nothing, just silence, until, a beat too late— "Ka-ching!" And finally the words—red-on-black, flashing in rapid succession on the screen: "Ready. Set. IPO."

"Welcome," Ted said, "to the corporate time machine."

I watched my uncle's nostrils flare in distaste, but his eyes never left the screen.

For the next eight minutes, Ted bombarded the man with a dizzying succession of bar charts, line graphs, statistics. There were recorded testimonials from CEOs, deliriously optimistic reports from investors, and ecstatic sound bites from CNBC and Bloomberg. An explication of the IPO process—from Registration Statement to Red Herring to Due Diligence to Effective Date—was punctuated by quick subliminal flashes of Jaguars and Chris-Crafts, Rolexes and houses on Long Island Sound. The whole presentation was slick, shameless, intentionally incoherent, crass, and utterly unethical. But it made Ted's central point—that you could buy corporate perform-ance in advance, reap decades of profits in a day, and walk away from the table before the future had any chance to disappoint.

With a final few clicks of the mouse—and a little synthesized voice bleating, "IPO: Tomorrow's Wealth Today" from the Har-man/Kardon speakers—the presentation came to a close. "So?" Ted asked as I turned up the lights. "What do you think, Reg?"

"What do I think?" My uncle looked somewhat dazed. "I think I'm confused—or else you are. I own a property management and de-velopment company. We're an old established family business. To borrow your metaphor, we are a chicken—and a rather fat one at that—not an egg."

"No, no, Reg. You misunderstand me. I don't want to take your chicken public. I want to sell you an egg—or part of an egg, at least—which you could quickly and easily turn around and sell at chicken prices."

Uncle Reginald raised an eyebrow. "Explain," he said.

Ted, overcome by his own enthusiasm, nearly jumped out of his seat. "Okay," he said. "Once upon a time, there was a little company called Stevedore Technologies. Remember the name, because in five years everyone on the planet will know it. A little tech startup, talent from the best firms in the business, privately funded so far, but going IPO in just a few days."

"And what do they make?"

"What?"

"What product does Stevedore Technologies manufacture?"

"Oh! Right! Nothing yet, but some amazing new electronic switching device that's going to revolutionize mass data handling on Internet servers."

"Internet?" A glimmer of interest appeared in my uncle's eyes, though he tried to hide it.

"But that's not the important thing. What's important is that the market's going to eat this up with a spoon."

Uncle Reg shifted in his seat. He was uncomfortable, clearly, but clearly not ready to leave yet, either. "Let me see if I understand you. You want me to buy shares of this company from you?"

"Better than that. I want to give you a chance to buy a big chunk of this company—say ten percent—at a substantial discount to the offering price."

The eyebrow again. "And why would you be so generous?"

"I won't lie to you, Reg. I got a temperamental genius-slash-founder-slash-CEO in the picture here. If I let him have his way, he'd keep doing private investor rounds of funding till the cows come home to roost. The market makes him nervous. Took lots of talking to get him to agree to an IPO, and now we got a takeover offer that's tempting him—"

"My brother's offer."

"Ah, you're better informed than you let on," Ted said. "Yes indeed, your own younger brother has made an offer for this company. But if Hawkings takes over Stevedore, there'll never be an IPO. Your brother will have this amazing money machine all to himself."

"So what is it you propose?"

"Okay, we're in what we call the Quiet Period now, and SEC regulations forbid me from making certain kinds of statements about the shares. But let me just say this: If I can line up one big investor to take a third of the shares of the IPO, I can give the genius-slash-founder-slash-CEO—Ben Fletcher, you'll meet him—I can give him peace of mind but still unleash—for him and for all of us—the rapid appreciative powers of the market."

"I'm afraid you'll have to translate."

"Okay, look, normally with an IPO we go out with thirty percent of a company into the market at, say, ten dollars a share. In this case, we'd sell you ten percent of the company at, say, eight dollars a share and go public with the other twenty percent at 10. So you instantly make a twenty-five percent return on your money! But once the other shares start trading, well, the SEC forbids me to make any promises, but the relative scarcity of tradable shares on the open market would tend to put even more upward pressure than usual."

"I see," my uncle said. "And what's the catch?"

"There is no catch."

"I'm not a fool, Mr. Witherspoon. There must be some sort of catch."

Ted smiled then and tapped his temple as if in admiration of my uncle's savvy. "Okay, there *is* a kind of catch. But a minor one: You agree to buy more shares in the aftermarket—at a premium. Now, don't get upset until I explain it to you. Number one: The number of shares you'll be buying *after* the IPO will be tiny compared to your initial investment, so your average cost-per-share will remain substantially below the initial asking price. Number two: By buying blocks of shares at, say, 12, then 14, etc., etc, you'll be helping to keep demand strong and the price of shares on the upswing, increasing the value of your entire stake in the company."

Uncle Reg seemed to grasp the logic of this. "But is this standard procedure?" he asked.

"That's the beauty of my world, Reg. There's no such thing as standard procedure anymore. So you see, everybody wins here. Ben gets his peace of mind. I get my IPO. You get a one-way ticket to Hog Heaven—not to mention bragging rights with your brother, since you'll own ten times as much of the company as he will."

This last point seemed to make an impact. Uncle Reg pursed his lips in thought and then asked: "How much would ten percent of this little company of yours cost?"

"Here's the figure we're working with." Ted wrote the figure on his notepad and slid it across the desk.

"That's an extraordinary amount of money," Uncle Reg said after a moment.

"All I can say, Reg, my friend, is that you've seen the charts. Priceline, Red Hat—granted, those were much bigger outfits, in a different league, but they would have been a steal at this valuation level before their IPOs."

My uncle stood up—as abrupt a movement as I'd ever seen him make. "Thank you, Mr. Witherspoon, for this lesson in New Economic lunacy," he said. "It's been very enlightening. I can return to Indiana now and confirm to my friends that everyone on Wall Street is indeed as mad as they seem."

"These are unusual times, granted. But people get rich by going *with* the markets, not by resisting them."

"I'll remember that, thank you."

"At least let me send over some papers, Reg—something for your lawyers to look at."

"You may send over whatever you like, Mr. Witherspoon—my lawyers love to look at papers—but I'm afraid I'm not interested in spending money like that on a fantasy."

"I'm sorry you feel that way, Reg. And you're right, it is a huge hunk of money. But the bigger the investment, the bigger the return—remember that." He stuck out his hand. "It was a pleasure meeting you."

"I'm sure it was," my uncle droned, reaching out to shake Ted's hand. But then he hesitated. "These papers," he said slowly. "You'll surely not want to send them to my brother's house. Perhaps you can send them to my lawyers' hotel. They're staying at the Sherry-Netherland."

An enormous smile spread itself across Ted's plump face. "Good point, Reg. I'll do just that."

"Your proposal will amuse them, I'm sure, quite as much as it did me. But now I must go. Good-bye, Mr. Witherspoon. William, Mr. Peritoni." And with a final sniff, he left.

The three of us said nothing for a few seconds. I could hear the fluorescent lights buzzing in the hallway outside. "Well," I said finally, "I guess that didn't go so well."

Ted laughed. "You got a lot to learn about this business, Will," he said. "It went beautifully. He'll be on board before the week's out."

"You're kidding."

"I never kid. Did you see his eyes, Will? Were you watching him watch the PowerPoint demo? He's in with it. He didn't care about anything he saw or heard except those charts. Well, that and the idea of screwing his younger brother. No, Will, he's heard all about this market on TV, just like everybody else, and he wants his share of it. You heard it here first: Once Reginald Hawking gets over the shock of the figure I wrote on that sheet of paper, he'll be back. Count on it."

"So you're saying that went well?"

"Couldn't have gone better. You're a genius, Will. Your instincts are great, even if you don't know it yet." He plopped down into his swivel chair and took a swig of coffee. "By the way," he said. "When do you leave for Texas?"

"On Friday. We're flying out on the Fletcher Broadcasting plane."

"And when do you get back?"

"Monday afternoon."

He looked surprised. "You're not leaving yourself much time before the IPO."

"Assuming it happens."

"Stop that. It'll happen. I'm certain of it now. And it's not as if you need to be here anyway. Just make sure you tell me before you leave how many shares I put aside for you. I'll do the rest. By this time next week, you'll be rich."

"I'll take your word for it, Ted."

"My word you can take to the bank. In the meantime, make nice with Eliza Fletcher and her father. Marry that girl and you won't *need* the Stevedore IPO."

"I'll do a lot of things for money, Ted, but marrying is not one of them."

"Yeah, right, of course. Go home and pack now. And don't forget your charm pills. If what I've heard about Fletcher Sr. is true, you'll need them."

I RENDEZVOUSED WITH JACK at our usual place in Trinity Church at the west end of Wall Street. We sat in one of the closed pews on the left side of the nave, where we knew we'd be past wandering range of the average tourist. "You gotta hand it to Ted," Jack said. "He knows human nature."

"Human nature, maybe," I said. "But I'm not sure he's right about my uncle. The man certainly didn't *look* on board to me."

"Tell you one thing," Jack went on. "Ted's got a very loose interpretation of Quiet Period. Not to mention a few dozen other SEC rules. But I guess I've learned to trust his sense of these things. It's gotten us pretty far already."

"I don't know," I said. "I sometimes wonder if the man is fully sane."

"Sane he isn't. But what's that old saying? 'In the land of the insane, the insanest man of all is king'—something like that?"

"Uncle Gil would know."

Jack laughed. "Yeah, he would."

I sat back in the pew then and looked up at the vaguely elegiac shafts of red and blue light streaming through the stained glass behind the altar. "You ever worry, Jack?" I asked.

"About what?"

"You know, about this. About all of it ending someday. I mean, it can't go on forever like this, can it?"

Jack stared at me. "That's the question I asked myself a year ago, when I was worth one-quarter what I'm worth today."

" 'History is for losers.' That's what Ted says."

"And has Ted ever been wrong?"

"Not yet."

"Then relax," Jack said. "This train is unstoppable. Just hang on and enjoy the ride."

"No matter who gets run over?" I asked, thinking of Uncle Gil and looking for reassurance.

Jack obliged. "We're all adults here, Will. Both your uncles are seasoned warriors in the business world, am I right? They know that everybody does what they gotta do to make their nut." He leaned over and punched my knee. "I better go now. Give me a call before you leave for Texas. And remember what I told you at the golf place yesterday: Don't overthink your swing or else you'll end up in the sand trap every time."

⌘

UNCLE GIL WAS at his computer when I walked into the Tribeca office later that afternoon. "Good God," he muttered as he stared at the screen. "This market will be the death of me."

"Down?" I asked.

"Down, up, down, then up up up. Every time I try to buy some Human Genome Sciences on a dip, it skitters up a few points and leaves my limit order behind. It's as if the market were taunting me."

"You're buying biotechs now?"

"I'm just playing. I have to admit that there's a certain excitement to all of this nonsense."

"I'm sure the tailors at Barney's would be interested to know you've come around to their way of thinking."

"Oh, I wouldn't go that far," my uncle said. "This is just mad money. I find myself with a few unexpected free hours this afternoon, so I'm amusing myself."

"Somebody break an appointment?"

"Yes. I was supposed to take Reginald and his lawyers to see a few bankers this afternoon, to talk about funding for this land development scheme of his, but the old stick-in-the-mud canceled on me, and won't say why. He's being very mysterious about it, too. My brother is becoming downright unstable."

This interested me. "When did he cancel?"

"He called just a half hour ago. Why do you ask?"

That would have been after our meeting at Pembroke Horton. Maybe Ted was right about him after all. "Just curious," I said.

Uncle Gil pushed himself away from his computer. "So, I assume you're all packed for your trip."

"Haven't even started. For the past two days, I've been working on my golf swing."

"I admire your priorities. Just don't forget to put in a good word for me with Fletcher Sr. I don't know if they talk to each other about business matters, but it couldn't hurt my cause with the son to have the father on my side."

"About that," I said carefully. "You're still sure this acquisition is something you want to do?"

I could feel his sudden stare like a heat lamp. "Why? Have you heard something?"

"It's just that it's an awful lot of money to spend on a company with, as you say, negative earnings."

"We seem to have switched identities, William. Now *you* seem to be the Nasdaq skeptic." He laughed. "No, Fletcher may go for the IPO—for the money—but to my mind he'd be making a mistake. And besides, this is about more than money. I have as little tolerance as anyone for the nonsense spouted by some of these New Economy apologists, but even I can see there's something to it. I'm a hopeless old dinosaur—too old to help invent the New Economy myself, but I can at least support those who can. As I've told you before, Stevedore is far too expensive at this level—I recognize that fact—but I'd like to buy it all the same. I think of it as my gift to the future, even if I overpay."

"That's very philosophical of you, Uncle Gil," I said, feeling a pang. "You might even say it's kind of noble."

"Come, Will," he said. "Spare me the flattery. And you've got packing to do, so I suggest you go back home and do it now."

Go back home, he'd said. Sometime over the past few months, the meaning of that phrase had shifted for Uncle Gil, as it had for me. It didn't mean Bloomington, Indiana, anymore. It meant "our home"—Uncle Gil's and mine. "I'll see you at dinner then," I said, and got out of there before I said something I'd regret.

CHAPTER XVII

⟳ THE TWO DAYS FOLLOWING OUR MEETING with Sir Reginald did pass with great swiftness, as I made ready for my journey to the Fletcher estate in Dorset. Uncle Gilbert, perhaps out of mercy, found little for me to do, but my other master, Theodore Witherspoon, made great demands upon my time. As it came out, he had been entirely accurate in his assessment of my elder uncle's hypocrisy. Sir Reginald was ready to play the joint-stock game after all, and now the two of them, along with Benjamin Fletcher and various associates, were deeply engaged in secret negotiations for the transfer of shares in Fletcher's project to the ownership of Sir Reginald Hawking. And though I knew that this particular outcome to the business would certainly be advantageous to my own interests, I did not relish being in league with my one uncle, for whom I bore no love, against the other, who had shown me much kindness. I attempted to console myself, however, with Jack's reflection that, in Finance, as in War, all sides understood that each would do what was necessary to win.

At dinner on the Thursday, Uncle Gilbert broached the topic of his own offer for the winch. "That pup Fletcher has put himself beyond my reach," Uncle Gilbert lamented as the three of us—Sir Reginald, Lady Dorothea, and myself—affected interest in our lamb chops. "He refuses all my enquiries, even when I send as my emissary young Will here, whom he counts among his friends. I fear he has rejected my offer and balks at informing me of his decision."

Sir Reginald cleared his throat. "I am, of course, no authority," he intoned with a self-satisfied smile, "but perhaps he has found your offer inadequate and has decided to sell shares after all. As I see it, Gilbert, one cannot gainsay the rapid appreciative powers of the market in these times."

Uncle Gilbert regarded him with startled eyes. "Why, Brother, you have been schooling yourself in the argot of the Alley, it seems. Wherever did you hear that wondrous phrase?"

"Oh, as you have oft pointed out, Gilbert, I know little of these matters, and merely parrot words I have heard other men utter."

"Hmph," Uncle Gilbert exclaimed. He eyed his elder brother for a moment before turning back to the consumption of his chop.

"Would it distress you much, Uncle Gilbert, sir," I asked then, "if Benjamin Fletcher did indeed go ahead with the joint-stock endeavour?"

He considered this for a few seconds, and I felt my other uncle's warning stare like a hot poker upon my cheek. "That's difficult to say," Uncle Gilbert observed finally. "For, after all, I stand to make a pound or two myself, should the shares come to the Alley and become subject to, as my brother so eloquently puts it, 'the rapid appreciative powers of the market.' Assuming that those powers do not turn against the shares."

"I have been made to understand," Uncle Reginald said, "that shares in projects such as this one nearly always appreciate in value."

"That has indeed been the case in most instances to date," his brother replied. "But as I have oft remarked to young Will here, the market is a fickle *Mistress*, who may withdraw her *Favours* at any time for no good reason."

My aunt, stiffening at this, spoke up. "Gilbert," said she, "I'll have to ask that you not use such colourful metaphors in my presence."

"I do beg your pardon, Lady Dorothea," my uncle said, with an apologetic nod of his head. "I own that, as a bachelor, I am unused to having ladies of your fine sensibilities at my table."

"That is obvious," said she, and pushed her plate of cucumbers aside.

"But to answer your question, Nephew, 'twould indeed distress me to lose this fight. For I begin to fancy the notion of myself as owner of such an Enterprise, playing a role in the making of the future, as it were. Call it vanity if you will, but an old man's vanity rivals that of even a woman."

(At which Lady Dorothea did cross her arms before her and sniff.)

"In any case," my younger uncle went on, "I cannot fathom why, if Fletcher and his banker have rejected me, they don't just say so. All of this secrecy and manoeuvring as it were behind the scenes—I suppose that's how business is transacted today, but I own I don't like it. In our day, men dealt with each other in a fairer and more open fashion, like Men of Honour. Is that not so, Brother?"

"True, Gilbert," Sir Reginald responded. "It is as you say."

"I suspect, in fact, that you in particular would find such ways of doing business distasteful, being no admirer of city mores."

"Indeed, for I am merely a country bumpkin, simple and naïve."

His brother did narrow his eyes at him then. "Do you mock me, Reginald?" he asked.

"I? Mock you? On the contrary, I merely agree with you. For yours has always been the wiser head in such affairs." And here a sickening smile did crease Sir Reginald's lips. "Is it not so, Brother?" he asked, patting his well-fed belly. "Is it not so?"

FRIDAY MORNING found me at the offices of Theodore Witherspoon in Lombard Street. "Ah, Will, my boy," said he as I entered. "You've come with your gold, I trust, for I know you leave today for Dorset and I must needs know how many shares to subscribe in your name."

"I've not yet decided precisely," said I. "But Jack Petroni has my money, and I'll instruct him ere I depart."

"Make sure that you do," said he, "and I'd advise you to take aboard as many as you can possibly afford."

"The endeavour looks bright, then?"

"As bright as can be. Sir Reginald, the crafty old dog, has agreed to all, as has our friend Fletcher. 'Twill proceed as planned on Tuesday."

I hesitated, then asked the question that had kept me wakeful all the night before: "Sir, I wonder, would it not be seemly to inform Gilbert Hawking of these matters, if all is decided? You might tell him at least that his offer for purchase has been rejected, even if you do not inform him of his brother's role in the alternative arrangements."

"Indeed not," Theodore Witherspoon said. "He must, of course, be informed before Tuesday. But we must keep him in a state of hopeful anticipation until the last possible moment."

"But why?"

"Because if he knows his offer's been refused, he might attempt to improve it! Adod, man, it took all my powers of persuasion to convince young Fletcher to go the joint-stock route with Sir Reginald. I don't want a sweetened offer from Gilbert Hawking to shake his resolve and play the deuce with my carefully laid designs."

"But does it not do my uncle harm to keep him thus ignorant?"

Mr. Witherspoon smiled. "Ah, is that what troubles you? No, you must not think in such terms. The time is ripe, Will; the Alley's appetite for projects like Fletcher's is at its keenest. If Hawkings were to purchase the project now, without bringing it immediate to open market, he'd live to regret it, for there's no telling what the project might be worth a year or two from now. Look at the Dive Bells, Will. A few years ago, there was no price too high to pay for a share of Drummond Bell; but now those same shares languish. No, 'tis best for all that the current design go forward, and thus that Gilbert Hawking be kept in ignorance."

I tried to convince myself of the soundness of this logic. There was no gainsaying that my Uncle Gilbert—by his own admission—was possessed of an old-fashioned turn of mind. Perhaps 'twould indeed be for his own good to keep him ignorant of this matter—something which he in any case suspected.

"And you need have no worries with regard to incurring your uncle's displeasure," Theodore Witherspoon continued. "Gilbert Hawking will never know of your rôle in bringing his brother to me. I've secured Sir Reginald's promise on that score."

So I would suffer no ill effects either, if the offer went forward. All would benefit—my Uncle Gilbert as much as anyone.

"But come," my mentor said. "Sir Reginald will be here directly to sign some documents. Have we any other business to settle before your departure?"

"None, sir. As I say, I'll have Jack bring you my purse before the end of the day." And I left then, not wishing to encounter Sir Reginald at the door.

I returned home to the Red Lion Square and completed my final preparations for departure. As I came downstairs with my small travelling bag in hand, I was met by Uncle Gilbert in the hall. "Know you where my brother has got himself to?" he enquired of me.

"Is he not with Lady Dorothea at Green Park?" I asked, answering his question with one of my own.

"Apparently not, for Lady Dorothea and her maid have just this moment returned from that place, and when I ask her, she says he told her only that he had some business to attend to." Uncle Gilbert twisted the locks of his full-bottomed wig. "He's up to something, I warrant."

Just then he seemed to take note of the bag in my hand. "So you're off, I see," said he. "God speed you, my boy. I know this journey means much to you."

"It does, sir."

"You'll do well, I know. For your good qualities—obscured as they sometimes are—will surely be valued by the lady *and* her father."

Then he surprised me by embracing me—an unusual gesture for him. "Is there anything else?" he asked then.

"Anything else, sir?"

"Is there anything you must tell me before you leave? Anything I should know?"

I hesitated, wondering if I might reveal just a bit of what I knew. But no, I had made my decision. There was no going back. "No, sir," said I. "I'll see you again in a few days' time, I hope."

"Good." Then he handed me a small purse. "For incidental expenses. Don't thank me, just take it." He embraced me again—exacerbating my misery—and saw me to the door.

Once upon the street, I sent Alfred off with the baggage. Then I called the boy Thomas Block and gave him a letter to deliver to Jack Petroni. In it were my instructions—to wit, to purchase as many shares of Fletcher's project as my fortune would allow.

Having thus thrown my bonnet over the highest windmill in the land, I besought myself a hackney coach and left my uncle's house.

CHAPTER 18

⌒ "I WANT YOU TO KNOW that I'm not at all impressed by the fact that we're boarding your father's corporate jet," I said to Eliza, as we boarded her father's corporate jet.

"Good, you're exhibiting learned behavior. I like that in a man." Eliza climbed up the embarkation stairs ahead of me. For a moment, her delicately curved, denim-clad rump swung before my eyes, and I felt the involuntary genital shudder of awakening Id. *Not now,* I commanded myself silently. *Not now.*

She stopped and turned back to me. "In any case," she said, "the only reason we're using this aircraft is because one of my father's VPs had to come to New York on company business. Under normal circumstances, I fly business class on a commercial airliner, like everybody else."

"Of course," I said. "Like everybody else." I looked down the line of small oval windows to the Fletcher Broadcasting logo on the tail. "And this VP, will he be flying back to San Antonio with us?"

"Yes, she will. She's probably aboard already."

She was. As we stepped into the body of the jet, a plump, fiftyish black woman put aside some papers, rose from her seat, and came up to meet us. "Eliza, it's been months," she said.

"Hi, Jaymee." The two women kissed. "Thanks for the lift."

"My pleasure. And this must be the guy we've been hearing so much about at the office." Jaymee swiveled my way and locked me in a pleasant but unmistakably assessing gaze.

"She's being nice to you, Will. Nobody's been talking about you at the office."

"Eliza's right; I'm lying," Jaymee said. "But we'll be talking about you from now on. I'm Jaymee Toland."

"Will Merrick," I said, shaking her many-ringed hand.

"I've known Eliza since she was six, so if you want to hear anything about the slacker drug addicts she used to date in high school, I'm the gal to see."

"Go to hell, Jaymee," Eliza said. "Don't you have any work to do?"

"Okay, okay." Jaymee headed back to her seat. "As a matter of fact, I have eighty-five pages of your father's nonsense to slog through before we get to San Antonio, so I'll be ignoring you for the entire flight."

"I can't tell you how happy I am to hear it."

"Hello, Ms. Fletcher." This was said—chirpily—by another woman who had appeared suddenly at my elbow. She was about six feet tall and aggressively blond. It took me a moment to realize that she was our flight attendant. "Is there anything you or Mr. Merrick would like?"

"Just coffee for me, Dana, thanks. What about you, Will? There's a full bar back there, unless Jaymee's been at it again."

"I'll take a beer."

"Any particular brand?" Dana asked.

"I don't know. Surprise me."

She brought me a Lone Star in a long-neck bottle—"for local color," she said.

"So you've really never been to Texas before?" Eliza and I sat ourselves at two swiveling captain's chairs that faced each other across an amoeba-shaped table. It was a nice plane.

"Never," I said. "I've heard rumors that it's big."

"Spare me." She took a sip of her coffee. "We'll be in the Hill Country, which is beautiful this time of year, if you like wildflowers. God, I can't wait to be back. After two straight months in New York, it'll be nice to talk about something other than valuations and vesting stock options."

"You're not afraid to be missing the last few days of preparation for your brother's IPO?"

"Are you kidding? That's why I picked this weekend to go home. Ben's a wreck."

"I know how he feels," I said.

She pressed her foot reassuringly against mine under the table. "You're stressed out about the IPO. I know you've got a lot riding on it. But you agreed to come with me anyway. Don't think it hasn't been noted."

"Excuse me, everybody," Dana called out then. "It's time for seat belts. We're cleared to fly."

As I buckled up, I asked Eliza: "So I get credit for giving your brother my life savings and then leaving town with you?"

Her look of blatant incredulity made me feel suddenly ill. "Tell me you put your life savings into Stevedore."

"Well, yeah, almost all. Why?"

She shook her head. "You guys all think you're invincible, don't you," she said. "But Texas is full of reckless cowboys. You'll fit right in."

It took us five hours to fly to San Antonio. Eliza spent most of the time reading, alternating between old issues of the *New York Times Magazine* and some novel with a fuzzy picture of a naked woman and a telephone on the cover. I tried to read my own book—*Golf for*

Dummies—but had a hard time concentrating. Maybe it was the implied skepticism in Eliza's comment, or maybe it was just being away from the hothouse exhilaration of New York City, but somehow I was becoming increasingly appalled by what I had just done—i.e., put $750,000 of my own money into a start-up technology company that made a product I did not understand and the market for which might or might not exist. Was I insane? Was everybody I knew insane? *Don't think about it,* I told myself sternly. *You've made your decision. Ted has everything under control.* But I couldn't head off the dread that was now seething in my stomach like a bad vindaloo. I tried to calm myself by watching the checkerboard of farmland pass beneath us—and somewhere over Ohio switched from Lone Star to single-malt scotch.

Just before our descent, Eliza put down her book and said, "Okay, you're about to meet my father, so I should tell you a few things to prepare you."

"I need a briefing to meet your father?" I asked.

From Jaymee's seat across the plane came a noise that seemed to be nasal or guttural in origin.

"Well, yes," Eliza went on. "At first impression, he strikes most people as an arrogant bastard."

"*Most* people?" Jaymee said.

I looked from Eliza to Jaymee and back again, trying to gauge their expressions. "But underneath the gruff exterior he's a pussycat, right?"

Jaymee made the noise again and Eliza said, "Well, no. He's pretty much an arrogant bastard all the way through. Your strategy should be to take whatever he gives you. Don't try to defend yourself, don't try to be clever, and whatever you do, don't think he's inviting you to banter. He's not. Just say 'Yes, sir' and 'No, sir' and you should be fine."

"I can see that my reputation as a sparkling raconteur is going to suffer in Texas," I said.

"See that? What you just did? You were being droll. It's a natural impulse with you. Suppress that instinct."

I stared at her for a few seconds, waiting for the telltale wink or smile. But she was serious. "Yes, ma'am," I said finally.

"That's the idea," Eliza said. "Now buckle your seat belt. We're about to land."

After a moderately harrowing descent, during which my mind helpfully reminded my adrenal gland that Texas was the wind-shear capital of the universe, we hit the tarmac and taxied to a stop in what looked like a parking lot for private aircraft. I slipped *Golf for Dummies* into my carry-on, released my seat belt, and followed Eliza and Jaymee to the door. "Bye-bye now," chirped Dana the giant flight attendant, giving me a reassuring pat on the shoulder.

The hot, damp wind hit me with a virtual thwok as I exited the aircraft. Balancing on shaky legs, I made my way down the steps to the tarmac, awash in the roar of aircraft noise. A shimmering silver Mercedes sat expectantly about twenty yards away. Two old men in suits stood beside it, one of them wearing a white cowboy hat. *Please let Eliza's father be the one without the hat.* I prayed silently. But the man Eliza ran to and threw her arms around was indeed the behatted one. Could be worse, I told myself—at least he wasn't wearing a bolo tie. I set my jaw a little tighter and marched over toward them.

"Daddy," Eliza said, with an unmistakable hint of Texas twang creeping into her voice. "This is my friend Will Merrick."

"Hello, Mr. Fletcher, sir," I said from behind Eliza.

"Come on over here, son, so I can shake your hand! You look like you think I'm gonna hit you!"

"Yes, sir," I said, stepping up and offering my hand. He grabbed it and shook it with a not unreasonable amount of force. Then, just as I was turning back to Eliza, he slapped me in a way that, in local parlance, would probably be referred to as "upside the head."

"There," he said. "You were right the first time! Never turn your back on me, son. Old Jaymee here'd be the first one to tell you that."

"I tried, Joseph, I tried," she said.

"Well, let's get in outa this heat while they load up the bags."

"Excuse me," I said. "If you don't mind, I'll just stay outside for a minute to make a quick call?"

Father and daughter shot me identical annoyed looks.

"I'm sorry. It shouldn't take long. I've got my cell phone."

"Fine," Fletcher said testily. Then the other old man, who was apparently the driver, opened the door to the Mercedes and the three of them climbed in.

I moved about ten yards away and punched in Ted's number. When I got his voice mail, I said, "Ted, it's Will. I'm in Texas now and . . . well . . . I've been thinking that maybe I want to go a little conservative on the Stevedore IPO. I know that Jack's probably given you my paperwork and my check already, but can I maybe revise it, to about half, say? Let me know. I'll keep the phone on. You know the number."

I hit End, pocketed the phone, and went back to the Mercedes. The driver opened the door again and I climbed into the blessed coolness of the passenger area next to Jaymee, with Eliza and her father across from us. Their conversation ended immediately. I leaned back against the soft leather of the rear-facing seat and stretched my legs.

"You like to golf, there, Will?" Fletcher asked after an awkward moment.

"Yes, sir."

"Any good? What's your handicap?"

"I don't really have a handicap, sir, except my own ineptness."
Damn it! I wasn't supposed to do that!

Fletcher was sneering at me, and I could see flashes of alarm in Eliza's eyes.

"What I mean, sir," I added quickly, "is that I'm a beginner, and not a very talented one."

"Well, fine, but we've got ourselves a tee time at six tomorrow. The club doesn't usually open till seven, but they like to be nice to me. So we'll have the course to ourselves."

"That sounds great," Eliza said, squeezing her father's arm. She was obviously delighted to see the old man, and looked younger and happier and less cynical in his presence than I'd ever seen her. It occurred to me, not for the first time, that there were two kinds of people in the world—those who lost their sense of irony when they visited their parents, sinking back into the earnest affections of childhood, and those whose sense of irony only intensified ("Yes, Mom, lime Jell-O *is* still my favorite dessert"). Which type you belonged to apparently depended on whether your childhood was happy or hellish.

Eliza squeezed her father's arm again and asked, "Who'll be playing?"

"It'll just be you, me, the untalented beginner here, and Laurence. He can't wait to see you, by the way. He'll be at the ranch when we get there."

"And when do we head out to the cabin?"

"Sunday morning. Laurence is going up with us, too. And I'm hoping his father will be able to meet us there."

"You'll like Laurence's father," Eliza said to me.

"I'm sure I'll like Laurence, too," I said.

"Laurence has a partnership in a white-shoe law firm, a three-stroke handicap, and a twenty-year-old crush on Eliza," Fletcher said, "so I doubt that very much."

I nodded. "Yes, sir," I said.

⬧

SOMERDALE PARK, which we spied from the carriage a full ten minutes before actually arriving there, was to my eyes an astonishment—

a great, three-storeyed, red-brick pile from the reign of the first King Charles, its roof sprouting more chimneys than a summer meadow does wildflowers. As we rounded the gravel approach to the massive front portico, I could but gaze upon the place in speechless awe. A score of excellent moulded-brickwork pediments crowned its bold cornice, aglow in the early twilight, which did give the whole an appearance of some jagged Alpine mountainscape.

"Home again," Miss Fletcher murmured as the coach rattled to a halt. I sprang from my seat and handed her out to the ground. "The soot and ill airs of London seem already a thing of the distant past. Do you not think so, Mr. Merrick?"

"I do," said I, though I own that, just then, I'd as soon have been choking on the soot and ill airs of London as breathing the sweet vapours of Heav'n, let alone those of eastern Dorset.

"Yes, yes, there will be time enough to wax rapturous about the air tomorrow," Colonel Fletcher intoned, coming up behind us. "But the hour grows late, and my appetite keen, so prithee make haste."

We entered the great house through a phalanx of curtseying housemaids and bowing footmen. "Mrs. Fletcher awaits us above in the front drawing-room," Colonel Fletcher continued. "It goes without saying that she is eager to see you."

We ascended the broad staircase to the first storey. As we entered what I took to be the "front drawing-room"—a luxuriously appointed hall that caught the butter-coloured late sun through its towering windows—a handsome and extremely well-formed woman threw herself upon Miss Fletcher's breast. "Eliza, dear," said she, "at last!" She looked hardly the senior of her daughter, with a soft rosy complexion and bright grey eyes. Watching these two beauties embrace, I felt a discomfort suddenly that perhaps I should have been ashamed of.

After this exceedingly affectionate greeting, Eliza took her mother by the hand and led her toward me. "Mother," said she, "this is Mr. Merrick, our great friend in London."

Mrs. Fletcher gave a smile then that dazzled me. "You are welcome in our home, Mr. Merrick," said she.

"I am honoured to make your acquaintance, Mrs. Fletcher," said I with a gallant bow, "and grateful for your hospitality. Your home is as charming as its occupants."

"Baugh!" Colonel Fletcher ejaculated. "We'll see what you say after a night in the damp of the back bed chambers."

Or after another hour in your *company,* I added silently.

"But here's someone else eager to greet the travellers," Mrs. Fletcher went on.

"Dear Laurence!" Miss Fletcher cried out.

A young man, appearing out of the shadows, attempted a bow to us, but Eliza tush-tushed the gesture and graced him with a warm embrace. This Laurence was a fine figure of a man—taller than I, damn him!—well-made and as handsome as I wished him ugly. He wore an exquisite bottle-green coat, a lace cravat, and a pair of leather country boots that looked as if made from the tanned belly-skin of a newborn calf.

"Come meet Mr. Merrick," Eliza said, pulling him toward me much as she had done her mother—as if I were the most fascinating specimen in the collection of Grisham College. "Mr. Laurence Carter, my oldest friend in the world, meet my newest, Mr. William Merrick, who has single-handed made London almost endurable for my brother and me."

"Well, sir," said he with a bow, "you have much to answer for, if you make the metropolis so agreeable to Miss Fletcher that you deprive us of her company here."

"She flatters me," I answered, "for 'tis Miss Fletcher herself who gives London all its lustre. Without her now, I'm sure th'entire city seems dull and lifeless."

"Bosh! Enough of this foppery!" said Colonel Fletcher. "We dine in a quarter hour, so you'd all do best to stow the pretty talk and make ready for the meal. Mr. Merrick, Josiah here will show you where to go."

Thus chided, we adjourned severally to our appointed rooms. Mine proved to be a chamber of prodigious proportions, with tall windows looking out across the gardens and the vast lawn to the forest beyond. Assisted in my preparations by this Josiah, I was soon out of my travel garb and into my new ensemble—one of Mr. Barney's finest efforts, I thought, as I examined myself in the pier-glass. I dismissed Josiah and spent a little time just walking about the room, examining its fine mahogany furniture and other appointments. Could I ever be at home in a place such as this, I wondered. I supposed I could, given enough time. I thought then of the business I had left behind in London. Even if all went as Theo Witherspoon predicted, would I ever be rich enough to be considered an acceptable match for Eliza Fletcher? If not, then what indeed was I doing there at Somerdale Park? A year from now, or two, would I and Eliza be coming here from our home in London for the shooting, the servants greeting us at the door as Mr. and Mrs. Merrick? Was I foolish even to hope for such an outcome?

The evening meal, which was served promptly at eight, proved an awkward affair. Colonel Fletcher seemed interested solely in the rapid and efficient consumption of his victuals (which, by the by, were very bad, quite inferior to the exquisite table the Colonel's son offered in London). Meanwhile, my other dinner companions spent most of the mealtime embroiled in a discussion of local Eminences—all of them, naturally, quite unknown to me—and precious little effort was made to include me in the general discourse. Watching this Laurence Carter engage the two ladies in conversation, I could only envy his ease and air of familiarity in that setting. His claim on the affections of Miss and Mrs. Fletcher had preceded mine (if indeed I had one) by at least a score of years. His deportment, moreover, was excellent, and his breeding obvious. Could I ever hope to make up this advantage? My mood blackening by the minute, I sat in silence and guzzled the indifferent claret.

After the ladies had retired, Colonel Fletcher conducted Mr. Carter and me to the game-room for brandy and cigars. There we stood at the hearth, beneath the mounted heads of hart and tusked boar, and attempted conversation on more manly topics. "So Miss Fletcher informs me that you are involved in financial matters in the City," Mr. Carter said to me.

"Yes, in my own small way. I assist my uncle, Mr. Gilbert Hawking. He is a wine importer of some prominence, and very much involved in what many are calling the New Finance."

"It must be fascinating for you," Mr. Carter observed, "for even here in sleepy Dorset we hear of the great doings in 'Change Alley, where fortunes are made from nothing as it were overnight. You must educate me in these matters."

"Do not be deceived, Mr. Merrick," the Colonel said gruffly. "Mr. Carter here feigns ignorance of these matters. But what he does not tell you is that his own father is Mr. Ezra Carter, and if the New Finance can be called a *Religion*, then Ezra Carter is one of its *High Priests*."

"Verily," said I, astounded. "I believe I know your father! For a short time I was employed by a broker, Mr. Theodore Witherspoon—who now, Colonel Fletcher, assists your son in his current endeavours—and while serving in that capacity I conducted a brief correspondence with a Mr. Ezra Carter, in connexion with some business. He was very kind to me."

"That is indeed a remarkable coincidence," said Mr. Carter. "And remarkable, too, that he was kind to you."

"I do believe he found my inexperience amusing. For I reminded him, he said, of his younger self."

"Ha! If you reminded my father of himself, you must have made an uncommonly favourable impression upon his mind."

Colonel Fletcher growled like an ill-tempered bear and said, "We'll see in due time exactly what kind of impression, for the man himself is to join us Sunday at the lodge." He coughed a phlegmy cough then and threw his cigar into the fire. "But that brings to mind tomorrow's shooting. Mr. Merrick, we rise early in this house, as Mr. Carter here can attest, so I suggest we all retire now for the night. Josiah will wake you at half past four, unless you wish to rise sooner."

"Half past four will be . . . quite convenient, sir," said I.

"Good. I intend that we be breakfasted and out in the wood by six." He stood before me then and, smiling, struck me another "good-natured" blow to the side of the head. "We'll see what kind of shot you are then, Mr. Merrick, eh?"

"Yes, sir," said I, ears a-ringing.

And with a swift, perfunctory bow, he bade us both good night.

CHAPTER 19

⚬ MY GOLF BALL skittered over the lush, carpet-quality green and fell into the ninth hole with a pronounced *plok*.

"A triple bogey," Joseph Fletcher said. "You're improving."

"Yes, sir," I replied. "Maybe I won't slow us down quite so much on the back nine."

"There won't *be* a back nine, son. My intent is to get out of this place before dark."

I saw Eliza and Laurence exchange a pained look. Feeling miserable, I retrieved my ball from the hole. It was bad enough, I told myself, that I was playing even more ineptly than I had with Jack at the pitch-and-putt course in New Jersey. But I also didn't like what I was seeing between Eliza and Laurence. I hated the wry smile she graced him with every time he made a knowing or witty remark. I hated the affectionate way one of them would tease the other when he or she hit a bad drive. And I especially hated the familiar and totally unselfconscious way she put her hand on his arm for support when she bent to retrieve one of her balls from the rough.

"We're heading back to the clubhouse," Joseph Fletcher announced then. "I think we all could use a cold drink and some lunch."

We climbed aboard one of our foursome's gleaming golf carts, leaving the caddies and our golf bags to bring up the rear. Old Fletcher insisted on driving, with Laurence in the seat next to him, so at least I was able to sit beside Eliza in the rear-facing backseats.

"It wasn't as bad as all that," she whispered, noticing my gloom.

"It wasn't?"

"It's not as if anybody's going to judge you on the basis of your golf game."

"Didn't I see you and Laurence snickering together when I sliced that drive off the sixth tee?"

"Well, it *was* pretty funny. You looked a little like Ed Norton in that old *Honeymooners* episode."

"Great," I said. "I'm sure every father would be thrilled to have Ed Norton as his future—" I stopped myself just in time.

Or maybe not just in time. Eliza's head turned sharply toward me. "His future what?" she hissed.

I fumbled a little before saying, "His daughter's future boyfriend."

She turned away again, looking back toward the caddies' cart. "You were going to say 'his future son-in-law,' weren't you."

The conversation in the front seat paused, so I couldn't answer without being overheard. Eliza and I sat in stiff silence until Laurence and Fletcher began talking again.

"You're getting a little ahead of yourself, aren't you?" Eliza asked quietly. "You think I brought you home to meet Mom and Dad before announcing the engagement?"

"I don't know what to think," I said honestly. "I'm totally confused here." We bumped along for a few more seconds, baking in the Texas sun, before I asked, "Would I be wrong if I thought that?"

She didn't answer. I turned to check her expression, and saw a thin line of sweat coursing from behind her earringless ear down the side of her long neck. "I've got a couple of decisions to make," she said. "Let's talk later."

"Is one of those decisions about Laurence?"

Her face was unreadable. "Later," she repeated.

After a few more minutes, we reached the clubhouse and took refuge in the air conditioning. "We'll have a drink in the bar room before lunch," Fletcher said. He led us into a place called, of course, "The 19th Hole" (as if to taunt me with the fact that it was really our tenth). After a word to the obsequious host, we were seated by some windows overlooking the crisscrossing arcs of water thrown by the sprinklers on the eighteenth fairway. We ordered our drinks and then Eliza and her father, seeing some old acquaintances across the room, went over to say hello, leaving Laurence and me alone at the table. The two of us sat in uncomfortable silence for a while, Laurence feigning interest in the specialty drinks menu. I kept thinking of what Eliza had said in Central Park when she first told me about Laurence, how she suspected he might be gay. If it was true, it certainly would ease at least some of my worries. "See anything interesting?" I asked hopefully.

"No," he said. "I'm not much of a drinker anyway."

"I like this furniture," I went on, fingering the scrollwork on the arm of my chair. "Is there much good antiquing down here?"

"You can get some interesting Mexican furniture downtown at El Mercado," he said. "I can steer you to a couple of the less touristy spots, if you'd like."

"How about music? I hear Austin and San Antonio have a lot of good music venues. Isn't K. D. Lang from somewhere around here?"

Before he could answer, our drinks arrived, and right after them Eliza and her father. "That was the Kendricks," Eliza explained. "Our neighbors when Ben and I were little. Haven't seen them in years."

"It isn't Mark Kendrick, is it?" Laurence asked. "Of Kendrick Nurseries?"

"That's the one," Fletcher said. "He's done pretty well for himself. You know him?"

"He's one of our corporate clients, though I've never met him."

The conversation went on about Mark Kendrick and other local celebrities for a while. My mind elsewhere, I excused myself and headed toward the men's room. I locked myself in one of the stalls, pulled out my cell phone, and hit the speed dial for Ted Witherspoon.

"Speak!" he barked after one ring.

"Ted! It's Will."

"Will! Nice to hear from you," he said, with smooth insincerity. "How's Texas?"

"Hot."

"Outstanding." I could hear him clicking his mouse in the background. "And what's old Fletcher like? As rich as they say?"

"Apparently. But listen, Ted, did you get my messages?" I had left him so many voice mails in the past twenty hours that I felt like a stalker.

"I did, Will. And I have to say they've left me deeply disappointed."

"It's nothing personal, Ted. I just thought I shouldn't expose myself so heavily on one deal."

"You're not going soft on me, Will, are you?"

"No, no, nothing like that," I said, though I wasn't sure exactly what he meant by "going soft."

"Well, good. Because I'm not gonna let you back out on this one. You want to get rich, don't you?"

"I just think—"

"You leave it to old Ted, okay?"

"But I don't want to put all my—"

"I said just leave it to me, okay?"

"It's my money!" I nearly shouted.

"And it'll be a hell of a lot more of *your* money come Monday at eleven o'clock."

"Monday? That's the day after tomorrow. I thought the offering was set for Tuesday."

"Did I say that? Well, scheduling, you know—wheels within wheels. So just take it easy, Will, okay? Your money's in good hands. But I gotta go now. Lots to prepare."

"Ted!" I shouted, standing up now in the toilet stall. "Ted?"

He'd hung up. I tried calling back, but he wouldn't take the call.

The rest room attendant—a young Latino with a carefully groomed mustache—was standing at the sinks. "Towel, sir?" he asked, holding out a fluffy white cloth the size of a tabloid newspaper. I wet my hands perfunctorily at the sink and took the oversize towel he offered, wondering if I might be on the other end of this transaction someday, after Ted had lost all my money. Horatio Alger in reverse—riches to rags—the second chapter of my American life. I handed the towel back to him and put a dollar in the saucer as I left.

I returned to the bar feeling rattled. "Damn it, son, you're as slow when you pee as you are when you putt," Fletcher said. "I'm hungry. Let's get lunch."

Fletcher signed the check and led us from the bar into the dining room. Halfway there, Eliza took my arm and steered me aside. "What did you and Laurence talk about while we were with the Kendricks?" she asked.

"Nothing much. Why?"

"He just asked me if you were gay."

"Never mind," I said. I looked at my watch. It was just past eleven. Still ten hours before I could credibly plead fatigue and go to bed. I closed my eyes for a second, manufactured what I hoped was a neutral smile, and girded myself for the coming ordeal of lunch.

AFTER ANOTHER INEDIBLE DINNER that evening at Somerdale Ranch, Eliza asked me to walk with her down to the stables. The moon was near full, and the pale wildflowers speckling the hillside seemed to glow around us as we walked—a spectacular effect, as if the earth were mirroring the star-pocked sky above. There was no wind, and we could hear the gentle gurgling of a brook in the distance. For the first time since arriving in Texas, I could understand why Eliza loved the place.

She took my hand and led me along the row of stalls. They were closed now, but we could just make out the quiet nickering of the horses inside. I breathed deeply, taking in the half-appealing, half-disgusting scent of straw and sweat and horse manure. On the door of one of the stalls was a mud stain the exact size and shape of a tennis racket.

"I bet you used to do this as a kid," I said. "Come down here at night to keep company with your horses."

She laughed. "Wrong," she said. "I was never one of those horse-crazy girls you read about in children's books. Maybe there was something lacking in me. I used to come down here to smoke cigarettes and flirt with the ranch hands."

"When you were ten?"

"Well, sixteen."

She was wearing blue jeans and a red sleeveless T-shirt with armholes just loose enough to reveal an occasional flash of black lace. I could imagine a fresh-faced, teenage Eliza driving the poor ranch hands to distraction.

"You're going to be nice to me now?" I asked.

She looked surprised. "When have I ever not been nice to you?"

"No comment."

We stopped beside a small pond and, in the moonshade of some live oaks, kissed for a few minutes—not passionately, but familiarly and affectionately, as the bats crisscrossed the sky above the water, silently eating mosquitoes.

"So, is it time to have that talk?" I asked.

"You want to talk? Now?"

"You said you would make some decisions, and then we'd talk."

She reached up and patted me gently on the cheek. "No, we're not going to talk now. We're just going to make out now."

But there was one thing I wanted to say. "Look, about that comment today—my slip about your father's future son-in-law? Well, I just want you to know that I'm sick of apologizing for making assumptions I thought I had the evidence to make. And whether or not you've been considering it seriously, I have, and I'm not ashamed to say so. And if you haven't, then please stop playing games with me and tell me the truth, okay? I'm tired of being pushed around by you, okay?"

She seemed startled by my vehemence—which I found a little startling myself. "Okay," she said. "You're absolutely right."

"I am?"

"Yes. I've been cruel to you."

"You have?"

"I know I've been going back and forth with you, and I apologize for that."

I felt a sudden impulse then to ask a question—*the* question. I suppressed it at first, but then—what with the night breeze and the scent of wildflowers and all those stars winking above—I gave in to it. "Eliza, what I'd like to do now is ask you if you would consider marrying me."

She turned away from me suddenly, releasing my hand, and started walking down toward the pond. She stopped right at the water's edge and put her hands in the pockets of her jeans. I followed and stood behind her. For a full minute, neither of us spoke. I heard only the tiny plops of what I imagined were frogs, fleeing the shore for the safety and silence of water.

"You really want to move so quickly?" she asked finally.

"It's been six months." When she didn't answer, I said, "I realize I'm not the best catch in the sea . . ."

"Oh, stop that, Will," she said. She turned and took my hands in hers. "I'm not quite ready to answer that question yet. Can you give me a night to think about it?"

"A night? Well, of course. I can wait a night." This was actually a more encouraging answer than I'd expected.

"I'd also like to discuss it with my parents," she went on. "If you don't mind."

I saw my prospects dim suddenly, like a three-way bulb that had just blown one of its filaments.

"Don't look so forlorn," she said. "The decision is mine to make. Besides, I think they like you."

"I can imagine how your father treats the people he *doesn't* like," I said.

She smiled and squeezed my hands. "Okay, then, we'll talk tomorrow. At the cabin. It's beautiful country up there, in the middle of nowhere—no phone, no TV, not even electricity. It'll be a good place to make a decision free of distractions."

"No electricity? Really? What about cell phone coverage?"

"If you bring your cell phone, I'll personally destroy it and you." She kissed me. "Sorry. I forgot about not being cruel. Besides, I don't even know if your phone would work out there. And it's against my father's house rules. The cabin is his place to be totally unconnected from the world, which for my father is pretty difficult."

I didn't say anything for a few moments, consumed with this new worry. How could I be totally incommunicado when my life savings and my entire family's fortune were riding on a deal that was set to go in thirty-six hours? I thought about what Ted had told me earlier that day: Your money's in good hands. Maybe he was right; maybe I should just let it go, cut myself loose and let Ted Witherspoon and the Nasdaq make me rich.

Eliza seemed aware of my qualms. "Come on, Will," she said. "It'll be good discipline." She insinuated herself closer to me at the edge of the water, leaning her head onto my chest. "It'll be like we're back in the 1600s or something. When hearts were pure and life was uncomplicated."

"Right," I said, holding on to her now as tightly as I could. "Pure and uncomplicated."

❧

THAT NIGHT I WENT to my room early—to allow Eliza and her parents time to have their "discussion." I lay in my comforting aerie of 320-threads-per-square-inch Egyptian cotton and stared at the blank ceiling, imagining the scene below. I saw the three of them sitting side by side on the distressed leather sofa in the game room, under the watchful eyes of the mounted deer and javelina heads on the wall. There is a quiet fire going in the fireplace, a little Scarlatti, say, playing in the background, three glasses of wine on the coffee table in front of them. Fletcher is seated in the middle, with a yellow legal pad in his lap, the page divided into two columns marked "Plus" and "Minus." Eliza and her mother sit on either side of him—matchingly beautiful bookends. They're discussing.

"I don't think there's too much to talk about here," Fletcher is saying. "The boy's obviously unsuitable."

"Joseph, you're being unfair," Eliza's mother says. "He's a very appealing young man."

"'Appealing' isn't high on my wish list for a potential son-in-law."

"Well, it is on mine," she replies tartly. "He's also quite good-looking, so put two points in the Plus column."

"Thanks, Mom," Eliza says.

Fletcher sighs, twirls the pencil a few times in his blunt fingers, and does as instructed. "But we've got to face the more substantial issues," he says. "Who is this Will Merrick anyway? Where does he come from? What's his family like?"

"I've only met his uncle," Eliza says. "But you'll be happy to know that he owns one of the largest gourmet wholesalers on the East Coast. It's called Hawkings—maybe you've heard of it. Not that that should matter."

"I think I *have* heard of it," Fletcher responds, with a certain grudging respect.

"His more immediate family is in Indiana. They own a business, too. Something in construction materials."

"Okay, but what about the boy himself? He wasn't all too clear on what the hell it is he does out there in New York. He says he works for his uncle, but then he also seems to be involved with Ben and this investment banker he's working with."

Eliza looks uncomfortable. "Well, his position is . . . fluid," she says.

"He's unemployed, in other words."

"No!" Eliza nearly shouts, straightening up. Her cheeks are coloring—God love her!—as she comes to my defense. "If anything, he's *over*employed. What he does is just a little hard to define."

"'Hard to define' is not good," Fletcher says, and here he writes a figure in the Minus column. "And he's a lousy golfer, which is a serious handicap in the business world," he adds, writing another number in that column.

"Fine, but let's get some of his assets down," Eliza interrupts, shifting her weight on the creaking leather. "He's intelligent, charming, energetic. He also has spirit."

"Spirit, eh? What's that worth in the marketplace? But I guess I'll just have to take your word for the other three." Fletcher makes an addition to the Plus column.

"Oh, come on, Daddy. You can do better than that."

The old man presses the end of the pencil against his creased lips. "Maybe so." After a moment, he carefully erases what he's written and replaces it with a figure somewhat higher.

"Also, he's passionate," Eliza says, somewhat self-consciously. "Give him a plus three for that. Maybe plus four." She smiles then, as if remembering something. "No, make it plus five, now that I think about it."

Fletcher clears his throat. "Well, seeing as this is the young man's own fantasy," he says, "I'll assume that that figure is substantially inflated. Let's compromise with the original plus-three figure." He writes it down.

Mrs. Fletcher jumps in then. "Benjamin seems to like him," she says. "So give him something for that."

"Fine, fine," Fletcher says impatiently, "but we have to face the serious question marks as well." He brushes the eraser curls off the legal pad. "You've known him a relatively short time, Eliza. I don't have to tell you that there are people out there who aren't above marrying for money. Are you one hundred percent certain that it's you this guy wants and not the Fletcher fortune?"

The muscles around Eliza's lips twitch imperceptibly. "Of course I am," she says. "There's nothing like that going on here."

Her father is watching her closely. "I hope you're right about that," he says finally. He writes nothing in either column. "Is there anything else?"

"Well, your own gut impression of him," Eliza says.

"Fair enough." He puts down the pencil, takes a white handkerchief from his pocket, and wipes his nose. With agonizing slowness, he puts the handkerchief back in his pocket, picks up the pencil, and then, huddling over the pad, writes something in one of the columns—I can't see which.

"Mom, too," Eliza says.

Mrs. Fletcher takes the pencil and legal pad from her husband and writes something down without hesitation.

Eliza looks down at the numbers, nodding ambiguously.

"And now you, Eliza," Fletcher says. "Your gut feeling. Be honest now."

She takes the pad and pencil from her mother. She turns to stare into the fire, showing the heartbreaking parabolic line of her cheekbone, the taut skin looking downy against the trembling backlight. She pauses a second—two seconds, three—before leaning over and writing on the marked-up page.

"Good," Fletcher says, a weariness creeping into his voice now. "Let's see what we've got."

"I have a calculator in my bag," Eliza says, getting up.

"That won't be necessary. Surely three educated adults can add up a few columns of numbers."

"All right," Eliza says. She sits again, moving closer to her father on the sofa. Mrs. Fletcher scoots closer on his other side. And then, as the fire crackles soothingly across the room, the three of them, heads together, lips moving, begin to calculate the arithmetic of my fate.

CHAPTER XX

THE FLETCHERS' WOODLAND LODGE proved a rough and rustick place, hidden away among the rolling hills of the area of Dorset and Hampshire known as the New Forest. Far from any modern thoroughfare, the site was attainable only by horseback or on foot, and even then only with considerable difficulty. Having become something of an urban creature during my brief tenure as a Londoner, I felt myself strange here—paradoxically, perhaps, since the landscape of alternating heath and forest was not unlike the sombre moors of the Devonshire I once called home.

Colonel Fletcher, who seemed equally contented here in the wilds as in the civilized parlours of Somerdale Park, conducted us, with apparent great pride, into the small stone structure. "This lodge is my Sanctuary," said he. "Here may a man live as simply as a shepherd, at one with Nature and far from the madding contrivances of modern life."

"Indeed, sir," agreed Mr. Laurence Carter. "It has been altogether too long a time since I have been in these hills. 'Tis as if my cares are already being lifted from my shoulders."

"Good, good," said the old man in satisfaction.

I, who in contrast felt my cares weighing on me ever more heavily the farther I felt removed from Temple Bar, nonetheless managed to make some equally banal utterance of my joy at being there.

"This being the wilds, however," the Colonel continued, "there are some sacrifices of comfort that must be made." And so saying, he proceeded to apportion the party to the available sleeping quarters.

"Well, it seems we two bachelors are to share a room, Mr. Merrick," said Laurence Carter, with what seemed a knowing glint in his eye.

At this juncture we heard a great knocking and hallooing at the open door, and into the lodge stepped a towering giant of a man in royal-blue hunting coat and leather breeches, with a broad, fur-trimmed hat that did lend him the appearance of an American bear. 'Twas Mr. Ezra Carter, of course, whose arrival had apparently preceded our own by several hours. He and the Colonel made a great noise over their reunion, each pounding the other upon the back with a force that would have sent two less hardy males into spasms of coughing.

"Father," Laurence Carter said, after all had had their fill of this welcoming ceremony, "this is a young gentleman I think you know."

The elder Carter looked upon me then with jovial, though questioning, eyes. "God damn me, sir, I think you are wrong, for had I encountered such a fine specimen of English manhood before today I surely would recall it."

"We have met through our words only, Mr. Carter, for I am William Tobias Merrick, to whom you offered such good advices by letter some months ago, when I did write to you in the name of my employer, Theodore Witherspoon."

After a brief moment of reflection, recognition dawned upon the features of the elder Carter's face. "Of course, of course!" he cried. "The young man who sought, as 'twere, to sell candles to the Master Chandler. I admired your spirit, as I recall, as well as your persistence. But how come you to be here, by God, in this forgotten precinct of the kingdom?"

'Twas all explained to him, after which explanation he said, "Remarkable! Though not so remarkable, perhaps, when one considers that the noble souls of any nation will naturally seek each other out." He turned to our host then and said, "So tell me, Joseph, is the young man as impressive in the *Flesh* as he is upon the *Page*?"

The Colonel stroked his moustaches and said, " 'Twould seem he is a better marksman with a pen than he is with a fowling piece. The lad's the worst shot ever to set foot in these hills."

Mr. Carter gave me a pleasant wink. "Don't you mind the Colonel, Mr. Merrick," said he. "He is forever out of countenance with the world, damn the old dog, though he has enough money to buy it three times over."

"Which is three times fewer than you can, Ezra," said Colonel Fletcher, "if what I hear tell of your current prosperity be true."

"Ha!" said the other. "You violate your own law forbidding discussion of business here—for which, I believe, you owe me the usual fine of ten pounds. But I will excuse you this once, for I am eager to go walking through the forest. 'Tis not for your company, after all, that I come here."

And at this we made ready to go out into the famously salubrious air of New Forest. Our party of six, followed by a brace of servants (for Colonel Fletcher's notion of living "simply as a shepherd" was one that perhaps did not bear close inspection), set out along an agreeable forest path. After some time, this path descended into chalky downs, which we traversed at a pace that might have done one of King William's regiments proud. Ascending again into a stand of wood, Miss Fletcher and I slackened our pace, so that we soon found ourselves quite left behind.

"I must rest a moment, Mr. Merrick," said she, though I suspect she was as capable as I of going on. "That fallen tree yonder would make an excellent place to catch one's breath."

"Or to quicken it," I observed, thinking of our previous night's conversation. Had she broached the topic of my proposal with her parents? Was this to be the moment my fate was decided? I led her to the tree, where, after much arrangement of her garments, we were able to sit in comfort.

" 'Tis lovely here, is't not, Mr. Merrick?" she asked. The exertion of our wandering had given her complexion a moist warm lustre. I noted with intense yearning the line of tiny droplets that clung, jewellike, to her shapely upper lip.

"Truly," said I, moving closer to her, "the scenery, particularly in this immediate vicinity, is uncommon lovely."

She frowned prettily and, turning her face toward me, said, "See here, Mr. Merrick, I have done my thinking, and have discussed certain matters with those dearest to me. Can you be serious for a moment, now that we are as far from the distractions of London as one can be, whilst I discuss with you certain particulars?"

I felt a jolt of excitement at hearing these words. All seriousness now, I said, "My lady, I can."

"Good." She folded her hands in her lap and said, "In our discourse of yesterday, you made no secret of the fact that the joining of our two fates in matrimony is something you desire above all things. Is this not true?"

"True it is, Miss Fletcher. For as I hope I made plain, to have you by my side as my wife would be the greatest happiness I could aspire to."

"And would this happiness be as *complete* as 'twould be *great*?"

"I'm not sure I understand you, Miss Fletcher."

"I mean to ask if you would be willing to make a sacrifice—a meaningful sacrifice—in order to attain this happiness."

"Anything at all, Miss Fletcher. You need only name it."

She unfolded her hands and said, "My father has a proposal to make you—one that I am not sure you will like."

This did surprise me somewhat, for I had assumed the proposal to be discussed would concern myself and the lady, not the lady's father. "I see," said I. "And that proposal would be?"

"He would have you come work for him—to leave behind your current endeavours and accept a position that's his to offer."

I was stunned into silence for a moment. I saw a great flash of light before my eyes, as of lightning. "You mean—" I began.

"I don't mean work *for* him, as in work directly *under* him, but in his company, Fletcher Broadcasting, a real full-time position. In other words, no more Ted Witherspoon and no more Wall Street."

I looked out across the rolling Texas hills. "But that's what I do," I said. "Wall Street is my career."

"It's been your career for all of a year. And this wouldn't involve moving away from New York. They've got a small cable subsidiary on Long Island, and they're looking to expand. He's willing to offer you a good, solid management position under the Director of New Business Opportunities."

"Well, I'm flattered, of course," I said, still feeling a little dazed. Then it occurred to me: "Wait a minute, is my accepting of this proposal a necessary condition of your accepting mine?"

"No," she said, "absolutely not. They're entirely unrelated."

"They can't be *entirely* unrelated," I said. "Why would your father offer me a job unless I was his son-in-law, or at least his son-in-law-to-be? He hates me!"

"He doesn't hate you, Will. True, he doesn't know you very well, but he's willing to take a leap of faith and give you a chance. I vouched for you."

"You did."

"Yes," she said. "I made a very good case for you. I told him about all of your very fine qualities that would make up for your lack of experience. But he does think it would be a good idea for you to get an MBA—you can do it nights, while you're working. But that means you wouldn't have time for your . . . unofficial market activities."

"While I'm working," I echoed, mind racing. Was this something I really wanted to do? Could I live without Wall Street, forgetting all about what I had thought of, for as long as I could remember, as my destiny? It would mean changing everything, rearranging all the furniture of my being. "Do *you* think I should do it?" I asked.

"Yes, I do. I mean, what you're doing now, it may be lucrative, but it's all a little makeshift, don't you think? A little unfocused?"

"What if I refused?" I said suddenly.

This seemed to sadden her. "If you refused, you'd refuse. My father would be angry, probably—"

"But what about you?" I grabbed her hands. "Let's say, for the sake of argument, I refuse your father's proposal. What about *our* proposal? You say they're unrelated. So why don't you give me *your* answer first? Will you marry me?"

She looked straight at me then, her delicate nostrils flaring defiantly in the piebald light, and said, "Yes."

Somehow this answer caught me unprepared. "Yes?"

"Yes, I will marry you. No matter what you say to my father."

"Really?"

"Of course."

I felt like the guy who pulls hard on a closed door, expecting it to be locked, who then nearly topples backwards when he finds that it opens easily. "Well then, yes!" I said. "Yes, I'll work for your father."

"Really?"

"Of course."

With a triumphant yelp, she pushed me backwards off the log to the soft bed of leaves on the slope behind us. Then she climbed on top of me and began kissing my neck.

"Damn it, Eliza," I said happily. "They'll come back looking for us! Your father will probably shoot me if he sees us like this!"

"We'll get married next week," she said, pressing her cheek against my chest. "My mother will be annoyed—she'll probably want some huge production—but I'll talk her out of it. I'd prefer something simple: City Hall, followed by a little reception at the ranch. If they want a big party, we could maybe let them go wild in the fall sometime. How does that sound?"

"Next week? Here in Texas?" I asked.

"Why not?"

"We're supposed to go back to New York tomorrow. Your brother's IPO is tomorrow."

"Screw my brother's IPO. Come on, Will. You're getting out of that game anyway."

She was right. Screw the IPO. And anyway, there was nothing about the actual event that required my presence in New York. My fate was in Ted Witherspoon's hands. "Can I invite my Uncle Gil to the ceremony?" I asked.

"Absolutely. We'll fly him in. Along with your family in Indiana— and that cousin you always talk about. What's his name?"

"Josh," I said. "I'd like Josh and Uncle Gil to be there. Everybody else can wait until the big reception in the fall."

She smiled. "So it's settled then?"

"It's settled." I craned my neck to kiss her on the scalp. "Eliza," I said, thinking suddenly of my little fantasy scene of the night before, and her hesitation at answering her father's final question. "Remember the night we went to Bedlam? In the cab afterwards, you said some things. But you know I'm not doing this for the money, right? You know I'd be marrying you even if you weren't rich?"

She reared back to meet my eye. "I don't *know* that," she said. "But I *hope* it. That's *my* leap of faith." She pulled away from me and sat up, elbows on knees. "In any case, if you're thinking of marrying me and then divorcing in a year with some big settlement, think again. Daddy's got a small army of lawyers on his payroll, and they know what they're doing. Wait'll you get a look at the prenup." She grinned at me, then got to her feet and said, "But we'd better catch up with the rest of them now. If I know my father, he'll have the Texas Rangers out looking for us within the hour."

⟨⟨⟩⟩

A PAIR OF BABY PIGS—tied up with twine and impaled from entrance to exit orifices on a metal spit—rotated over a glowing pile of mesquite chips on the massive stone fireplace behind the cabin. Two young cowboys fussed over them, slathering their flanks with marinade and rearranging the sprigs of rosemary in their mouths. It was late afternoon. The Fletchers, the Carters, and I sat at the slate-topped picnic table, eating Texas wildflower salad. Eliza sat beside me, her thigh pressed against mine under the table. The edges of the red-striped canopy fluttered languidly above us in the sweet-smelling Texas breeze.

"We used to hunt javelina up here when I was a shaver," Joseph Fletcher was saying. He picked a piñon nut out of his dentures. "Nowadays, they only let you take two a year, but back then we'd shoot three in a day and have the boys roast 'em up just like those sucklings over there."

"Good eating, javelina," Ezra said, "if your cook knows what he's doing."

"Course, it wudn't so crowded up here when Ezra and I would come up." Fletcher's Texas accent was intensifying now that we were out in the hills. "These days we've got people living two miles over on one side and three on the other. Gotta be careful what you shoot at or you might hit somebody's Rottweiler."

"Can javelinas be as aggressive as wild boar?" I asked, trying to contribute.

"Hoo, you better believe it, son. They're not so big as boar, but they can be mean as hell if they're cornered."

I nodded, pleased with this little exchange. It was my first utterance all weekend to which Joseph Fletcher had responded with something other than scornful incredulity. I felt that my presence there was becoming, if not accepted, at least tolerated. Eliza hadn't told her parents yet about the results of our talk, but I think they could sense what had happened by the way we were acting with each other. Taking another slug of wine (a 1996 Escondido Valley Sangiovese), I returned Eliza's thigh pressure and told myself that maybe, just maybe, I could someday fit in with these people.

The feast went on for the rest of the lazy afternoon, the wildflower salad followed by the suckling pigs, black-eyed peas with a cornmeal crust, prickly pear relish, and a Jack Daniel's pecan pie with honey-and-cayenne-pepper ice cream. Even the food was getting better, I thought.

After eating our fill, we all retired to our various amusements. Laurence walked across the lawn to sit in the shade of a live oak and smoke a cigar (his only vice, as far as I could tell). Eliza and her mother, meanwhile, went inside on some pretext or other, and Fletcher went off to badger the caretaker about a problem with the cabin's roof. Seeing me left alone at the picnic table, Ezra Carter said, "Hey, Will, how about you join me in a game of horseshoes? There's a pit behind the barn where we used to play as kids."

"Sure," I said, thinking that it couldn't hurt to develop a friendship with one of the biggest venture capitalists in Austin, no matter what direction my career took.

"Take it easy there," Ezra said as I stumbled getting up from the table. That flash of light appeared before my eyes again. Ezra was gripping me by the elbow. "A bit too much indulgence at table, perhaps?"

"Perhaps so," said I. "But I am quite recovered now. Thank you."

Turning from me, he had a word with one of the servants, and then, after fortifying ourselves with a dram of cider, we made our way down to the bowling area of which he spoke. The game had already been prepared for us—the pins arranged at one end of the small clearing, the balls piled neatly at the other.

"So, Mr. Merrick," my companion began. He took up one of the balls and tested its weight. "'Twould seem you have prospered much since last we communicated. As I recollect, you were but a broker's apprentice then, and now you seem quite the man of consequence, if your attire does not lie."

"I have had my share of good fortune during the past months, sir, 'tis true. However, as I think you yourself wrote in one of your letters, the opportunities for success in the current climate are numberless."

"Yes, I did so write." He wound himself up and sent the ball hurtling down the green. It struck the pins with considerable force, sending all but one tumbling. "And yet I fear this climate, as you call it, may be turning stormy."

"In what way, sir?" I asked.

He removed his coat and handed it to one of the servants. "This passion for *Engines* of all types now seems overdone," he answered after a moment. "Water-Engines, Drainage-Engines, Engines for the Simple Destruction of Unwanted Structures, &c. &c. Each projector claims his project will change the world, and there are hundreds, even thousands, who believe him, and thus send the shares of his project ever higher." He launched a second ball down the green, toppling the last pin. "But changing the world," he went on, as the pins were reset, "and prospering from that change, are two very different things."

"But I understood from Theodore Witherspoon that you were among the most enthusiastic supporters of these new projects," said I, feeling the first twinges of trepidation in my chest.

"And so I was—and am still, though I am more cautious of late.

Share prices now exceed all reason. And the man who says that no price is too high is a man who will eventually come to realize he has overpaid. Your bowl, Mr. Merrick."

Feeling somewhat light-headed now, I removed my own coat, took a ball in hand, and bowled it, missing the pins entirely.

"Damme, man, you must provide me with more competition than that," said he.

"I wonder, sir, if you are familiar with the winch project of the Colonel's son, Mr. Benjamin Fletcher."

"So it may be said, since I have a financial interest in it."

These words did bring me some relief. "You think it a worthwhile endeavour, then?"

"As Benjamin's godfather, I have felt certain . . . obligations," he said hesitantly. "You must bowl again, Mr. Merrick."

"Yes, of course." I bowled a second ball, with the same outcome as the first.

"I can see the game does not amuse you, sir," he said, "and I think I know why." He regarded me thoughtfully for a moment. "There is something I'd like to show you. Would you take a short ride with me?"

" 'Twould be my pleasure, sir."

"Good." He signalled to the footmen to indicate that we would play no more and began walking toward the small stables. "This should require but an hour of your time," said he. "Come along."

Scarce ten minutes had passed before we were mounted and descending the wooded highlands toward the chalky downs. " 'Tis largely Crown land here," said Mr. Carter as we rode. "The first King William set it aside as game reserve, and so it remains wild, even to this day."

"I see, sir," said I, though my taste for such trivial discourse at that moment was anything but keen. I could not help but wonder what this man wished to show me. His reluctance to endorse the younger Fletcher's project did give me pause—for Ezra Carter, as was well known, was no man's fool.

After a time, we passed through a copse of yew and came upon a group of ruined structures. Two stone cottages, their thatched rooves stove in and overgrown with water horsetail, had collapsed into the waters of a peat-stained stream, and beyond them an old barn, likewise long disused.

Yet again, I felt that flashing before my eyes, and swooned in my saddle.

"You sure you're all right, Will?" Ezra asked, concerned.

"Fine, fine," I said, shaking the dizziness from my head.

We rode around the barn and brought our mounts to a halt at a small collection of troughs and holding basins, above which rose a rusted windmill tower. At the base of the tower stood some even more rusted machinery—a squat circular pump of some kind. "They were still working this place when Joe and I were boys," Ezra said. He dismounted and tied the reins of his horse to the windmill frame, so I did the same. "Some old Mexican and his sons—Morales, his name was. Funny old bastard who liked to do magic tricks. I say old, but he was probably ten years younger than I am today." Ezra circled the base of the windmill, kicking at the machinery. "This was his baby, this thing. Had it brought over all the way from Houston. Probably spent a good chunk of money on it, too."

"What exactly is it?"

"A gas-powered water pump—state-of-the-art when he bought it. Worked fine for a while, though the windmill worked fine, too, most days of the year. But old Morales had to have his fancy pump."

He knelt and smeared some of the grime away from the pump's flaking label.

"So what happened?" I asked.

Ezra got to his feet again. "The damn thing kept breaking down, and his sons kept forgetting to bring out the gas to run it. Then one day they needed to replace a part and it turned out the manufacturer had gone belly-up and nobody else made anything similar. So they went back to using the windmill."

Ezra came around the end of the pump and put his hands on my shoulders. "The point is, Will, the pump was good, but it wasn't good enough. And that's the way it's always gone with technology. Some innovations change everything for all time; some are just transitional or marginal and get superseded almost as soon as they hit the market. And it's never easy to tell the one from the other."

I opened my mouth to speak, closed it again, and then said, "You think Fletcher's switching technology is the latter."

He squeezed my shoulders and then let his hands fall. "Ben's my godson," he said. "But I like you, Will, and I wouldn't want to see you get hurt. My firm has done a lot of research into this shit, and it's our belief that Stevedore's technology won't make it, and when the market realizes that, they're gonna get creamed."

"Does Ben know this?" I asked.

"Ben and I never did get along, but I talked with him a few months back. Naturally, he thinks we're wrong."

"But you're not wrong."

He stared at me for a few long seconds before saying, "No, son, I don't think we are. And I wonder if Ben really does. Truth be told, I think the reason he went with this Pembroke Horton guy is he knew that the big boys would've told him to take a hike, or at least wait until he had some actual paying customers."

I looked away, toward a crow perched on the top of the windmill. Could this really be why Ben had finally agreed to the IPO with Ted—because he knew his technology was a loser, because he knew he could probably make at least something off it while the market still threw money at new technology no matter what it was? "Mr. Carter?" I said. "You came to the cabin in an SUV, right?"

"Yeah, my Cadillac Escalade. Joe doesn't like it—he says it spoils the trail—but fuck if I'm gonna ride horseback all the way out here from the roadhead."

"Can I borrow it? I think I need to get to the nearest phone."

He took a set of keys from his pocket and handed them to me. "There's a phone in the Escalade, though you'll have to ride up to the ridge behind the cabin to get a signal. And don't tell Joe about the phone or he'll skin me alive."

"Will you excuse me?" I said, taking the keys from him.

I rode back to the cabin as fast as the horse would take me. Laurence, having finished his postmeal nap under the live oak, was inspecting a broken stair leading to the cabin's porch. "What's the hurry?" he asked as I rode up.

"Can you do me a favor?" I dismounted and handed him the reins. "Can you just take care of this horse for a few minutes?" I rushed over to Ezra's Escalade and climbed in.

"That's my father's," Laurence shouted.

"He said I could borrow it." I started the engine, spun the vehicle into a quick 180-degree turn, and started along the rough track toward the ridge.

I pulled the cell phone from its dashboard cradle and powered it up, but all I got was the "Looking for Service" message on the LCD. Frustrated, I threw it down onto the passenger seat and looked at my watch. It was an hour later in New York. Ted would still be in his office, but his assistant Mary had probably gone home, meaning he'd pick up the phone himself. This was good, since he'd probably told her to fend off all calls from me. Maybe I could reason with him now.

Finally, just as I got to the top of the ridge, I heard the phone emit a strangled little beep, indicating the presence of a signal. I grabbed it and punched in Ted's number. He answered on the first ring. "Ted, it's Will."

"Will, boy, how the hell are you?"

"Ted, I want out of the Stevedore IPO. Completely out."

"You still on about that? Why don't you get your panties untwisted and let me do my job. You're a goddamn old woman, Will."

"It's a bad company, Ted."

"There's no such thing in this market."

"I've got it on good authority—from Ezra Carter."

"Ezra Carter?" There was a second of static-filled silence. "You been calling Ezra Carter behind my back, Will?"

"No, he's here. I've met him. It's a long story, but he says that Fletcher's switch isn't any good."

"It doesn't really matter if it's any good, Will. Why can't you get that concept?"

I took a breath and said, "I could call my Uncle Reg and blow the whole deal, if you make me."

"Oh, there's been a development there," he said. "Seems somebody told your Uncle Gil about my deal with his brother, and he was so pissed he kicked old Reg out of the house. So I got him and his fine lady in a hotel room."

"What hotel?"

Ted laughed. "You crack me up, Will, you really do. And don't bother asking Gil or Jack either, because they don't know. Now, goddamn it, Will, you're starting to annoy me. If you want my advice, just let it go. There's nothing you can do about it." And at this he hung up.

I tossed the phone onto the passenger seat and put my head down on the steering wheel. I had been set up, I thought. I'd let myself be set up, and I'd allowed my eldest uncle to be set up too.

I looked at my watch again. Theoretically, I could still get back to New York before the IPO happened. If I drove straight to San Antonio, I could probably get to the airport in time for a late flight to New York. If not, I could drive on to Houston and get the first direct flight in the morning. It might just get there in time for me to do something. If I acted now.

Eliza was standing alone on the porch when I arrived back at the cabin. "Internal combustion engine," she said as I got out of the SUV. "My father's not going to like that."

"Eliza, I've got to get back to New York right away."

The smile ossified on her face. "Oh?"

"It's a business thing," I explained. "Something's come up."

"Come inside for a minute," she said. She grabbed my hand and pulled me into the cabin. She led me into the front bedroom, closed the door, and sat me down on the spongy bed. "Now what do you mean you have to go to New York?" she asked.

I hesitated, thinking it wasn't a great idea to tell her my intention was to back out of her brother's IPO. But I had no choice. "I just learned something about Stevedore, about the prospects of their technology." I explained to her what Ezra had told me, and how Ted was refusing to let me pull out of the deal. "I've got every bit of my net worth tied up in this offering. This could ruin me."

"But what about your uncle?" Eliza asked. "Why can't you call him and have *him* take it up with Ted?"

"I can't. Uncle Gil doesn't know about my role in the Stevedore IPO."

"How can he not know? I thought he was involved too?"

And so I had to explain it all to her—how we'd been forced to maneuver around my uncle's takeover bid to make sure the offering went through as planned.

"Wait," she said, still standing over me. "You lied to your uncle so that the IPO could happen?"

"I didn't lie, exactly. But Ted decided that Uncle Gil shouldn't know about the alternative arrangements until the last possible moment. Besides, it was for his own good."

"You deceived your uncle? For the sake of a business deal?"

"I know how it sounds, Eliza," I said, getting up from the bed. "But I had to weigh the advantages and disadvantages—"

"Get out," she said icily. She turned away and walked toward the window, her arms folded tight against her chest.

"We'll talk when I get back, okay?" I said. I followed her and took her shoulders in my hands. "I'll explain it all to you."

"Get out, Will," she repeated, shrugging my hands away. "Don't say another word. Just leave."

I'll fix this, I told myself. I'll go back to New York, get that mess settled, and then take care of this one. I'll make her understand that I had made the only sensible choice—for everyone. "I'll fly back here on Tuesday," I said. "On Monday night, if I can. I'll call you." But she didn't answer me.

I ran into Ezra on my way out of the cabin. "You get a signal up there?" he asked, hitching his horse to the front handrail.

"There's a complication," I told him. "I've got to get back to New York. Listen, I have no right to ask this, but can I borrow your Escalade to get to an airport?"

"Shit, son, that's my ride back to Austin!"

"It's totally unreasonable of me to ask, I know. But I have no choice."

"You know where you're going?"

"I assume if I follow the track, it'll get me back to a road."

He took a big handkerchief out of his pocket and wiped his forehead. "Oh, fuck it," he said finally. "I'll get one of the staff to pick it up at the airport when you're done. Just make sure I get the thing back. And go now or you won't reach the paved road before dark."

I didn't even go back into the cabin to get my clothes. It wasn't necessary—everything besides my toiletries case and an extra pair of jeans was back at Somerdale Ranch. And besides, I didn't want to run into Eliza again. So I climbed back into the Escalade and set off.

The sun lay low now above the western ridge, bathing the landscape in amber light. Ezra Carter's bay, Escalade—a sturdy beast, well suited to the terrain—proved a speedy one as well, and I made good progress. By my rough calculations, I could reach Southampton within a few hours. From there, a Night Coach might take me on to London—though I was uncertain whether such a thing as a Night Coach from Southampton even existed. If not, could I ride all the night myself upon this mount and reach London by morning? I knew not, nor had the time to wonder. I would, in any event, make the attempt.

Twilight came, the sky over the Dorset wastes turning a luminous violet-blue, but still there was no sign of any principal road to Southampton. Could I have somehow gone astray? I brought the horse to a halt and looked about myself. The light was failing rapidly now, the moon not yet risen, and the land was filled with a spreading darkness. Beneath me, my mount breathed heavily already, the heat rising from his slick flanks.

Shifting into gear again, I headed down a steep decline into a barren wash. Here the track seemed to disappear after a few minutes. I groped the Escalade's dashboard for the fog lights, found the switch, and turned it. A tunnel of light broadened in front of me. In the distance, I saw the continuation of the track, like a pale yellow line squiggling up the other side of the wash.

Accelerating, I sped up the small ridge, the engine and my own wild frustration roaring in my ears. At the crest, I gunned the engine, but then the land fell away beneath me, and I was airborne. Not fear but incredulity filled me as I felt poor Escalade, muscles straining against the emptiness, turning in the air, turning, toppling over, and my own body floating from his saddle as the darkling heath rushed swiftly toward my head.

JANUARY

PROFIT/LOSS
STATEMENTS

CHAPTER 21

⚭ *"IN READING THE HISTORY OF NATIONS, we find that, like individuals, they have their whims and their peculiarities; their seasons of excitement and recklessness, when they care not what they do. We find that whole communities suddenly fix their minds upon one object, and go mad in its pursuit; that millions of people become simultaneously impressed with one delusion, and run after it, till their attention is caught by some new folly more captivating than the first."*

I close the book and sit back against the unforgiving slats of the stout wooden chair. Above me stretches the vaulted ceiling of the New York Public Library's main reading room—a triptych of pink-tinged clouds bubbling optimistically into baby-blue skies. It's early afternoon on a day not unlike the one depicted on the ceiling, though the sunny weather hasn't kept the crowds from the reading room. I'm sitting at the very last table in the room, between a perpetually sighing college coed and an emaciated, unwashed, woolly-bearded man who scribbles feverishly into a series of dog-eared notebooks. Together, we make a triptych of our own—Melancholia on one side, Dementia on the other, me in the middle. And what mental condition do I represent, I wonder. Hubris? Foolhardiness? Regret?

Leaning forward again, I turn the spine of the red clothbound book I've been reading: *Extraordinary Popular Delusions and the Madness of Crowds*, by Charles Mackay, L.L.D. It's a remarkable document, one that is apparently famous among those losers for whom (according to Ted) history serves as a guide. It's a 150-year-old cautionary tale, a classic, and one that's probably on the shelves of every bookstore and public library in the city. Why, I ask myself, was I not aware of this book a year ago? Why had no one ever told me about it?

And it's a good thing they hadn't. Because if they had, I might never have become rich.

"Beware of stories with obvious morals," as Ted used to say.

I should explain:

Let me go back to where I left off—March 2000, the south-central Texas hills, my desperate attempt to get back to New York in Ezra Carter's Escalade. It was a stupid move on many different levels. Being deep into my own "season of excitement and recklessness," I had neglected to buckle my seat belt, and ended up driving off what amounted to a small but significant precipice. I wasn't seriously hurt, but I did break two ribs and put a sizable gash in my forehead. My upper lip was so swollen from the impact of the air bag that for two days I bore more than a passing resemblance to Donald Duck.

While I was laid up in the hospital in San Antonio, the Stevedore IPO went forward in New York. Helpless to alter my fate, I followed the story on CNBC from my bed. Shares of Stevedore went out at twelve dollars a share and, as I watched, more than doubled—to 25 7/8—by the end of the trading day on Monday. By late Tuesday, they'd tacked on another six dollars.

I called Ted at about three o'clock EST. This time, he took my call. "So, will you let me sell now?" I asked him.

"Are you willing to do what I tell you?" he answered.

I hesitated only a second before saying, "Yes."

"Outstanding. Here's what we'll do: You can't sell yet, but we have ways of locking in your gains no matter what happens. You okay with that, Rockefeller?"

"Whatever you say," I told him.

"Good." He paused a second and said, "I'm a professional, Will. And professionals don't lose in the market. Remember that."

Not long thereafter, the Nasdaq tanked, pulling shares of Stevedore down with it.

Everyone knows the rest. After taking repeated hits over April, May, and June, the market recovered somewhat over the summer, sending the Nasdaq over 4000 again. Many people who had been pummeled by the downturn, thinking the correction was over, resumed their optimism. Shares of Stevedore started climbing again, luring many investors back in.

But not me. When Stevedore hit 20 again, I sold all of my stake and even took a modest short position in the stock—which proved a wise move when, a few weeks later, three separate analysts downgraded the company on the very same day, sending the stock price plummeting again.

We made a fortune on Stevedore. I did; Jack did; Ted did. Ben, of course, didn't become one of the self-made billionaires of the era, but he'd protected himself. When the company went into Chapter 11, he salvaged what he could and moved on to "other projects."

Even my Uncle Gil did well. Ted's assurances notwithstanding, he'd found out about the part I'd played in undermining his takeover bid. Sometime in late March, feeling betrayed by Stevedore and everyone associated with it, he'd negotiated a buyout of his interest in the company. Rumor has it he was also shorting the stock—out of spite—when news of the downgrades hit the street, so he, too, actually *made* some money on the company's misfortunes.

In fact, the only person who really suffered financially—besides, of course, the millions and millions of investors who held on to their stock in Stevedore and other tech companies while the market sank—was Uncle Reg. Being contractually obligated to keep his shares and options for a set period, he was helpless to save himself when the market turned ugly. Before it was over, his real-estate company also went into Chapter 11, and he lost the mansion in Indiana. Last I heard, he was accepting loans from his other brothers to tide him over.

I, meanwhile, kept shorting every tech stock I knew, on Ted Witherspoon's advice. And on December 31, 2000, as the market continued heading south, my net worth—on paper, at least—surpassed $2 million for the first time.

Of course, I had other, more serious losses. . . .

"So, is the wedding off?" I asked Eliza when she came to pick me up the day I was released from the hospital in San Antonio. A huge Latino nurse was pushing me in a wheelchair out to the parking lot. Eliza walked beside the chair, wearing a yellow sundress (she dressed differently in Texas, I'd noticed) and deep-green sunglasses that she seemed reluctant to take off. I suspect she didn't want to look me in the eye.

"Is it?" I asked again.

"You're very young," she answered—with a chilly crispness that told me she didn't want to talk about it in front of a three-hundred-pound orderly.

We got into a Ford Explorer I'd never seen before. After an embarrassing moment in which she had to help me buckle my seat belt (my right arm was in a sling and I couldn't twist to grab the belt with my left hand without sending shock waves through my battered rib cage), we started out of the parking lot. I waited until we got on the interstate before saying, " 'Young' means reckless but capable of change, right?"

She snorted at the windshield. "No, actually, 'young' means selfish and amoral and deeply untrustworthy."

"But capable of change," I insisted.

"I don't know about that."

I noticed then that we'd passed the exit back to Somerdale Ranch. "Where are we going?" I asked.

"To the airport. Your stuff's in the back."

So that was that, I thought. Not that I didn't deserve it. But I felt obliged to at least defend myself. "I honestly felt that I wasn't doing him any harm," I said. "Ted swore that he'd be better off not knowing."

She jerked the steering wheel to the right and hit the brakes, bringing us to a shuddering stop on the gravelly shoulder of the interstate. Then she pulled up the parking brake with the force of a rodeo rider pulling the rope tight around a calf's ankles. "Jesus Christ, Will, Ted swore that? *Ted* swore that it would be best for you to betray the man who fed and sheltered you, and you just went along?" She shook her head. "No, Will, that's too easy. You can keep lying to yourself if you want to, but I don't want to listen anymore."

I couldn't answer. I looked out across the dusty Texas wasteland, at the kind of heart-sinking encrustation of Day's Inns and Taco Bells and Jiffy Lubes that clings to the outskirts of every urban area in the country. Eliza was right, of course; I was lying to myself—and had been for months now. "I didn't know what I was doing," I said finally. I fingered the stitches in my forehead. "I don't deserve you. I love you, but I don't deserve you."

She took off her sunglasses and stared at me. Cars were passing fast on the highway beside us, the Explorer rocking explosively each time one blew past. "I repeat, you're very young," she said finally. Then she released the parking brake and pulled back onto the roadway, setting off a symphony of dopplering horns from cars in the middle lane.

We didn't speak again until we stopped at the departing flights drop-off area. "There's a flight to Houston leaving in forty-five minutes," she said. "From there, it should be easy to get to New York. I assume you'll get a seat."

"So that's it?" I said bitterly. "I don't get a second chance?"

"No, Will, you don't." She held out her hand then. In it was the pair of lightbulb earrings I had given her in the Japanese restaurant back in January. "I think I know now—finally—what had been bothering me all along about you. You're just not a serious person, Will. I don't mean to be brutal here, but I've got to say that, in my opinion, you have no idea what's really important. Yet. And that's fine, I guess. I don't think you're a bad person. I love you, too, damn it. You're a very lovable person. You're just not what I'm looking for in a life companion."

"Yet?"

She sighed. "Please don't keep hoping," she said, in a less forbidding tone. She put the earrings in my hand and closed my fingers around them. "Go out and play the game for a few more years— you're good at it, and you'll probably make a fortune. On the other hand, you might lose your shirt. Either way, it won't matter as much as you think."

Easy for you to say, I thought.

"Easy for the rich girl to say, right?" she went on, clairvoyantly. "Don't think I don't realize that. But who ever said life was fair?" She leaned over then and kissed me on the forehead. "Here's a little bit of advice, though. The key to any game is knowing when the game itself ends and the real stuff begins. I think you have trouble with that concept." Then she pointed at the airport doors. "Better not miss that flight."

We got out of the Explorer and Eliza retrieved my suitcase from the back. "Please don't call me when we're back in New York, okay?"

"Well now I feel totally demoralized," I said.

"Good. Demoralized is a good start. It was excess cockiness that got you into this mess in the first place." She hugged me—just hard enough to make me gasp from the pressure on my ribs. Then she climbed back into the Explorer, tooted the horn, and drove away, leaving me alone on the baking pavement.

I looked down at the earrings in my hand. Lightbulbs. They caught the Texas sun, flashing like two good ideas in a cartoon. Feeling dizzy now, I thrust them into my pocket and turned toward the entrance of the terminal.

And so I returned to New York—only to find that my old life with Uncle Gil was as closed to me now as my new one with Eliza. "He doesn't want to see you, Will," Mrs. Popper said to me at the doorway to the Madison Avenue apartment. I had been standing out there for five minutes, trying to get my keys to work in the locks. But apparently he'd changed them while I was gone. "He feels you've betrayed him," she went on. She looked at me with her eyes damp but her formidable bulk immovable in the doorway. "He's sent your things over to Jack Petroni's apartment. Mr. Petroni is expecting you."

This shouldn't have come as a shock to me, since Uncle Gil had refused to speak to me every time I'd tried calling from the hospital. But somehow I had hoped he wouldn't react this way. "Is he really angry?" I asked.

"He's miserable, as we all are." She looked behind herself before adding, in a whisper, "Make it up to him somehow. Don't ask me how, but just try." Then she closed the door and locked—snap, snap, snap—all three of the Medico deadbolts.

That was ten months ago. I'm in my own apartment now. It's a very nice place—a high-ceilinged three-bedroom overlooking the Promenade in Brooklyn Heights, for which I am extravagantly overpaying, despite the market crash. Meanwhile, both Jack and I are working for Ted Witherspoon in a more official capacity at Pembroke Horton. It's just not the same anymore, though, and I've been thinking of leaving. What with my Uncle Reg's mega-lawsuit against the firm, I'm regarded with some suspicion there now. And to be honest,

I think Ted might be losing his edge. He's still out there trying to flack tech IPOs. It's as if he doesn't want to admit that the world has changed. So he's doing exactly what he always made fun of other people for—the old-school doomsayers who refused to believe in the boom when it was happening before their eyes; he's clinging to an outdated paradigm, fighting the market. It's kind of sad, actually. Like everything else about what I now regard as my former life.

As for Uncle Gil, I haven't seen him since the day I left for San Antonio—haven't even heard from him. Until now.

Pushing aside the Mackay book, I unfold the printout of the e-mail I received from my uncle that morning:

Will—
I'd like to see you. Would you be interested in coming here to
the apartment today after lunch? Two o'clock sharp. We'll
have coffee.
                                        —Gilbert Hawking

A shred of hope, it seems to me. He wants to have coffee with me. I look at the clock hanging over the return desk across the crowded reading room. Plenty of time to get from 42nd Street up to Madison and 75th. I won't even take a taxi; I'll just walk. Another in a line of small acts of contrition.

❧

'TWAS EXACT AT TWO O'CLOCK I found myself before the house on the Red Lion Square. Straightening my hat and wig—and saying a little prayer under my breath—I stepped up to the door and knocked. Alfred, supercilious as ever, appeared and informed me that I was expected.

In shame, I entered what until late had been my own home, and was conducted to the drawing-room. My uncle was already seated within, in the great carved oak chair that looked so quaint in the milieu of those modern digs. He wore the selfsame grey coat and chestnut periwig as when I had first seen him but a year and a half earlier. Now, however, the lines about his face and mouth were deeper, his face thinner and more pale. "Good day to you, sir," said he, rising from his place and giving a stiff little bow.

"Good day, Uncle," said I, with an awkward answer to his bow. "I trust I find you in good health?"

"Oh, tolerable good, tolerable good. And you?"

"In body, Uncle, quite well, having recovered fully from my Dorset injuries. In spirit, however, somewhat less well."

This piqued his curiosity. "You have experienced some reversal in the Alley, then?"

"No, no, quite the contrary, in fact. For, as you know, in the Alley one man's *Misfortune* is oft another's *Boon*."

"Oft, perhaps, but not always. Indeed, there has been quite enough misfortune to go around these past months, with shares looking dear at ten guineas that once looked cheap at eighty. 'Tis the vast majority, I daresay, who now find their fortunes in need of mending."

"While it affords me little pleasure to say so, Uncle, I can report that I am among the minority who have come through this past year with my fortune unscathed."

He harrumphed and looked down at the snuffbox he twiddled in his hand. Then, with a tiny smile on his face, he said, "As am I, Nephew. Thanks, in part, to your perfidy, which did me far more good than harm."

It seemed he gave me here an opportunity. "Uncle," said I, rushing up and kneeling before him, "I know not what to say in my defence. I can only beseech you—"

"Tush, tush, sir, get up. I insist you rise, for I must tell you straight off that the forgiveness you seek is one I am not ready to grant."

This last remark did come to me as might a sharp blow to my brain-case. "It does grieve me to hear it, sir," said I.

"Will you rise, then?"

I did, feeling chastened and quite miserable, my hopes dashed as suddenly as they had been raised that morning by his letter.

"Having said that, however, there are *degrees* of forgiveness," he began, but then stopped himself. He picked up a copy of some pamphlet and threw it peevishly in my direction, so that it fluttered to the floor at my feet. "Look here, Will Merrick, you have hurt me to such an extent as I never thought it possible for a man of my . . . *Curmudgeonliness* to be hurt. I took you into my house—took you to me almost as a son— only to find myself done brown, and you a Bosom-Serpent, candle-holder to that rogue Witherspoon and my own treacherous brother."

"No one can understand your feelings more completely than I, sir—"

"You manoeuvre behind my back, *against* my interests—for you knew my intentions with regard to Fletcher's project."

"Oh sir, but 'tis even worse than you think. I must make a clean breast of't. For even before the matter of Fletcher's winch came to the fore, I deceived you elsewhere, using your capital to raise funds of my own without your knowledge."

"Yes, yes, I am aware of that, too."

This took me by surprise. "You know of those matters?" I asked.

"Of course," said he. "A man who does not speak to his banker is a fool, no matter how many underlings he employs as his agents. Cardozo keeps meticulous records of the comings and goings in his establishment, and while he naturally had no knowledge of what was taken and restored to my strongbox, it requires no special genius to infer the obvious. One who requires access to a strongbox twice in a day has quite clearly taken something from it on the first visit, used it, and returned it on the second."

So much for the perfection of my plotting, I reflected. "Then you know the full extent of my treachery toward you, Uncle. And I have no excuse to offer but my own blindness, my own selfishness. If only there were some means by which I could heal this breach . . ."

He held up a hand. "Stop, stop, sir. For you must not say what you do not mean."

"But, sir, I mean every word I have uttered."

"Truly?" said he.

"B'm'Faith, sir, I mean it truly. For if there were anything, no matter how difficult or injurious to myself, that I can do . . ."

"There is," said he.

"There is?" I was dumbfounded now, but suddenly shot through with hope. "But how?"

My uncle took hold of his lapels and gave them a sharp yank. "I assume your own record-keeping is quite as meticulous as Cardozo's. I would require, therefore, that you calculate the summe of all your profits earned upon my capital from the day you were admitted to my household until the day you left it. Then you will write me a draught upon your own bank for exactly half that figure."

Lawd, but this man did never cease to leave me planet-struck! "You ask me to buy my way back into your affections, then?" I asked.

"Precisely, for *Fair Words butter no Parsnips*, sir. Of course, there's the matter of compounding—initial gains being employed to generate subsequent gains—but I am a reasonable man and am willing to overlook such complexities." He looked upon me then with an air I recognized from his business negotiations. "Do you agree to these terms, sir?"

Here I felt no hesitation whatsoever. I stood up straight and pronounced the words: "With all my heart."

"Good," said he, clearly delighted with himself, though not wishing to show it. "I imagine your calculations will require some time, what with the need to refer to your records, &c. &c. We can reconvene on the morrow, if convenient."

"I'Faith, sir, I have in my breast-pocket a small book—I call it my Palm-Book—in which are writ all of my financial particulars. If you but give me an hour, I could make the calculation without delay."

"Excellent," said he, rubbing his hands together in the fashion that was once so familiar to me. "You may retire to the back parlour for this task. I'll see that Alfred provides you with whatever pen and parchment you require."

And so it was done. After something less than an hour, I rejoined my uncle in his drawing-room. "I have the draught here, sir, made out in your name."

"I trust you have been all honesty in your figuring."

"As best I could, Uncle."

He took the draught from my hand and looked at the figure enscribed upon it. "Adod, sir, you must be some manner of *Financial Prodigy*, for this figure is most impressive."

"I have done well, Uncle," said I, with a small blush. "With your assistance, however unwitting it was."

He looked up at me then. "You no doubt expect that I'll tear up this draught."

" 'Twould pain me if you did, Uncle," said I, with (I think—I *hope*) total sincerity.

"Good, for I'll not tear it up! Do you hear me, sir? And pray do not think that this draught wipes the slate clean between us. You must square accounts with me in ways that gold can play no part in."

"To do so is my greatest wish, Uncle—and more than I deserve."

He nodded once and said, "Then give me your hand on't." I did, with the greatest relief and joy—so that I nearly shook that good old man's arm from its socket. "Let us part now," he said then, letting go my hand and rubbing his shoulder with amusement in his eyes. "And if you are not otherwise engaged on Sunday, I'd like you to return and share a meal with me here. 'Twould gladden Mrs. Popper's heart, for she says I have no more appreciation for her belly-timber than does a *Toad* for a *Toccata*. Your accustomed appetite for her victuals will please her no end after all these months."

"So it shall be done, sir. On Sunday next."

"Good," said he, waving me off with a poorly concealed smile. "Now go away, Will, before I think better of an old man's foolishness."

And at that, Reader, I left my uncle's house. I returned to the streets of my beloved London with a purse lighter than it had been in many a day. But my heart, it must be said, was lighter still, for I reckoned the start of my new life—my *true* life—as having commenced on that bright and cold January afternoon. And as I made my way along the High Holborn in the direction of that great unfinished business of St. Paul's—with the sharpers and the mountebanks, the moth-eaten quacks, the eager sellers of plate and sweetmeats, the ale-drapers and punks of the trade, all seeking to drop fools' pence into knaves' pockets—I could but wonder if ever I would truly understand anything at all, let alone that ever-mysterious sequence of transactions we know as Modern Life.

EPILOGUE

⌒⌒ "HAS ANYONE EVER TOLD YOU that you drive like a high-school English teacher?"

Josh Dooling—his hands on the wheel in perfect ten-and-two position—looked over at me with a puzzled expression on his face. "What's that supposed to mean?" he asked.

"Just that there's a certain . . . punctiliousness to the way you drive," I said. "Perfectly conjugated. No dangling participles or misplaced modifiers."

"You're making no sense again, Will," he said, as he made the turn onto Spring Lake Road.

"There! That turn you just made—like an impeccably diagrammed sentence. Signal, quick rearview check, smooth hand-over-hand motion, perfect alignment in the receiving lane."

Josh took a deep breath and then said, "Okay, two things: A, nobody teaches sentence-diagramming anymore, and B, what's your point?"

"Excuse me, but A, you taught *me* sentence-diagramming, back when you were coaching me for the PSATs, and B, I'm just making an observation."

"An observation?"

"You're getting old, Josh. Thirty-one."

"I *feel* old," he said. "The whole world feels old now."

It was a sunny afternoon in October, the trees clustering around the passing farmsteads brushed with the first faint gildings of creamy yellow and mottled gold. I was in Indiana for my eldest brother's wedding—Lucy Skymartin had finally said yes—and Josh and I had decided to drive out to the lake north of Bloomington where we used to vacation as kids. We were supposed to be getting fitted for our ushers' tuxes that afternoon, and we hoped that our being no-shows would annoy both my brother *and* his bride. If the new times weren't what they were just then, it would have felt like old times. I was even broke again, almost.

I picked up the day-old *Wall Street Journal* from the floor of the car. "So what are you buying these days?" I asked him.

"I'm not buying anything these days. Who can *afford* to buy anything? Even you can't afford to buy anymore. Besides, there's just no joy in it anymore for me. First the bubble bursting, then September 11. Game over, man." He downshifted the five-year-old Nissan as we came around a curve in the road. "I'm surprised you can still work up the enthusiasm."

I reached for the lever beside my seat and reclined the back a notch or two. Josh was right, of course—the joy of it *was* gone, and it probably wouldn't be back for some time. We'd all woken up from our collective dream—that dream of flying, of limitlessness, of invincibility—only to be confronted, just a few months later, by a nightmare that drove it all home. We learned that even the real stuff—even concrete and steel—can dissolve away before our eyes, and that what we consider normal or even conceivable on any given day is only a thin sliver of the spectrum of possibility. Disasters come in all degrees of magnitude, and we recognize the minor ones as minor only when everything suddenly, brutally, becomes much much worse.

"It was amazing," I said after a moment. "When everything opened again the week after? I was a wreck, still shaking from everything that had happened, but some of the traders at Pembroke seemed to pick up right where they left off. Talk about thick skins. It was kind of inspiring actually. Or at least reassuring. As I lost all the money I had made the whole previous year." I looked over at him. "But you know, as I sat there, taking an absolute beating, I couldn't help finding it all strangely satisfying. As if I knew it needed to happen, for me to move on." I laughed then and said, "I really blew it."

"You did," he said, and I could see he understood me—that I wasn't talking about my financial debacle. "I could see it coming. In your e-mails. You talking about how you could get around your uncle's takeover bid—I should have said something. I blew it, too, I guess." He shook his head. "You're lucky Gil forgave you."

"Believe me, I know it," I said.

"What about Eliza? Have you talked to her?"

"I call her. Even though she tells me not to. But it's not going to happen there, Josh. She says she can't trust me."

"Smart girl," he said. "You dating anybody else?"

"Yeah, I've gone out a few times. Some nice women, too. But it's not the same. All of them seem to share the same fault—they're not Eliza." I brought the seat back to vertical. "I miss her," I said.

Josh said, "I know."

I turned to the stock tables in the *Journal*. "Okay, Josh, you say you're not buying, but what are you following? I know you can't be ignoring the market."

Josh shrugged. "Oh sure, I'm following a couple things—beaten-down techs mostly. Ariba, Nokia, a few fiber companies."

"Hey, did I ever thank you for that tip on Level Three Communications? I bought it at 40, which was already way off its all-time high. Now it's at 4."

"It'll come back," he said sheepishly.

"Not in my lifetime." I put down the paper and watched a farm pass on our right. "It really does seem like history now, doesn't it? Like some sepia-tinged memory of long ago? I mean, we knew it wasn't real, even when we were in the middle of it. And now it's as if we can't even imagine what was going through our heads, how we could have acted as if nothing else really mattered. But it wasn't just about greed, right? It was about vision and freedom and taking the world by the balls. Right?"

After a pause, he said, "For some people it was, I guess."

Just then we passed a landmark that released a jolt of recognition from some obscure corner of my brain. "Wait! Stop! Stop here!" I shouted.

Josh looked as if he thought we might have hit something. "What is it?"

"Turn into this driveway ahead. I know this place."

He turned as instructed, driving the Sentra up a dusty dirt lane to a collection of nearly dilapidated farm buildings. "Stop there, at those old beehives."

We got out and the June heat enveloped us instantly. I ran up the grassy slope to the collection of stacked white hives. They were empty and disused, several toppled over on their sides, the burst screens erupting from the wooden frames. "I came here once as a kid," I said to Josh, who stood at the periphery of the hives as I walked through them. "There was a guy here harvesting honey. Odd old guy, he made a bee beard for me—you know, when the bees swarm all over somebody, so it looks like he's wearing an apian jumpsuit or something? Scared the shit out of me."

"I imagine it would," Josh said, indulging me.

"I wonder if he's still around. This was probably fifteen years ago, and he seemed old to me then, but I was just a kid. I guess he could've been in his early fifties or so." I lifted a rusty smoker from the ground and sniffed it. "Let's go knock at the door."

I ran down the slope again and headed to the main house, Josh following. I took the three porch steps in one leap and knocked on the door. After almost a minute, a man in his twenties, wearing sandals and a Chicago Bulls T-shirt, opened the door. "Yes?" he said through the screen.

"My friend and I were just driving by, and I remembered that I came here once, to this farm, when I was a kid—I was interested in the beehives—and there was a farmer here then—old guy with thatchy gray hair—and, I don't know, I was just wondering if you knew what happened to him."

The man laughed. "Yeah, I know what happened to him. Come in." He held the door open as Josh and I stepped into the kitchen. The interior surprised me; it was new-looking and well-kept, with modern appliances and artificial marble countertops. "He's in the den," the man said, and led us through the house to a room off the dining area. Inside, an old man sat in front of a computer screen with his back to us.

"Hey Ellroy. You've got visitors."

"Just a second. I just want to finish something here."

The younger man shrugged in our direction. "Ellroy's my grand-dad, and he's addicted to E*TRADE."

"There," the old man said with satisfaction. He clicked the mouse and turned in his swivel chair toward us. It was the same man I remembered—a little older-looking, but the same bulbous nose and unruly nest of hair. "Just made a hunnerd dollars in ten minutes on Merck, God be praised. So what can I do you for?"

"Sir," I began, feeling embarrassed now, "you won't remember me, but I came here one day as a boy—fifteen years ago, when we were vacationing at Spring Lake down the road. You were out with the hives and you made a bee beard for me."

"Oh sure, sure, I remember you." He chuckled and looked up at his grandson. "This was the kid who fainted."

"Oh man," the grandson said. "You're famous in our family. Ellroy here has told the story a hundred times if he's told it twice."

"Gave me quite a scare. I thought you'd dropped dead right there on the lawn. Took me a few minutes to bring you around, as I recall."

"I'm glad you remember," I said. "You don't keep bees anymore, I see."

"Oh no, no," he said. "Couldn't make any money at it. So I give it up a few years ago. Now I make money here"—he swept his wrinkled hand over the computer keyboard—"trading."

"And you, um, do all right with that?"

"Oh, I lost a bundle when everybody else did. Most of my retirement account—which means I won't be headin' to Tahiti anytime soon! But I'm doin' okay lately, playing the daily swings. And the Good Lord is smilin' on me *this* week. I can do no wrong."

We ended up visiting with the man for just a short time. There really wasn't much connection between us, after all, and the conversation became strained after a while. But old Ellroy seemed genuinely touched that I had stopped by, and as we left he pressed a baggieful of his wife's homemade Toll House cookies on us. "God bless you, boys," he said as we left, "and stop by anytime."

Back on the road, Josh and I were silent for a few minutes as we systematically ate our way through the whole bag of cookies. When they were gone, Josh cleared his throat and said, "Okay, Mr. Market Visionary, is that a buy signal or a sell signal? An old farmer daytrading from the family farmstead. Is it a sign that we haven't learned a thing, that there's still more irrationality to be drummed out of us? Or is it the first faint indication of healing?"

I licked the melted chocolate from my fingers. "I wish I knew, dear coz, but I have no idea," I said. "That's why they call it a market."

ABOUT THE AUTHOR

GARY KRIST is the author of the novels *Chaos Theory* and *Bad Chemistry*, and two story collections, *Bone by Bone* and *The Garden State*. He reviews books regularly for the *New York Times, Salon,* and the *Washington Post Book World* and frequently writes satirical op-eds for the *New York Times*. He lives in Bethesda, Maryland, with his wife and daughter.